Materi... Girl 2:
Labels and Love

Material Girl 2:
Labels and Love

Keisha Ervin

www.urbanbooks.net

Urban Books, LLC
78 East Industry Court
Deer Park, NY 11729

ISBN 13: 978-1-60162-458-1
ISBN 10: 1-60162-458-1

First Printing August 2011
Printed in the United States of America

10 9 8 7 6 5 4 3 2

This is a work of fiction. Any references or similarities to actual events, real people, living, or dead, or to real locales are intended to give the novel a sense of reality. Any similarity in other names, characters, places, and incidents is entirely coincidental.

Distributed by Kensington Publishing Corp.
Submit Wholesale Orders to:
Kensington Publishing Corp.
C/O Penguin Group (USA) Inc.
Attention: Order Processing
405 Murray Hill Parkway
East Rutherford, NJ 07073-2316
Phone: 1-800-526-0275
Fax: 1-800-227-9604

Material Girl 2:
Labels and Love

By
Keisha Ervin

Dedication

This book is dedicated to all the material girls in the world in search of their very own material boy. He's only a few feet away. Just close your eyes real tight, click your heels three times, and he will appear.

Acknowledgments

To my Heavenly Father, you are my guiding light. When I can't depend on anyone else in this world, you are always there for me. Nobody loves me like you do, and I will continue to praise your name.

To my baby, Kyrese. You have been workin' my nerves lately with this whole preteen thing you're going through, but I couldn't see myself on this earth without you. I love you so much. (Kissing your face right now.)

Locia, as time and years pass, our friendship contin ues to grow and become stronger. I pray that we have twenty more years of friendship together. I love you more than you love a good clearance sale, cheapskate. LOL!!

To all of my family and friends. I love you all.

To Carl Weber and the entire Urban Books staff. You all have been nothing but good to me. I sincerely appreciate your hard work and diligence.

Brenda Hampton, what can I say? You are not only my agent but one of my close friends. Your words of wisdom and all that you have accomplished inspires me. I love you dearly.

Most important, to all of my fans, thank you so much for riding with me. Your e-mails, messages, and tweets mean the world to me. Without you all, there would be no me. You all are the reason I continue to write, and I love each and every one of you from the bottom of my heart.

Acknowledgments

Keisha Ervin Contact Info:

keisha_ervin2002@yahoo.com,
www.keishaervin.com,
www.facebook.com/keisha.ervin,
www.twitter.com/keishaervin, and
www.myspace.com/keishaervin

"Some people come into our lives and quickly go. Others stay awhile, make footprints on our hearts, and we are never, ever the same—"

Anonymous

"Beep me 911 or call me on my cell phone. I'll call you back to see what you gon' tell me."
Missy Elliot, "Beep Me 911"

"Okay, now, I know you ain't doing it like you used to but just 'cause you one step away from being in the welfare line don't mean we have to starve to death," Tee-Tee complained as soon as his cousin Dylan sat down for breakfast at The City Diner.

Dylan loved going to The City Diner. Coupled with their wide variety of comfort foods, she thoroughly enjoyed the whimsical way in which it was designed. The diner was filled with old movie and music memorabilia, the 1950s-style booths, tables, and a jukebox.

"Tee-Tee, shut up. I got enough going on to be dealing wit' you and your nonsense. It's too damn early." Dylan took off her purse and set it down in the empty seat next to her.

"Uh, ah, did slumdog just read me?" Tee-Tee looked at his and Dylan's best friend Billie, appalled.

"Yeah, honey, you just got served," Billie nodded, tryin' to be hip. "Does anybody still say that?"

"No," Dylan shook her head.

"Anyway," Tee-Tee flicked his wrist, "Miss Unfashionably Late, I know you're a recessionista now, but I know you *not* shoppin' in the Miley Cyrus collection at Wal-Mart." He curled up his lip and looked Dylan up and down.

"What?" Dylan gazed over her outfit which she thought was cute. She wore a black fitted fake leather jacket from Forever 21, wife beater, white jeans, and motorcycle boots. Her accessories consisted of a green scarf, gold watch, skull ring, and a black hobo-style purse.

"You are such a hater, but anyway, how are you, my love?" Dylan turned her attention to Billie and patted her on the arm.

"Good," she cooed. "I am so excited to go on my honeymoon," Billie clapped enthusiastically.

"I know you are. Where are y'all going again?"

"India, Italy, Japan, and Rome. We'll be gone a month."

"Can I come too?" Dylan half joked.

"Nigga, no." Billie laughed. "I have been married to my husband for two months, and we have yet to spend a moment alone. I can't wait to get the hell up outta here."

"Them li'l critters you call kids gon' have a fit. You know they can't live without they mama," Tee-Tee took a sip from his glass.

"They will be all right." Billie crossed her legs. "Their father is watching them and say something else about my kids and see don't I reach across this table and stab you in the neck with this fork." She held it up.

"And I thought marriage would soften you," Tee-Tee said, then chuckled.

"Actually it has," Billie smiled. "Guess who I invited over for New Year's Eve?"

"Fantasia's brother Teeny?" Tee-Tee exclaimed over the moon.

"No." Billie looked at him as if he were crazy.

"Don't be lookin' at me like that. If I wasn't married, Teeny could get it."

"Oh my God, I can't. It's too early in the morning for your foolishness." Billie hung her head and laughed.

"Well, who is it?" Dylan asked.

"Cain and Becky," Billie replied.

"What the fuck was on yo' mind?" Tee-Tee drew back. "Bitch, was you high? We don't like them."

"I know, but the kids want they daddy there, so I couldn't just invite him and not her," she explained.

"Shit, why not? I would've," he countered.

"That's 'cause you're ignorant," Dylan chimed in.

"You damn right I am," Tee-Tee shot sternly. "That skank wouldn't be up in my house. I mean, c'mon. Am I the only one that remembers Becky was your husband's mistress while y'all was married?" He looked back and forth between Dylan and Billie.

"Hell, naw, I haven't forgotten," Billie replied. "I'm just over being mad, besides, I gotta new man. I ain't trippin' off Cain and his floozy."

"Yous a good one, honey, 'cause er'time I see ha we'd be fightin'." Tee-Tee bobbed his head like a ghetto girl.

"Me and you gon' be fightin' if you don't leave my friend alone," Dylan warned.

"Well, ain't you fcisty this morning." Tee-Tee gave her a sly grin.

"I swear to God I can't stand you," Dylan laughed.

"Well, you know y'all are invited," Billie continued on.

"We better," Tee-Tee shot. "If Pam and Tommy Lee can come, I know we invited."

"You are a damn coon." Billie playfully pushed him in the arm.

"I'm pregnant!" Dylan blurted out, unable to keep it bottled in anymore.

"Oh my goodness." Tee-Tee placed his hands in front of him as if to say "freeze." "Oh my goooooodness. We having a baby!"

"You have *got* to be kidding me." Billie rolled her neck and folded her arms across her chest.

"What?" Dylan looked at her perplexed.

"You know you really had me fooled. I'm up here thinking you have changed, and you pregnant by State."

Dylan rolled her eyes to the ceiling. Billie was always jumping to conclusions. She never took the time to learn all of the details before reacting. Little did she know but Dylan and Billie's brother, Angel, had slept together the night of Billie's wedding.

"And you think it's funny? Bitch, you must have me fucked up. Let me go before I have to choke the shit outta this ho." Billie grabbed her purse, scooted back her hair, and stood up.

"Billie, sit yo' ass down," Dylan demanded from across the table. "I am *not* pregnant by State."

"Well, who, then?" Billie retook her seat.

Dylan licked her lips nervously and swallowed.

"Angel."

"Oh, hell to the no!" Tee-Tee wagged his finger. "You done stole my man, and you gettin' ready to have a baby by him. Just shoot me now!" He pounded his fist on the table.

"You are so dramatic." Dylan rolled her eyes.

"Hold up," Billie jumped in. "So you mean to tell me you pregnant by my brother, Angel?"

"Yes." Dylan closed her eyes and nodded.

"And can't nobody else be the daddy?" Billie questioned, still skeptical.

"No." Dylan shook her head.

"Nobody?" Billie pried.

"No!" Dylan shrieked.

"Okay." Billie put her hands up. "I believe you."

"Damn, was I that much of a ho?" Dylan looked at both Billie and Tee-Tee.

"Yes!" they both exclaimed in unison.

"Y'all ass ain't shit." She shot them both an angry look.

"No, we speaks the truth," Tee-Tee objected. "Shit, yo' ass was about to be the female Wilt Chamberlin."

"Fuck you." Dylan gave him the middle finger.

"No, thanks. My man already did this morning." He batted his eyes.

"Ugh, don't make me throw up again. I already have twice this morning." Dylan smacked her lips together as if she had a bad taste in her mouth.

"Okay, let's get focused here," Billie interjected. "How far along are you?"

"Two months," Dylan answered.

"Whoa." Billie's eyes grew wide. "So that means that you and Angel did the oochie wally oochie bang bang during the weekend of my wedding."

"Actually, the night of," Dylan responded.

"Wow." Billie shook her head dazed.

"So the million-dollar question is . . ." Tee-Tee placed his right elbow on the table and leaned forward, "does he know?"

Dylan winced. "No."

"Ooooooh, scandalous," Tee-Tee snapped his fingers.

"Why haven't you told him?" Billie asked.

"'Cause it's already weird between us," Dylan said after a pause. "I mean, after we smashed—"

"Speak English," Billie waved her hand cutting her off.

"Fucked, made love, had sex," Dylan said loudly. "He basically told me it was a wrap, and that we would never be, so what do I do? Call him and say, 'Hey, how you doing? Did you hear Heidi from the Hills had ten surgeries in one day, and oh, by the way, I'm pregnant'?"

"Girl, don't she look faaaaaaaaabulous," Tee-Tee added.

"No, more like a hot mess," Dylan disagreed.

"Fuck all of that." Billie waved her hands. "When are you going to tell him?"

"Soon, of course. I'm just tryin' to find the right time," Dylan responded hesitantly.

"Girl, you better tell that man. Nothin' good ever came from keeping something a secret. I learned that from watching *Days of Our Lives*. Especially not no shit about no baby," Tee-Tee cautioned.

"Okay . . . you just got really deep," Dylan said in a *Valley Girl*-like tone.

"I know, and now I have a headache." He massaged his forehead.

"Look, there's no time like the present. The longer you wait, the harder it's gonna be," Billie said.

Dylan took a deep breath.

"I guess. I just have never been this scared before in my life." Dylan buried her face in her hands.

"Why?" Billie asked, concerned.

"'Cause I'm still in love with your brother, and what if he don't want me to have it?" Dylan swallowed the tears that were rising in her throat. "Could you imagine anything worse?"

"Yep," Tee-Tee nodded with a faraway look in his eyes. "A Coogi sweater with matching pants."

"Anyway," Billie tuned up her face, "if I know anything, I know my brother. He gon' want you to keep it."

"I hope so," Dylan said optimistically.

"Look, quit stalling and call him," Billie persisted.

"Okay." Dylan dug into her purse and pulled out her phone. "I'll be back." She pushed her chair back.

Outside the restaurant, Dylan stood on the sidewalk. The chilly November air kissed her face as she held the phone in her hand. In a year's time, life for Dylan Monroe had changed drastically. She'd gone from trips around the world, designer dresses straight from the runway, and A-List soirees, to weekly runs to Wal-Mart and clearance-rack clothes. She was now catering the parties she used to attend. She'd found the love of her life, heavyweight champion of the world, Angel Carter. But after having a torrid affair with her newly married, ex-fiancé State, she lost Angel.

After nearly a year apart, she and Angel rekindled their romance at Billie and Knox's wedding. Dylan hoped that night would be their chance for a new beginning. But Angel still wasn't able to forgive and forget, so he made it clear once and for all that what they once shared was a thing of the past. Heartbroken, Dylan accepted their fate but still held out hope for them in her heart. All the signs for their relationship pointed to over, but somehow, fate stepped in, and now, she was carrying his child.

Nervous as hell, Dylan looked over her shoulder to see if Billie and Tee-Tee were watching her. Of course they were. Turning her head, Dylan took a much-needed deep breath and found Angel's number in her address book. Reluctantly, she pressed send. A second later, the phone began to ring.

Damn, why couldn't his line be busy? she thought, holding her breath.

Three rings later, her call was sent to voice mail. Knowing she would never build the courage to call him again, Dylan decided to give him the news via voice mail.

"Hey . . . it's me, Dylan," she spoke softly. "I know we haven't spoken in a while, but I really need to talk to you." Dylan paused and tried her best to swallow the baseball-sized lump in her throat. "Umm . . . I'm pregnant, and I'm scared. I just . . . really need to talk you, so call me as soon as you get this message."

Dylan took the phone away from her ear and ended the call. She hadn't realized it when she was on the phone, but her entire body was shaking. She prayed that Angel would call back soon, because if not, she knew that she would be on pins and needles for the rest of the day every time her phone rang.

One thousand, five hundred and ninety-three miles away in sunny Malibu, California, Angel sat on the side of his bed in nothing but a pair of Armani Exchange boxers. Exhausted, he yawned and rubbed his eyes, then picked up the X10 remote control which controlled almost everything in the house. Using the remote, he opened the curtains. The view of the Pacific Ocean was right before his eyes. Angel sat and watched as the waves crashed onto the shore, while reminiscing about the night before. He and his girlfriend of two months, Milania Fairchild, had made love in every position imaginable. They'd even made up a few of their own.

She was a little-known Victoria's Secret model with no children and no hidden baggage. She was an all-around good girl with a heart of gold. He enjoyed her company tremendously, cherished the way she made him laugh, and the fact that she was able to take his mind off Dylan was an added bonus. They'd messed around a year and a half before but nothing serious ever popped off between them due to the fact that Angel couldn't hide his true feelings for Dylan any longer.

But now they were officially a couple, and life for Angel was good. He'd finally come to terms that what he and Dylan shared was over. He could no longer dwell on the past and the moments they shared, although deep down inside, a corner of his heart still ached for her. Angel looked over his shoulder and found Milania, who he thought was asleep, staring back at him.

She'd been admiring his toned back. Milania looked at him and winked. Angel was by far one of the sexiest men she'd ever laid her eyes upon, and in her industry, she'd seen a-plenty. But there was something about Angel that set him apart from the pack. Maybe it was his confidence or his cocky swagger that attracted so many women to him. No, it was his boy-next-door charm.

One glimpse at Angel's beautiful smile or one look into his smoldering brown eyes and you were trapped. His skin was a tantalizing shade of warm honey. He was six feet two and 220 pounds of pure muscle. He rocked a bald head and goatee. Across his chest was a tattoo that read "Death before Dishonor" and along the right side of his body beginning at his shoulder and ending at his ankle was a tribal tattoo.

"What you over there thinkin' about?" she asked, feeling cream build inside her panties.

"Nothin'," he lied. "Just tryin' to wake up. I'm still tired as hell from last night."

"Really?" She smiled deviously. "Would you like some more?" She removed the covers and revealed her flawless five feet eleven svelte physique.

Angel unconsciously licked his bottom lip. Milania was built like an Egyptian goddess. Her skin was a silky shade of butter pecan. Long, raven locks of black hair cascaded over her shoulders and down her back. She didn't need a stitch of makeup to enhance her beauty. Her doe-shaped eyes, high cheekbones, and Cover Girl smile were all she needed to turn a man on. The winter-white lace bra and bikini panties she wore only added to her sex appeal.

"As a matter of fact, I do. Come get in the shower wit' me." He got up and made his way to the bathroom.

"You ain't said nothin' but a word," Milania beamed, getting up too.

As Angel turned on the shower and got in, she began to peel off the straps of her bra, but as the first strap came down, Angel's cell began to vibrate. Milania stopped dead in her tracks, considering if she should take a quick peek. For the past two months, she'd wondered if she was the only woman Angel was seeing. Now was the perfect opportunity to take a glimpse at his contacts and call log and find out. Quietly, she crept around the bed and picked up his phone.

Blindsided by the name on the screen, Milania had to catch her breath so she wouldn't hyperventilate. *What the fuck does she want?* Shaken, Milania took a rapid glance over her shoulder to make sure the coast was clear. Seeing that it was, she pressed ignore, sending Dylan to voice mail. *This bitch ain't gon' get in my way this time,* she hissed as the icon showing Angel had a voice mail message popped onto the screen.

With the sound of water running in the background, she pressed one and listened to Dylan's message. Flabbergasted by the news, she stood paralyzed. Her heart was beating a mile a minute. *This can not be happening,* she thought, freaking out. *No way can this bitch be pregnant. If Angel finds out, he will surely end things with me and go back to her. I can not lose him again. If I do, all of my hard work will go down the drain. The media won't be fascinated with me. The paparazzi won't clamor for my photo. I won't get anymore free swag, and most important, my plans of being Mrs. Angel Carter will no longer exist. Okay, Milania, think.* She ran her free hand through her hair. *You just need a li'l more time to solidify your relationship before he learns that she's pregnant.*

"What's takin' you so long? You get lost?" Angel yelled from the shower, causing Milania to jump.

Her whole entire body was shaking.

"No, here I come!" she yelled back, praying he didn't hear the panic in her voice.

Milania looked down at the phone realizing she had to make a decision and quick. *Fuck it,* she said to herself. She knew that what she was about to do was fucked up and morally wrong on so many levels, but getting put on nowadays wasn't as easy for everybody as it was for Amber Rose. Some chicks had to work a li'l harder, suck a li'l bit more dick, give up a lot more pussy, show even more ass and play a lot more games to be famous.

Now was Milania's time to shine. She would be Hollywood's new "it girl," and Angel Carter was her meal ticket to making all of her dreams come true. Without hesitation or a blink of the eye, she erased the message and any evidence that Dylan had called. Pleased with her choice, Milania stripped down to her birthday suit and smiled. Angel was hers, and she was willing to do any and everything to make sure things stayed that way.

"I can't believe that muthafucka!" Tee-Tee spat with his hand on his hip.

He and Dylan were inside of Macy's picking out an outfit for her to wear to Billie's New Year's Eve party.

"I mean, it's been three weeks since you called him, and his ass ain't called and said nothin'?"

"I found it odd too at first, but I guess he just doesn't wanna have anything to do with me." Dylan tried to seem nonchalant about the situation as she slipped on a dress.

For the past three weeks, she'd put on the illusion that she was this strong, independent woman who didn't need a man, meaning Angel, by her side. But really, when no one was around and all she had was herself to be with, she felt sick, like the air God breathed into her lungs had escaped. She felt bamboozled, hurt, pissed off, unwanted, shut out, forgotten, and alone.

It wasn't like she had a mother who she could lean on. Her mother, Candy, couldn't even be put in the classification of a mother. She was like the anti-mother. Candy could've easily been the spokesperson for the worst mother in the world. She didn't even teach her her ABC's. One of Dylan's many nannies did. Yet still crying on her cousin's shoulder was something she wasn't willing to do. Yes, the pain in her chest felt like she was being constantly stabbed, but Dylan had to live and stay focused for her baby.

Regrettably, with each day that passed, that notion became harder and harder. For Dylan, being pregnant only brought on an added stress that she didn't need. She was already dealing with the fact that her bakery, Edible Couture, which had only been open six months, was failing miserably. Every day it became increasingly harder for her to pay the store's rent and the rent on her town house. Bills were piling up to the ceiling, and sooner than later her bakery would have to close. If that was Dylan's fate, she didn't know what she was going to do.

"It's okay if he don't wanna have nothin' to do with you, but what about the baby?" Tee-Tee continued to go off. "The baby don't have nothin' to do wit' y'all mess. It didn't ask to be brought into this world," Tee-Tee snapped outside the dressing-room door.

"Just please give me his number so I can cuss his ass out."

"For the one-hundredth time, no!" Dylan stepped out to view herself in the full-length mirror.

She couldn't even tell that she was pregnant. The tell-tale signs only came through in her face and breasts.

"But why?" Tee-Tee whined. "I'm so good at it. Plus, his ass deserve to get a tongue-lashing."

"I know he does, but it's just not worth it." Dylan examined herself from head to toe and side to side, hoping Tee-Tee would drop the conversation, because she was starting to feel claustrophobic.

"Okay, I know that having a baby changes people's views on life, but you are not gon' sit up here and pretend that you are not fazed by his behavior."

"Honest to Prada." Dylan raised her hand as if she were giving the Hippocratic Oath. "I'm okay. I mean . . . I'm not okay." She looked off to the side. "You know what I mean. I just have to learn how to deal with having this baby on my own," she swallowed, looking down at her feet.

"If you say so," Tee-Tee replied and zipped up the back of her dress. "By the way, have you talked to Billie?"

"Yeah, like a week and a half ago."

"Has she talked to him?" he inquired.

"We really weren't able to get off into all of that. She and Knox had to get on their flight to India." Dylan felt a heat wave rush over her body.

"So is he coming to the party?" Tee-Tee probed further.

"As far as I know, no," Dylan said, fanning herself with her hand. "I gotta sit down."

"You okay?" Tee-Tee took her by the hand and led her back into the dressing room.

"No, I feel like I gotta throw up."

"Ughh. Just don't do it on me." He scooted back.

"Shut up." Dylan grimaced, fanning her face with her purse. "I don't think I wanna go to the party," she pouted.

"Why?"

"'Cause I look like a fat pig." Dylan picked at her dress.

"No, you don't. You're barely showing, and you gotta come. It's gonna be fun, and we gon' be the flyest chicks up in there. Well, I know I am 'cause a bitch like me is about to show her ass while I still can before this baby come." Tee-Tee popped his lips.

"Oh, Tee-Tee, I'm so sorry." She rubbed his arm. "I haven't asked you anything about how the adoption is going."

"It's going. We're going through the homestudy process now," he sighed.

"What's that?"

"It's a written report by a social worker where basically the social worker does an intensive background search, finds out our motivation toward adoption, etc. Afterward, the social worker gives their summary on us and their recommendation."

"Well, if you need my help with anything, just let me know."

"I will, and by the way, bitch, you betta work! That dress is fierce on you!" He snapped his fingers.

Dylan looked down at the dress. It was an all-black sheath dress by Rachel Roy.

"Thanks, my love. I like it too, but this is just way too expensive."

"Girl, this dress is a steal!" Tee-Tee looked at her crazy. "It's only ninety-nine dollars."

"Yeah, like I just got ninety-nine dollars layin' around." Dylan wrinkled her brow.

"Well, you ain't gon' be coming around me lookin' crazy, so I'll buy it for you."

"No, it is not that serious."

"Girl, boo, I got you."

"Tee-Tee, thank you," Dylan said, hugging him around the neck.

"And you deserve a phone call from yo' deadbeat baby daddy," he eyed her sternly.

"Well, we can't always get what we want." Dylan looked down at her stomach somberly and rubbed her belly.

"If we ever come close again . . . I know what I'll say then."
Tevin Campbell, "Can We Talk"

2

New Year's Eve had arrived and Billie's party was in full swing. For the past hour, she'd been running around the house like a chicken with its head cut off. There were a million things going on at once. The chef was preparing a five-course meal. The party planner was decorating and setting the table. Billie's kids, Kaylee, Kyrese, and Kenzie were running around like wild banshees, and Tee-Tee and Bernard hadn't stopped arguing since they arrived.

Also to Billie's dismay, her ex-husband, NFL star Cain, and his reality-show wife Puss 'n Boots aka Becky had arrived. Puss 'n Boots had been there for almost an hour, but Billie still couldn't get past her attire. The chick looked like pop star Kesha on crack. Her overly dyed blond hair was fried and stringy. She'd bedazzled her right eye with blue rhinestones in the shape of a star. And her barely-there outfit consisted of a hot pink leotard, black tutu, lime green lace tights, and yellow combat boots.

Billie wanted to slap her for coming around her kids, let alone her new husband, Knox, dressed like that, but Billie wasn't going to let Cain and his bimbo wife ruin her holiday. She had too much to be thankful for. She had three gorgeous kids and a yummy new husband who she loved more than life. Knox was the husband she'd always wanted Cain to be. He was selfless, calm, understanding, and toe-curling good in bed. Half of their honeymoon was spent inside their hotel room. Knox was everything she wanted, and more.

"Babe," Knox reached out and took her hand, "sit down and chill out. Why you runnin' around so much?"

"'Cause it's still a lot to be done. The table isn't finished being set, and the food is nowhere near being done," she sighed, rubbing her forehead.

"That's what you hired all these people for, remember? They're the ones that are supposed to be stressin', not you."

"But—"

"But nothin'," Knox cut her off.

"No, babe, seriously, I really need to go check on the girls and make sure they haven't gotten anything on their dresses." She tried to walk away again.

"The girls just ran past me. They're fine. *You* the one that need to calm down."

"I feel like if I'm not involved, it won't be done right. I just want everything to be perfect."

"And it will be, as long as you're here," he guaranteed, smiling.

Billie couldn't help smiling too. Knox always knew how to lift her spirits. Plus, his dashing good looks didn't hurt. He was six feet three of mouth-watering sweet vanilla milkshake. His charming smile, luscious brown hair, and debonair style reminded her of Robin Thicke. Billie couldn't get enough of him. He was a mixture of the boy next door and a hood boy from the block.

"How do you do that?" she asked with a pleased expression on her face.

"Do what?" He held her close.

"You *always* know when to say the right things to make me feel better." She hugged him, then kissed his lips.

"You better stop before you make my dick hard." Knox massaged her ass.

"I like it when you talk nasty to me, Daddy," she grinned.

"And I like that dress you wearing even more." He ran his hands down her hips.

Knox couldn't get enough of his wife. To him, she was the sexiest woman on earth. Billie was a perfect size twelve, five feet eight, diva with diamond-shaped eyes. Whenever she smiled, a slight glimmer of a dimple graced her left cheek.

"Come on." He took her hand. "Let's go say hello to our guests."

"Do we have to?" Billie whined.

"Yes, now bring yo' ass." He dragged her into the living room.

"Huh!" Billie groaned as she overheard Tee-Tee and his husband, Bernard, arguing.

Tee-Tee and Bernard were total opposites. Tee-Tee was loud and flamboyant, whereas Bernard was reserved and thugged out to the fullest. He rocked a mouth full of gold teeth and on a daily basis, he donned strictly white tees, jeans, and Tims.

"Why er'time we go out you gotta embarrass me, huh? You ain't always got to show yo' ass, Teyana," Bernard whispered, hoping no one would overhear.

"Bitch, you mad?" Tee-Tee jerked his head back. "I can't help it if I'm a diva." He sashayed around in a circle so he could put his sexy outfit on full display.

Tee-Tee was rockin' the hell out of a skintight, snake print, spandex dress, and nude Louboutin heels.

"If that dress was any shorter, you'd be arrested for crack!" Bernard spat.

"My last man didn't pay $10,000 for these silicone missiles for nothin!" Tee-Tee mashed his breast implants together. "Hell, how you think I pulled you? Now you wanna act brand-new 'cause you put a ring on it. Chile, please, I'm servin' fish, honey, and this here ain't trout!" He snapped his fingers in the air.

"You are actin' like a real bitch right now," Bernard fumed, folding his arms across his chest.

"What? Is *that* supposed to hurt me? I don't care about you callin' me a bitch as long as you put a *Miss* before it. Now *this* is me." Tee-Tee posed like a mannequin. "Teyana aka Tee-Tee aka The Original Suzanne Sugarbaker all day er'day, so if you don't like it, then, oh . . . well." Tee-Tee twirled his index finger in Bernard's face.

"You know me, I'll be on to the next one on-on to the next one." He sang doing the ole school dance called the Prep.

"Teyana, now you stop that!" Bernard stomped his foot. "You ain't gotta show out like that. You know I love you. You my ride-or-die chick. What I say in my vows? *Lie together, cry together, I swear to God I hope we fuckin' die together.*"

"Boy, stop before I have to take my panties off," Tee-Tee grinned softening up, "wit' yo' fine ass."

"See. This is the reason I didn't want to come in here," Billie turned to Knox.

"Be easy, Ma. They're your family," he laughed.

"Unfortunately," she pouted. "All I know is I'll be glad when Dylan gets here." Just then, the doorbell rang.

Billie's maid Zoila answered the door.

"Mrs. Christianson—" Billie's maid called out.

"Zoila," she snapped, stomping her foot. "How many times do I have to tell you it's Mrs. Townsend? I'm only Mrs. Christianson on paper. To the world and for business purposes, I am still known as Mrs. Townsend, okay?"

"I sorry." Zoila replied in broken English.

Knox stood by Billie's side utterly embarrassed. The fact that Billie wouldn't take his last name made him feel less than the man he was. And it really messed him up that she would even want to keep her last husband's surname after the way he dogged her.

"I came to tell ju that jur brother is here," Zoila continued.

"What?" Billie said shocked.

"What up, big sis?" Angel came around the corner with his arms held out for a hug.

"What are you doing here?" she asked, walking into his embrace. "I thought you were gonna be in Vegas."

"Nah, I couldn't bring in the New Year without my family." He hugged her tightly.

"I wish you would've said something," Billie said, thinking of Dylan who would be arriving any second.

"I wanted you to be surprised."

"Oh, I'm surprised all right." She hugged him back.

"Let me reintroduce you to someone." Angel stepped to the side. "You remember Milania, right."

Billie's eyes grew wide like saucers. *So this is why he been playin' Dylan to the left, 'cause he got a new chick.*

"Hi," she quickly spoke. "Umm, we need to talk," Billie said, turning her attention back to Angel.

"Uh . . . ah . . . what the hell is *he* doing here?" Tee-Tee sashayed over to them, wagging his finger in the air. "I thought you said he wasn't coming."

"That's what I thought."

"Damn, did I do something? 'Cause y'all actin' like I'm the Grinch who stole Christmas." Angel looked around confused.

"Nigga . . . don't . . . act . . . stupid!" Tee-Tee waved his index finger like a snake ready to spit venom.

"Tee-Tee, calm down." Billie pushed him back. "I got this. Angel, it's not that we're not happy to see you."

"Speak for yourself," Tee-Tee said underneath his breath.

Billie cut her eyes at him and said, "It's just that considering everything that's going on—"

"Everything like what?" Angel asked, still puzzled.

"Baby," Milania chimed in, "why don't we just go? It's obvious we're not wanted here."

"My brother's always welcome," Billie interjected, shooting her the evil eye. "Now, if you'd like to stay, champagne and caviar are being served in the other room."

"A'ight, but we need to talk," Angel said, still perplexed by everyone's odd behavior.

"Oh, we will," Billie reassured him.

Once Angel and Milania were out of view, Billie raced up the steps to her bedroom. She had to stop Dylan from coming before she got there and had her heart ripped from her chest. Billie quickly dialed her number but got no answer. After trying five more times, she sat on the edge of the bed, wondering what to do next when she heard the sound of the doorbell ring.

"Shit!" she shrieked, making a mad dash for the door.

Billie hit the steps and saw Zoila walking toward the door.

"I got it!" She raced down the steps in six-inch heels.

"Okay," Zoila shrugged.

Out of breath, Billie smoothed down her dress and opened the door. "Hey, girl. What you doing here so early?" She poked her head through the crack of the door.

"What are you talkin' about?" Dylan eyed her baffled. "I'm late, and why are you huffin' and puffin'?" She tried to come inside.

"We gotta talk," Billie whispered, pushing her back.

"Bitch, are you high? If you don't let me in . . ." Dylan tried pushing past her again. "It's cold."

"Listen," Billie whispered.

"Who you talkin' to?" Angel said from behind.

"Huh?" Billie spun around, slamming the door in Dylan's face. "That was . . . one of them damn Jehovah Witnesses." She placed her hand on her hip. "You would think 'cause it's a holiday they would have the day off."

"Billie, open the goddamn door!" Dylan banged her fist on the door.

"Is that Dylan?" Angel looked at his sister.

"You know what?" She raised her hand and slapped her thigh. "I think it is." She swallowed hard. "I'll get it. Why don't you go back in the living room with the others?"

"I'm good." He pushed his sister aside and opened the door.

"What the hell is yo' problem?" Dylan yelled expecting to see Billie but instead, came face-to-face with Angel's warm brown eyes.

"Angel," she said, taken aback by his presence.

A mixture of anger and lust raced through her veins. She wanted to slap him and fuck him all at the same time. Dylan knew that one day they would see each other again, but to see his face and be so close to him that she could reach out and touch him took the wind out of her. Nothing had changed about him. It had only gotten better. Angel was drop-dead gorgeous. The sight of him alone caused her pussy to cream.

"Come in." He extended his hand.

"I'm good." She rolled her eyes, remembering how he'd played the fuck outta her by not responding to her message.

Bypassing him, she entered the house and spotted Billie.

"So *that's* why you were actin' so crazy?" she asked, referring to Angel.

"Yeah," Billie whispered, pulling Dylan by the arm. "I tried callin' you. As a matter of fact, why don't you come upstairs with me so I can show you these Manolo's I bought the other day."

"Nah, I think me and Angel need to speak first. I got a couple of things I need to get off my chest." Dylan unbuttoned her coat, revealing the form-fitting Rachel Roy dress she wore underneath.

Angel's forehead immediately scrunched, almost causing his eyebrows to meet. Dylan had always been curvaceous, but in the months since he'd last seen her, her body had blossomed in all the right places. Her breasts were more than a mouthful. They were plump and juicy like two ripe melons, and her hips and ass rivaled Jessica Rabbit. He wondered what had brought on this sudden weight gain. Dylan prided herself on being a size four.

"You wanna come with me upstairs," she tilted her head toward the steps.

"Yeah, 'cause we most definitely need to talk."

Inside the twins' room, Dylan closed the door behind her. She'd promised herself that the next time she saw or heard from Angel that she would give him a piece of her mind.

"You got something you need to tell me?" he eyed her suspiciously.

"No, the real question is, what's going on wit' you? I mean, I know we're not together anymore, but I expected more from you than this."

"More from me like what?" He looked at her sideways.

"So you really gon' stand there and pretend like you don't know what's going on?" Dylan shot him a look.

"Yo', just tell me what the fuck is going on. 'Cause all y'all got an attitude wit' me like I've done something wrong."

"Umm . . . you have!" Dylan yelled. "I leave you a message damn near two months ago tellin' you I'm pregnant, and you don't call me back and say nothin'."

"Pause." Angel held his hand up. "You did *what?*"

"I left you a message tellin' you I was pregnant, Angel. Like, please don't try to play me like you ain't get it," she shot.

"I didn't. If I did I would've called you back. C'mon, man, you know me better than that," he reasoned.

"I thought I did." She shrugged her shoulders, shaking her head.

"So let me get this straight. You tellin' me that you're pregnant?" Angel asked.

"Yes," Dylan groaned.

"And how many months are you?"

"I'll be four months on the fifth," Dylan sucked her teeth. "The baby is due June fifth."

"And the baby's mine?" Angel questioned in disbelief.

"Yes!" she yelled, annoyed.

"You sure?"

"Are you fuckin' kidding me? Of course I'm sure." Dylan rolled her neck. "Let's not forget you ran up in me the night of your sister's wedding without a rubber."

"I'm just sayin' . . . shit, a nigga gotta be sure these days. Hell, you heard 50 Cent's song 'Have a Baby By Me, Baby, Be a Millionaire.'"

"You know what? Fuck you." Dylan pointed her finger in his face like a gun. "I ain't gotta put up with this shit." She turned to leave.

"Quit actin' like a fuckin' brat." Angel reached out and grabbed her hand, pulling her back.

There they stood, chest to chest, exchanging breaths. Old feelings and past memories flooded both of their minds. Angel gazed down into Dylan's hazel eyes. She was pretty as hell. No, fuck that. She was gorgeous. Everything about her screamed top-notch bitch from her golden skin to her full, luscious lips.

Dylan was a risk taker. She never conformed to what everybody else was doing. She created her own path. Her numerous tattoos and rocker chic haircut proved it. She was nothing short of a sexy, glamorous, free-spirited version of Rihanna. A part of Angel wanted to say fuck her and keep it moving, but then he wondered if by chance he leaned down and kissed her lips, would they still taste the same on his tongue . . . when the door swung open.

"Baby, we might have to have two flower girls for the wedding 'cause your nieces are just too cute." Milania entered the room, shocked to find him standing there with Dylan.

"I didn't know you weren't alone," she said, her heart thumping loudly.

Dylan stepped back and looked at Angel with shock and horror in her eyes.

"You gettin' married?"

"As a matter of fact we are," Milania answered, taking her place by Angel's side.

"I don't believe I was speaking to you," Dylan shot with an attitude.

"Regardless of who you were talkin' to, I answered the question." Milania arched her eyebrow and gave Dylan a look that said, "and what?"

Dylan stood speechless. A mixture of emotions flooded her body. She wanted to smack the shit out of Milania, choke Angel, scream, cry, but the rising chunks of vomit in her throat reminded her that in a couple of days she would be four months pregnant and didn't need the added stress.

"So, honey," Milania wrapped her arm around Angel's waist and smiled, "you wanna introduce me to your friend?"

"Uhhhhh, Milania, this is Dylan." Angel shook his head tryin' to gather his thoughts. "You remember her, don't you?"

"Your ex, right? Wow, I've heard so much about you." Milania eyed Dylan up and down with a look of disgust in her eyes.

"Is that right?" Dylan glared at Angel, surprised.

"Well, somebody had to be his shoulder to lean on after all the drama you put him through." Milania dug the knife in deeper.

"So you told her our business?" Dylan's chest heaved up and down.

"Yo', it wasn't even nothin' like that—" Angel tried to explain.

"You know what? It's cool." Dylan put her hand up as if to say, "stop." And with that being said, she turned and left the room feeling dizzy.

"It was nice meeting you again!" Milania grinned.

As carefully and as quickly as she could, Dylan raced down the steps. It seemed as if her body temperature had gone from 98.6 degrees to a scorching 103 in a matter of seconds. Sweat beads dripped from her forehead, and she couldn't stop her hands and legs from trembling. She had to get outside. Some fresh air would do her good.

After grabbing her coat and purse, she turned the knob on the front door. She could hear Billie call out to her in the distance, but Dylan couldn't turn back now.

She didn't even get into her car. She needed to become one with the wind. Heartbroken, she ran as far away from Billie's house as she could when suddenly she couldn't run anymore. The pink vomit in her throat had returned and was fighting to find a way out. Unable to suppress it, Dylan held her stomach and threw up next to a payphone.

"Why'd you tell me this . . . were you lookin' for my reaction?"
Anita Baker, "You Belong To Me"

3

Emotionally beat down, Dylan entered her South St. Louis townhome and slowly walked up the steps one by one. The sound of her dog, Fuck'em Gurl, barking from her kennel, caused her head to hurt. Not only did she have a throbbing headache, but Dylan couldn't get the sound of her voice saying, "You gettin' married?" out of her head.

Somehow, she never thought she'd utter those words to Angel. She always figured she'd be the one saying, "I do" to him. But life was known for throwing you lemons when all you really wanted was apples. Inside of her kitchen, Dylan placed her clutch on the countertop and stood aimlessly. A part of her wanted to submerse her misery in a pint of Edy's Double Fudge Brownie ice cream, while the other side of her wanted to run upstairs to her room and burst into tears. Neither would solve the problem, yet both options seemed sufficient enough for the situation. Unfortunately for Dylan, the liquid currently building in her eyes won.

Before she knew it, a storm of tears covered the skin of her face, and she realized that from that day onward she would be embarking on her new frontier alone. Angel wouldn't be there to hold her hand or kiss her lips along the way. Now, due to his impending nuptials, Dylan was forced to set fire to any feelings she harbored for him and grow twenty inches tall overnight. Only the notion would be easier than the actual deed.

How in the hell could Angel . . . my Angel . . . be engaged to that . . . that broke-down Selita Ebanks, she wondered as a tear slipped into the corner of her mouth. *He belongs to me.*

"Well, Dylan, you have been broken up thirteen months. When did you think he'd move on?" She spoke out loud to herself as she leaned down on the countertop and cupped her right hand underneath her chin.

"I wonder how long they've been together. Wait!" she shot up.

"What if he was fuckin' her when we slept together? Naw," she shook her head profusely, wiping her eyes. "Angel wouldn't do no shit like that or would he?"

But whether Angel dicked her down while he had a chick was the least of Dylan's worries. Any fantasy or hope that her pregnancy would somehow bring them back together had diminished as soon as Milania opened her big mouth. All of her dreams, wishes, yearnings, and prayers were flushed down the toilet like shit. Just as Dylan's feet began to scream, "Bitch, get me outta these heels," her doorbell rang.

"Who is it?" she yelled from the top of the stairs.

"CoCo and Chanel!" Tee-Tee yelled back.

"Use your key. I don't feel like walkin' down the steps!"

"I swear a pregnant bitch ain't shit," he groaned, digging through his Hermès Birkin bag.

"What are y'all doing here anyway?" she said once he and Bernard made it up the steps. "Why ain't y'all still at Billie's?" She turned her back and wiped her face.

"We had to make sure you wasn't over here on suicide watch." Tee-Tee took off his coat.

"Plus, it's New Year's Eve. We couldn't let you ring in the New Year alone," Bernard added.

"Oh," she said, still trying to pull herself together.

"And plus, Billie's bad-ass kids was gettin' on my damn nerves," Tee-Tee said, putting his stuff down.

Dylan stood quietly and didn't respond.

"I know you ain't actin' funny. What you actin' all weird foe? Ohhhhhhhhh," Tee-Tee figured it out. "'Cause Angel's back in town, and he makes you all anxious like a lesbian at a makeup counter."

"No," she laughed.

"Well, what is it then?" He kissed her cheek and noticed she'd been crying. "Gurrrrrrrrrl." He made her face him. "Don't be over here cryin'."

"I'm okay," she sniffled.

"No, you're not."

"But I will be." Dylan tried her best not to cry. "What's that in them bags?"

"Food, I'm hungry as hell," Bernard answered.

"Awwwwww, y'all really are my bitches."

"You know we got you, boo." Tee-Tee smacked her on her ass.

"And we wanted to gossip," Bernard added.

"Yes, honey!" Tee-Tee flicked his wrist in the air. "So for starters, did you see what Becky had on?"

"Who is Becky?" Dylan eyed him, perplexed.

"Puss 'n Boots, gurl."

"Aw, yeah, I always forget that she has a real name. But no, I wasn't there long enough to see her outfit." Dylan sat on the couch and removed her heels.

"Guuuuurl, homegirl looked worse than them queens on RuPaul's Drag Race."

"Hell, naw, really?" Dylan giggled.

"Yes, gurl. Now forget the preliminaries. Let's get down to the red of the meat. What happened between you, Angel, and Milania?"

"He claim he didn't get the message—"

"That's some bullshit," Tee-Tee cut her off, rolling his eyes.

"Right," Dylan agreed. "I don't believe his ass either."

"So did you tell him you were pregnant?"

"Yep."

"What he say?"

"He asked if I was sure it was his." Dylan screwed up her face, pissed off once again by the thought.

"Weeeell . . ." Tee-Tee shrugged his shoulders.

"I know, I know. I was a ho," she laughed.

"I'm just sayin'," he laughed too.

"Here, sweetie," Bernard handed her a plate full of Thai food.

"Ooh, this looks good. You know, I bet y'all didn't even bring me dessert." Dylan batted her eyes.

"We did, and don't be tryin' to get off the subject. Back to the story, trick," Tee-Tee demanded.

"Oh, where was I?"

"Angel asked you was the baby his." Bernard sat down.

"Oh yeah, right after I chin checked his ass about coming to me like that . . . it was weird." Dylan gazed off into space.

"How?" Tee-Tee asked, dying to know.

"'Cause we kinda just stood there for a minute lookin' at each other, and I swear it was like he was gettin' ready to kiss me."

"Scandalous," Tee-Tee snapped his fingers.

"Then Cruella De Vil entered the room and ruined everything." Dylan took a bite of her food.

"You mean Angel's fiancée, Milania," Bernard commented.

"So y'all know?" Dylan rolled her eyes, chewing.

"Yes, honey," Tee-Tee slapped his hand on her thigh. "As soon as you left, homegirl made the announcement in front of everyone."

"Wow. What did Billie say?"

"Gurl," Tee-Tee cracked up laughing, "Billie almost fainted. The chick was livid. I was afraid for my life."

"Me too," Bernard nodded. "I thought girlfriend was gon' have a Teresa Giudice moment and flip over the table."

"Are you serious?" Dylan asked astonished.

"Yes. From the look on Billie's face, I could tell she wanted to say, 'Fuck New Year's Eve,' and send everybody's ass home," Tee-Tee cracked up laughing.

"Wow, that's crazy," Dylan chuckled.

"She told me to tell you that she was gon' call you as soon as everybody leaves," Tee-Tee said.

"Shit, my ass might fuck around and be asleep. I want nothin' more than for this day to be over." Dylan's bottom lip trembled.

"Awwwwww, pooh-pooh, don't you let that mutha-fucka make you cry." Tee-Tee wrapped his arm around her shoulder. "I know you're hurt."

"No, I'm not," Dylan pouted, wiping her eyes.

"Yes, you are, and it's okay to have wanted y'all's relationship to work, but Angel has moved on. Now it's time for you to do the same. Right now, the only thing that matters is him taking care of his seed."

"And if he don't, we gon' sic the state on his ass," Bernard joked.

"Or better yet, Gloria Allred," Tee-Tee up'd the ante.

"Y'all ass is silly," Dylan held her chest, laughing.

"I told you we got you, boo. We're like Victoria's Secret Wonder bra—we lift each other."

The ten-minute ride back to the Four Seasons Hotel seemed like an eternity for Angel and Milania. She'd tried conjuring up a conversation with him, but her words only landed on deaf ears. Angel was so transfixed on the news of him becoming a father that he couldn't think straight. The entire ride home he replayed his and Dylan's conversation over and over again in his mind. He couldn't even front a part of him was happy about the news, but the other side of him was pissed.

He'd finally come to terms with his unresolved feelings for Dylan, torched them with a match, and never once looked back. He'd settled on being with Milania. With her, he'd found the answer to all his problems. She was his distraction, his place of comfort, his wife-to-be, but now, he had to break the news to her that Dylan, his first love, the one chick who held his heart in the palm of her hand, was pregnant with his child.

Angel didn't know how he was going to tell her, or more important, how she would react. Hell, the news hadn't even settled into his brain yet. He could only imagine how she was going to feel. As they entered the Presidential Suite, Milania admired the layout. The suite consisted of a comfortable living area, a dining room with seating for six, an adjoining pantry, powder room, and an exceptionally spacious master bedroom.

"Well, that was fun," she said sarcastically, throwing her Marc Jacobs patent leather flap bag on the sofa.

For her, the party was an absolute bore, with a capital B. She couldn't get away from Billie and her group of minions fast enough. To her, they were nothing but a gaggle of uppity snoots. On top of that, the whole night Billie kept giving her the stink face. The Bay Area hood chick in Milania wanted to throw shade back, but because Angel was there, she kept her attitude on reserve.

"Soooooo," she spun around on her Dior heels and faced him.

Angel stood at the minibar with his back turned, fixing himself a drink.

"Now that we're alone, do you mind tellin' me what you and ah . . ." she snapped her fingers, "what's her face was doing in your niece's room by yourselves?"

"Yo', let's not do that. Her name is Dylan," Angel snapped unintentionally.

"Okay . . . ah . . . uh." Milania chuckled, taken aback. "I'm not even gonna go there." She licked her bottom lip furious.

"Man, come on, you know her name." He looked at her. "We all know her name. You might as well get use to sayin' it now."

Milania folded her arms across her chest.

"And what the hell is *that* supposed to mean?" She rolled her neck.

Smothered in anxiety, Angel downed the glass of vodka and slammed it down hard on the bar.

"It means she's pregnant!"

"And?" Milania screwed up her face.

"And she gettin' ready to have my baby, so that mean she gon' be around."

"You're kidding me, right?" She pretended to act surprised. "Wait, you mean to tell me that you're actually serious? So, Dylan," Milania made air quotes with her fingers, "tells you she's pregnant by you and you just take her word for it?"

"Yeah, Dylan wouldn't lie about no shit like that."

"I'm sorry, but isn't she the same chick that fucked her ex behind your back?"

"Look, we ain't even gotta go through all of that. The baby is mine point-blank, it is what it is."

"You can stop wit' the attitude. I'm just tryin' to look out for you," Milania countered. "'Cause the last time we started gettin' serious, she got in between us and you broke things off. Now here she comes again! I don't know about you, but I'm not tryin' to see me wit' out

you again. And I'm especially not tryin' to see her play
you out like a fool for the second time.

"Dylan," Milania stressed, making air quotes once
more, "is a snake; she's a liar and a manipulator, and I
will bet everything, including my engagement ring, that
that baby is not yours!"

"Nobody's playin' me. Yeah, Dylan did her dirt, but I
think I know her a li'l bit better than you do." He stepped
past her.

"Wow." Milania threw her hands up, stunned. "Should
we just call the engagement off now 'cause you going
mighty hard for a chick who ain't shit!"

"I'm not going hard for nobody." Angel spun around,
heated. "I'm just tellin' you what it is! I love you!" He
took her by each of her arms and held her close. "And I
wanna marry you . . . not her." Hearing himself say that
out loud stung Angel's heart.

"But the situation is what it is. She's pregnant, and
we have to find a way to deal with it if we talkin' about
living the rest of our lives together. So what I'm sayin'
is . . . is this something you gon' be able to deal with it?"

Milania gazed off to the side and willed herself to
cry. She'd come too far to back out now. For the past
two months, she'd sat idly by, playing the role of the
supportive girlfriend. Angel never had to want for anything. She cooked his food, swallowed his dick, rubbed
his feet, whateva, you name, she'd done it. And her
hard work of sweet-talking him and hypnotizing the
dick was rewarded with the ultimate payoff—a ring.

"I just thought I would be the one having your first
child," she sniffed, lying through her teeth.

Milania would rather chew on hand grenades then
ruin her shape by having a baby.

"Now, because of her, I don't get that opportunity."
She looked up at him somberly and blinked so a tear
would fall.

"Yo', don't even think like that." Angel kissed her forehead.

"But it's true." Milania up'd the ante by burying her face into his chest and shrugging her shoulders profusely.

"I understand what you sayin', but none of that matters to me. We can have as many babies as you like. I just want us to be OK. Tell me we gon' be OK." He pushed her head back so he could look at her face.

Milania swallowed hard and willed herself not to laugh. She couldn't believe her guilt trip was actually working.

"We gon' be okay," she whispered.

"Tell me you love me."

"I love me," she giggled.

"Aww, okay. Somebody got jokes."

"I'm just playin'. You know I love you."

"Prove it." He kissed her so hard that she couldn't breathe.

But Milania loved it when he got rough; the rougher the better. They were there in the middle of the living area, and Milania and Angel went at it like two wild animals. Clothes were flying everywhere as their tongues tangoed in each other's mouths. Fully naked, Angel anxiously forced her to the floor. With Milania on all fours, he quickly put on a condom and inserted himself deep within her walls. A heart-pounding thrust from his pelvis caused her to scream out his name.

"Angel!" Milania moaned, overwhelmed by his size and force.

Angel was a ravaging beast. When making love, he took no mercy, only prisoners. In that moment, he was like a hungry lion searching for his prey and Milania was his victim. Her smooth caramel skin taunted him. He couldn't touch it or kiss it enough. Thrusting his hips, he dug deeper inside her warmness in search of something that would make him feel whole again. Something that would take away the uncertainty of his day. But what he often searched for he never found. With Milania, it was all pleasurable but never fulfilling, so Angel took both of her legs into his hands and flipped her over. Milania's glazed-over eyes gazed back at him. Her eyes pleaded with him to give her more.

Panting, she parted her legs wider, aching for him to reenter her again. When he did she came alive. Every time he plunged his massive, hard dick inside her wet pussy, whimpers of satisfaction fled from her soft lips. Matching his rhythm, Milania rocked slowly to an imaginary beat. The plush carpet burned her butt, but that only added to her experience.

Feeling a nut build in the tip of his dick, Angel arched his back and leaned over Milania. Gripping her hands tightly, he suffocated her with another spellbinding kiss. Angel was moving at such a fast pace that Milania could no longer keep up. Her body was succumbing to the height of sexual bliss. With one more gratifying push and pull of gravity, Angel and Milania released a roaring scream into the otherwise quiet atmosphere. Reeling from their romp, Angel fell over onto his back. His shoulders brushed against Milania's as they collected their breath.

"That was sinful." Milania ran her tongue across her top lip.

"I agree." Angel breathed heavily.

After a brief moment of silence, Angel turned his head and looked at Milania.

"So what now?" he said.

"What do you mean?"

"You gon' ride wit' me or what?"

"I guess . . . I mean," Milania rubbed her forehead. "This whole situation is just out of control. I really just feel at this point that since Dylan is gonna be in our life that she and I should just sit down and get to know each other."

"I don't know about that." Angel shook his head.

"What? Is there something else I should know?" She cocked her head back.

"Nah, I just don't know if Dylan gon' wanna do all that."

"Well, hey, at least I'm puttin' it out there."

"Look, I'll see what I can do." Angel pulled her on top of him and hugged her.

With her face pressed up against his chest, Milania smiled like a Cheshire cat. As long as she kept her scorned fiancée act up, she'd have Angel wrapped around her finger. The next thing on her list was getting Dylan out of her life for good.

"First the Fat Boys break up, now every day I wake up, somebody got a problem with Hov."

Jay-Z, "Ain't No Love"

4

For most women, being pregnant was an exciting adventure. They're filled with excitement and patiently awaiting their bundle of joy, but Dylan honestly couldn't wait for the process to be over. She desperately wanted to be a part of the beaming expectant mothers' club, but Dylan still wasn't even sure what type of mother she would be.

What if she turned out to be an even worse mother than her own? She and her mother Candy weren't even on speaking terms due to the fact that Candy stole $50,000 from her trust fund in order to launch an edible dildo company entitled Eat a Dick. But not speaking to her mother was nothing new. Throughout her entire life, her relationship with her mother had been strained. Candy loved only a few things in life: her whisky, her men, and her money. Dylan, somewhere in between all of that, tried her best to fit in, to no avail.

Because of her mother, Dylan had little to no relationship with her father growing up. She only got to see him twice a year because Candy was determined to pay him back for divorcing and leaving her for a younger woman. Candy would never admit to anyone, not even herself, that she was the reason her marriage went sour. She never acknowledged anything that she did wrong, especially the deep scar of betrayal that she'd etched in Dylan's heart.

When Dylan was five, Candy and her father divorced, and after that, Candy remarried five times. Because of her innate ability to be alone at the age of ten, Dylan was almost molested by one of Candy's many boyfriends. After that, most mothers would have tried to clean up their act but not Candy. Three weeks later, they were in another city, and Candy was under a new man. To escape her mother's craziness, by the time Dylan was thirteen, she was going to nightclubs and smoking weed.

After years of being subjected to Candy's lifestyle, when she turned eighteen, she moved in with her father permanently. Sadly, they only had a few years together before he died and left Dylan with a multimillion-dollar trust fund. Her father was the CEO of his family's well-known brewery company. By the age of twenty-eight, Dylan blew the entire thing.

So, suffice it to say, the last thing Dylan wanted to do was suck at being a mom. She wanted to be like Clair Huxtable or Gloria from *Modern Family*, superstylish and sexy. But every time Dylan looked in the mirror, all she saw was a blob.

From the time she woke up to the moment her head hit the pillow at night she felt blah. Whenever no one was around she found herself crying. She didn't even get excited when it was time for her monthly doctor's visits. This was not how she envisioned herself as a soon-to-be mother. The only thing that seemed to make her a little happy was perusing Web sites like Shopbop, Neiman Marcus, and Bergdorf Goodman. But that happiness faded once she remembered that even the clearance department was too pricey for her.

That afternoon, after a long, uneventful day at the bakery, she came home to find Angel, of all people, on her steps. He was the last person she wanted to see but was the one person who made her remotely want to smile. Dylan stepped out of her used 2006 Saturn Ion and into the crisp air and inhaled deeply. She was not in the mood for no bullshit. Plus, she was tired and ready to lay the hell down. Her feet were killin' her, and she could almost swear her ankles were swollen.

Angel stood up and dusted the back of his Levi jeans off. He and Dylan immediately connected eyes. A smile a mile wide etched across his heart. He hated that she had that affect on him even after all the time that had passed.

"What's up wit' you?" he asked, gazing down at her face.

Remember you do not like him. He is the enemy, Dylan thought.

"You're a sexy beast of a man, and I salivate over you when I'm eating prime ribs."

"What?" he grinned, caught off guard.

OMG, did that really just happen? she thought, clasping her hands over her mouth, paralyzed in embarrassment. *Just pretend like you're asleep. Just pretend like you're asleep.*

"You a'ight?" He eyed her suspiciously.

"Yeah, why wouldn't I be?" Dylan played it off like nothing had happened.

"Yo', you buggin'," Angel chuckled. "But, uh, I just swung through so I could check on you. You know—see if you was good."

"I'm fine, you?"

"I'm good," he laughed.

"What the hell is so funny?"

"You."

"Me?" she pointed at her chest. "I didn't I know was a joke."

"No, but your uniform is," Angel continued to laugh.

A year and half ago, Dylan would never have been caught dead in a uniform unless she was doing some sort of sexual role play.

"You are such a hater," Dylan grinned, waving him off. "There's nothin' wrong with my uniform."

"I'm just fuckin' wit' you. You doing yo' thing, Ma. I'm proud of you." Angel stared deep into her eyes, wondering if the feelings he secretly harbored for her would ever fade away.

"Business good?" he asked trying to remain neutral.

"You know it's wintertime and I am four months pregnant, so I think I should be going in the house before I catch hypoglycemic." Dylan did her best to avoid the conversation. She didn't feel like explaining that she blew at being an entrepreneur.

"You mean hypothermia?" he eyed her.

"Yeah, that too. You coming in?"

"Nah," Angel shook his head and laughed. "I just wanted to check wit' you real quick. I got a conference call wit' my agent in thirty minutes."

"Oh, okay," Dylan responded slightly disappointed.

"But I did wanna find out when your next doctor's appointment was."

"At the beginning of next month. We'll be learning the sex of the baby. What—you wanna come?"

"Of course. I wouldn't miss it for the world."

"Good," Dylan gave him a warm smile.

"I want you to understand, even though I'm gettin' married—"

"Ugh, please, don't ruin the moment," Dylan cut him off, covering her ears. The last thing she wanted to talk about was Angel getting married.

"Nah, seriously," he pulled her hands down, "you and the baby are my number-one priority."

"I don't think Milania would appreciate you sayin' that."

"Milania understands. As a matter of fact, she's fully on board and wants to be involved."

"*Involved?*" Dylan screwed up her face. "Involved like what?"

"Chill. She just wants to have lunch wit' you so y'all can get to know each another better."

"I know enough about Miss Thang. I'm good."

"C'mon, Dylan, for me." He held her hand close to his heart.

Dylan knew deep down inside that his romantic gesture really didn't mean a thing, but for a split second, she imagined that Angel was still hers and that in that moment he would take her into his arms, kiss her on the lips passionately, and they would ride off into the rosy sunset. But then, reality kicked in and she remembered that he was in love with another and she was four months pregnant and miserable.

"Okay. I'll go, but she better not start trippin'."

"I promise she won't." Angel kissed her on the cheek. "This is gonna be good for all of us."

"Mmm-hmm, we'll see."

Out of everything in life outside of her man, her Louboutins, and her friends, Billie loved her children the most. They were her pride and joy, and if need be, she would gladly lay down her life for them. Billie stood in front of the window, patiently awaiting their arrival. It was Sunday, and the kids were returning from their routine weekend trip to their father's house. She couldn't wait to see their little chubby faces. Finally, Cain's car pulled up. Billie couldn't get to the door fast enough. Seconds later, after Cain hugged and kissed the kids good-bye, they were walking through the door. Billie's children were absolutely adorable.

The twins, Kenzie and Kaylee, were nine going on thirty. They possessed their mother's timeless good looks and sharp tongue. Both girls' skin was the shade of roasted almond butter, and they both had long, wild, curly brown hair. Kyrese, on the other hand, was eleven with the color of rich cocoa. He rocked a low cut and a diamond stud earring in his ear.

"Hi, Ma," he spoke.

"Hi. How was your weekend?" Billie kissed him on the cheek.

"It was all right. I mostly just played the game by myself."

"Oh," Billie replied, hoping that Cain would've done something productive with him.

"Well, what did you two ladies do?" Billie turned to her daughters.

"Where do I begin?" Kaylee put down her overnight bag in an overly dramatic way and stood back on one leg. "Mama-Mama-Mama-Mama. Giiiiiiiiirl, let me tell you! We been tryin' to rock wit' this whole custody thing on the strength of you, but yo' girl, Becky, is trippin'."

"Trippin', like what?" Billie said, ready to pounce.

"Mama," Kenzie joined in, "the chick must think she Alicia Keys 'cause she done went and did the unthinkable. Now brace yourself. Wait for it, wait for it," Kenzie did her best Steve Irwin impression. "She asked us to call her 'Mama.' Boom! There it is, I said. It's out there, can't take it back."

"Oh, *no*, she didn't." Billie drew her head back.

"Oh, *yes*, she did." Kenzie rolled her neck.

"But don't worry, Mama. We shut that mess down like a bad Ferris wheel," Kaylee assured her. "I told her, 'Look-a-here, lady,'" she stomped her foot and pointed her finger. "My mama is at 5555 Fifteenth Street. And as far as we are concerned, you ain't nothin' but a stranger up in this house."

"Okay, y'all go on upstairs and put yo' stuff up," Billie fumed. "Mama gotta wreck shop."

Once the kids were out of sight and out of earshot, Billie went into the kitchen and dialed Cain's house number.

"Hello?" Becky answered.

"I always knew you had a screw loose, but apparently you missing a nut and a bolt too—" Billie hissed, "'cause you done lost yo' damn mind."

"Excuse me?" Becky snapped.

"Oh, honey, you're excused! Let me make one thing clear so we never have to have this conversation again! Kaylee, Kenzie, and Kyrese are my kids! Not yours but mine! I pushed they bad asses out so I at least get the consolation prize of them callin' *me* mama, and not some jump-off that done finagled her way into becoming my ex-husband's wife! If you want somebody to call you mama, have yo' own damn kids! Better yet, go get you a monkey, a parrot, something! Train one of them muthafuckas to call you mama 'cause these over here got one mama, and that's me!"

"You know what, Billie? It's obvious that you're jealous of me. But I'm not tryin' to take your place as their mother. I'm simply tryin' to bring us all closer together. So if you want to continue to build a wedge between our two families, then go right ahead."

"Bitch, you can stop it wit' all the blended family bullshit. 'Cause I ain't Sheree, and you for damn sure ain't Jada." Billie referred to Will Smith's ex-wife and current wife.

"Whateva. I don't have time for this. Tell the kids we love them, and we'll see them this weekend," Becky hung up in her ear.

"Heffa," Billie spat, hanging up the phone as well.

"That's the same thing I said," Kenzie shook her head,
entering the room.

Anxiously awaiting Milania's arrival, Dylan sat alone
by the window at Bar Italia sipping on lemon water.
Homegirl was twenty minutes late and with each second that passed Dylan grew more and more pissed
off. Hell, she didn't even know why she was there. She
didn't owe Milania a damn thang. To her, the chick was
nothin' more than a jump-off searching for her next
come up and Angel was her victim. Dylan couldn't even
imagine their so-called relationship going the distance.

If they made it to the altar and actually got married,
pigs were sure to fly. *But then again, maybe the sleaze-
bag does genuinely love him,* Dylan thought as a black
Lincoln Town Car pulled up to the side of the curb causing passersby to stop and stare and a slew of paparazzi to
arrive out of nowhere. Just like in a horror film, the hairs
on the back Dylan's neck stood up as Angel's faithful
driver, Tony, who once used to chauffer Dylan around,
opened the door for Milania. Unconsciously, Dylan held
her breath as Milania stepped out into full view.

Dylan would never admit to anyone, but in terms of
fashion, the chick was killin' the game. The Michael Kors
black feathered mink peplum jacket, spandex skirt, and
Christian Louboutin double platform pumps were off
the chain and most definitely something Dylan would've
gravitated to when she had the funds to splurge. After
stopping and taking a few photos for the paps, Milania made her way inside the restaurant while talking
on the phone. As the hostess guided Milania to their
table, Dylan imagined that the blue and white striped

oversized slouchy T-shirt, jeggings, cuffed high-heeled booties, and cross body bag from H&M she wore was straight from the runway. But the closer Milania neared and the faster Dylan's heart began to race, the less confident she became.

"Yeah, I'm here. Let me handle this real quick and I'ma call you back. Okay, doll, smooches." She blew a kiss into the phone before ending the call.

"Hello," Milania spoke energetically as she sat down and took off her Versace shades.

"Hi," Dylan responded, unable to take her eyes off Milania's zebra print Lauren Merkin clutch.

"Luv the shoes," Milania pointed down at Dylan's feet.

"Thanks," Dylan replied, caught off guard by her kindness.

Maybe this bitch ain't the tin man after all. Maybe she does have a heart.

"Yeah, I have some just like it except mine are designer and not the knock-off version, of course."

I wonder if I would go to jail for stabbing a ho, Dylan pondered.

"So how are you?" Milania said to Dylan while waving to someone she knew across the room.

"Good, you?" Dylan responded dryly.

"I'm wonderful, planning for the wedding. You know how that is . . . oops, sorry, you don't. But look, enough about me. First off, thank you for coming."

"Yeah, I've been waiting for like half an hour."

"Really?" Milania said sarcastically.

"Yes, really," Dylan snapped back. "And what's up with the photogs?"

"Please, believe the paparazzi is the least of your worries, but that's neither here nor there." Milania placed her elbows onto the table and clasped her hands together. "I invited you here because I wanted to make something perfectly clear so that you and I are on the same page. I don't like you, I will *never* like you, nor do I want to get to like you. As a matter of fact, I can't stand the sight of your face."

"Excuse me?" Dylan glared at her with venom in her eyes as the paparazzi took pictures of them through the window.

"Oh, honey, you're excused, but let me explain something to you. This is you," Milania placed her left hand down low.

"And this is me," she raised her right hand high. "Whateva you and Angel had going on is over. He's with me now and nothin' about that is gonna change unless I want it to, so you," she pointed her index finger at Dylan, "and that baby of yours, need to kick rocks wit' open-toed shoes on. And I know that you think your li'l cutesy girl antics are gonna bring him back, but they're not. Sweetie, you're a joke to us. We sit up and laugh at you. But see, I actually have a heart. 'Cause I honestly feel sorry for you. Sometimes I say to myself, Lord, please help that poorly, cheaply dressed woman."

For a second, Dylan sat there thinking, *Is this really happening?* Because no way did Milania invite her to lunch to cuss her out. *This chick must have a death wish, or better yet, is plain crazy,* Dylan thought. But once she realized that what she was experiencing was real and not a bad dream, Dylan instantaneously kicked into cuss-a-bitch-out mode.

"Look, bitch," Dylan placed her shoulders back. "I don't give a fuck about you likin' me. 'Cause frankly, I don't like you either. As a matter of fact, who are you?"

"I'm a Victoria Secret model, thank you very much," Milania retorted, squinting her eyes.

"Bitch, you in the catalog on page 97 of the clearance section modeling a mock turtleneck. Don't nobody know you," Dylan frowned.

"It don't matter if nobody knows me. They will once I'm Angel's wife. And at the end of the day when it's all said and done, you're the one pregnant lookin' stupid wit' no man, no nothin'."

"Don't you know I eat bitches like you for breakfast?" Dylan leaned forward and glared in Milania's eyes. "And if you really think for one second that Angel is gonna marry you, then you're dumber than you look. You're nothin' but a rebound, and once Angel realizes what a gold-digging skank you are, he's gonna drop yo' ass like Buck got dropped from G-Unit. Now get the fuck outta my face, prostitution whore. Spandex hurts my eyes."

"Are you done?" Milania replied sarcastically to try to make Dylan believe that her words didn't sting.

"I was done the moment you walked yo' stank ass up in here."

"Check, please." Milania signaled the waiter, grabbing her clutch. "Consider this a favor. Lunch is on me," she dropped a stack of money on the table. "Now, stay the fuck away from Angel," she shot over her shoulder, walking toward the door.

"Have you figured out what you'd like, ma'am?" The waiter asked with his notepad out.

"Tell me, do you all have public humiliation on the menu?" Dylan asked in a daze.

"Yes, honey, I had it for an appetizer."

"Feels like I'm broken and you're not here to fix me up."
K. Michelle "Fallin'"

5

Milania sat with the window slightly cracked, puffing on an L as the car took leave from the restaurant. DJ Khaled's "All I Do Is Win" bumped loudly from the speakers. To most, the catfight she initiated with Dylan would've been a dumb move, but every move Milania made was calculated and never out of character. The dispute wouldn't push her and Angel apart, but bring them closer together. Milania was willing to bet money on it. And, yeah, Angel would suffer from her devilish ways, but everything Milania did was for his own good.

With Dylan out of the way, he'd be more focused on their impending nuptials, therefore, helping elevate her status and career, which was blowing up by the day. Milania had offers coming in from everywhere. She'd been the cover girl for *Harper's Bazaar*, *Cosmopolitan*, and *Complex* magazine. She'd even become Marc Jacobs's new muse.

Nearing the hotel, Milania put out her blunt, dowsed herself in perfume, and popped a piece of Spearmint gum. Angel hated smokers. As Tony helped her carry her shopping bags up to the suite, Milania prepared herself for the performance of her life. With her room key out, she placed it in the door and thought about the one thing in life that would make her actually cry, which was being poor.

By the time the door was open and her right foot had crossed the threshold, a stream of tears graced her lovely face. To Milania's surprise, she found Angel standing in the middle of the living area talking on his cell phone with an angry expression on his face. *Damn, that bitch didn't waste no time, did she?* Milania thought. But when Angel turned and noticed the tears sliding from her eyes, any worries that Dylan had got to tell her version of the story first was put to rest when Angel said, "Ay, let me call you back. My girl just walked in upset. What's with the tears?" he asked, ending his call.

"I tried so hard to get along with her, but she was just so nasty." Milania rushed into his arms, sobbing.

"What happened?" Angel held her close.

"I told her that at first I had difficulty dealing with the fact that you and her were having a baby, but that now I was on board and wanted to be a part of the experience any way I could. I even went so far as to go to City Sprouts and buy the baby some things," she pointed toward the door at the bags.

"But she wasn't having it. She called me a prostitution whore and said that she didn't like me, that I was a rebound, and that you weren't really going to marry me."

"Word?" Angel asked furiously.

"Yes," Milania wailed.

"Hold up," Angel released her from his hold and dialed Dylan's number.

She answered on the first ring.

"I was just about to call you," she said taking off her black peacoat.

"Yo', when you met up wit' Milania, did you call her a prostitution whore?"

"I sure as hell did."

"I thought the whole point of y'all gettin' together was so y'all could try to get along?"

"Umm, it was, but—"

"But nothin'," Angel shouted, furious. "That shit wasn't necessary."

"Hold up," Dylan's upper lip curled. "Who in the hell do you think you're talkin' to? She's the one that came to lunch wit' an ole aggressive-ass attitude, actin' all high saddity like I owed her something!" she yelled into the phone, snapping her neck.

"Yo', you can go head wit' all that neck poppin' and lip smackin' you doing," Angel barked, knowing her all too well. "All I was tryin' to do is get both of you on the same page for the sake of this baby, but you can't even be adult enough to do that."

"You know what? I ain't got time for this BS," Dylan scoffed. "You gon' sit up here and chastise me like I'm a fuckin' child over a bitch you've known five seconds! She's the one who came at me crazy, and you damn right I called her a prostitution whore, a skank, and a bitch too! Fuck her and fuck you! Now get the fuck off my line!" she snapped, mashing the end button on her cell phone.

"Stupid bitch make me sick. I wish I wasn't pregnant so I wouldn't have to deal wit' her ass or him." Dylan shook her head trying her best not to cry but a bucketful of tears had already begun to spill down her cheeks.

Seeing her in tears, Fuck'em Gurl ran over to Dylan and stood on her hind legs so she would pick her up, but Dylan wasn't in the mood, so she ignored her.

"I can't believe that he would even have the audacity to believe her word over mine. I just wish this shit would be over already," she sniffed, wiping her nose. "I can't take this shit anymore." She held her head back and cried.

Everything seemed to be falling down around her at once. Her business was failing miserably, therefore affecting her livelihood. Disconnect notices swarmed her mailbox daily. Hell, Dylan didn't even have health insurance. Every time she visited the doctor, she paid out of pocket, and she'd be damned if she'd ask Angel for a dime with the way he was acting.

And sure, Tee-Tee or Billie would gladly give her a loan, but Dylan couldn't bear looking like a failure to them once again. That, coupled along with how she would provide for a child she wasn't even sure she wanted and a baby father who she loved more than life itself who was acting like a goddamn fool was too much to handle.

If Dylan could, she would gladly fall asleep and never wake up again. But just when death became the best solution to her problems, a sharp pain raced throughout her lower stomach. Writhing in pain, Dylan slowly made her way over to the bed to call 911. It felt like she was having the worst menstrual cramp anyone could experience in life, and with each second that passed the feeling got worse.

Oh God, please help me, Dylan said, doubled over in agony as she felt a warm sensation slide down her leg. She couldn't handle the realization that she might lose the baby. Yes, for months she'd secretly loathed the baby, but now she felt nothing but worry and regret.

An hour later, Dylan lay nervously in a hospital bed with an IV in her arm and a heart monitor on her belly awaiting the emergency room doctor's return. A million and one thoughts ran through her mind, like, what if the baby had died or if it were still alive, would it have brain damage or Down syndrome. Deciding the best thing to do was take matters into her own hands, Dylan did the one thing she hardly ever did: pray.

Hey, God, she closed her eyes and pressed her palms together. *How are you? I pray that all is well 'cause it's surely not with me. Look, Big Guy, I know that I don't talk to you that much, but please, I'm askin' you, please don't let me lose my baby. And I know that you're probably rollin' your eyes at me right now and sayin' to the überfabulous Lena Horne, this chile better make up her mind 'cause an hour ago she said that she didn't want it. But God, I do. I really, really do. I want my baby more than I want a pair of Giuseppe shoes. This baby is all I have, and I promise I'm gonna do right by it. Just please, please, don't take my baby. I love you more than I love Prada, amen.*

Opening her eyes, Dylan inhaled deeply and hoped that God would answer her prayers when the door opened. She hoped it was Billie and Tee-Tee. She'd called them right after dialing 911. Instead, she found the doctor.

"Hey, Doc, got any good news?" she asked on pins and needles.

"Well, Dylan," Dr. Crane looked over his chart. "Your cervix is closed, and I don't see any evidence of a rupture or miscarriage."

"Thank you, Jesus." Dylan gave a great sigh of relief. "So what was that warm liquid that came out of me?"

"Just a little pee," Dr. Crane said with a laugh.

"Oh," she placed her hand on her chest, appalled.

"But I'd like to do an ultrasound just to make sure." He gave her a warm smile.

"Cool . . . but you might wanna know before you go down under that I haven't had a proper bikini wax in months, so it might be like *Thrilla in Manila* down there."

"Okay," Dr. Crane laughed, leaving the room.

"Dylan!" Billie rushed past him frantic with Tee-Tee two steps behind her.

"Hey," she smiled.

"Are you okay?" Billie gave her a big bear hug.

"Yeah, the doctor just told me that I was fine."

"Good. Girl, you had me worried sick." Billie playfully hit her on the arm.

"Me too," Tee-Tee popped his lips. "'Cause I was about to be mad as hell if I was gon' have to take back all that stuff I done bought for that baby."

"Tee-Tee, what in the hell have you bought my baby?" Dylan asked, intrigued.

"None of yo' damn business. You'll find out when we have the shower."

"Billie, did you call Angel like I asked you?" Dylan asked.

"Yeah," Billie answered. "He's on the way."

Although Dylan was upset with him, she knew that he deserved to know what was going on with the baby.

"So tell me, girl, what the hell happened when you met wit' Milania today." Tee-Tee sat at the end of the bed.

"Ooh, yeah, I wanna know too." Billie took a seat in a chair.

"I swear to God, y'all, the only thing I hate more than drugstore makeup is that bitch," Dylan said with a sudden fierceness.

"What happened?" Billie asked, dying to know.

"That heffa is playin' Angel for a fool. She never wanted us to get along. Her mission was to get me alone so she could tell my ass the fuck off."

"What she say?" Tee-Tee drew his head back ready to cut a bitch.

"First of all, I think the bitch told the paparazzi where we were meeting," Dylan pointed out.

"Are you serious?"

"Yes, so you know every gossip rag in America is going to know that I'm pregnant now."

"That's a mess, but tell us what she said," Tee-Tee insisted.

"She told me she ain't like me and some shit about her being up here," she raised her left hand up high. "And me being down here," she placed her right down low.

"Oh no, she didn't," Billie gasped.

"Oh yes, she did. She said that she and Angel sit up and laugh at me and that they feel sorry for me and that Angel is hers and that nothin' about that is gonna change unless she wants it to."

"Get the . . ." Tee-Tee inhaled deep. "Outta here."

"Yes, ma'am, that bitch was out for blood."

"Wow, I knew there was something about her that I couldn't vibe wit'," Billie confessed.

"I'm tellin' y'all, I can't stand her. It's like I'm Jennifer Aniston, and she's Angelina Jolie. And I so wanna be Angelina Jolie," Dylan whined.

"Oooh, friend." Tee-Tee rubbed her thigh.

"Do you know that that trick called me . . . oh my God, this is so hurtful." Dylan fanned her eyes so she wouldn't cry. "A poorly dressed woman."

"Oh, hellllllll, no! I'ma kick her ass," he fumed.

"Bitch had the nerve to sit up there and talk about me while her neck lookin' like Kimora Lee Simmons and shit." Dylan fumed with anger.

"What her neck look like?" Billie egged her on, laughing.

"Like a pack of pork sausages," Dylan replied.

"Yo' ass is silly!" Tee-Tee laughed too.

"So what my brother have to say when you told him?" Billie quizzed.

"Oh, baby, I didn't even get a chance to tell him anything because as soon as I got home he was on my phone tellin' me off too," Dylan's nostrils flared.

"You're joking, right?" Billie said in disbelief.

"No, that heffa went home and lied on me, and your brother, for whatever reason, ate that shit up. I didn't even get a chance to explain myself. I was so pissed off that I went off on him, then hung up. Right after that, that's when my stomach started to hurt," Dylan said visibly upset.

"I'ma tear his ass a new one as soon as he step foot in here," Billie assured her.

"Don't say nothin' to him, Billie. It's not even worth it."

"Oh, but I am."

"When I see him, I'ma say somethin' to him too," Tee-Tee crossed his legs. "To me, he's the reason why you're in here in the first place. Angel should've known better than to call you wit' that mess."

"You're right," Dylan nodded. "But I've been under a lot of stress lately. It could've been a number of things that made me go in the hospital."

"I still blame him. But on a brighter note, I got good news, y'all. The home study process of the adoption is over!"

"Good. So everything is straight?" Billie made sure before she got her hopes up.

"Yes, and the adoption agency has found us a baby already!" Tee-Tee raised his hands in the air and waved them around.

"You're kidding me?" Dylan beamed.

"No, the girl is seven months pregnant, and she's having a girl," he cheered.

"Oooooh, Tee-Tee congratulations!" Billie hugged him.

"Thank you. We are sooo excited." Tee-Tee grinned from ear to ear.

"I am too," Dylan cooed. "That means we're going to be new mommies together."

"I know, gurl, I'm so happy! But anyway, y'all want something?" Tee-Tee rose from the bed. "I'm gettin' ready to go get me something to drink."

"Get me a bottle of water, please." Billie went into her purse and grabbed a dollar bill.

"You want something," Tee-Tee asked Dylan.

"No, I'm good."

"All right. I'll be right back."

Standing at the vending machine, Tee-Tee inserted his money into the machine and pressed E10 when he noticed Angel getting off the elevator.

Dirty dog, Tee-Tee snarled, rolling his eyes.

"What's going on, Tee?" Angel approached him with a look of worry on his face. "Is she okay?"

"Mmm-hmm." Tee-Tee eyed him up and down.

"Is the baby cool?"

"Yep." Tee-Tee stood back on one leg and popped his lips.

Angel let out a sigh of relief, unaware that Tee-Tee had beef with him.

"Good. What room she in?" Angel asked.

"Angel," Tee-Tee placed his hand on his hip, "we not cool."

"What?" Angel screwed up his face.

"Did I stutter? You heard me," Tee-Tee replied mockingly.

"Yo', I ain't got time for this." Angel waved him off, not in the mood for a bunch of back and forth. "Just tell me what room she's in."

"So you can yell at her some more? I think not," Tee-Tee checked him. "Personally, I don't see why she wanted Billie to call you in the first place. 'Cause if I were her, I wouldn't want to have shit to do wit' yo' ass."

"Well, you ain't her," Angel shot back.

"You damn right I ain't." Tee-Tee countered. "That girl has been going through hell, and all you've been concerned with is yourself. Do you know how hard all of this has been on her? She loves you beyond belief and although she doesn't talk about it, I know seeing you with another woman has been torture. And although it's been over between y'all for some time now and my cousin knows she will never get you back, she's still been tryin' to make things right with you. And what do you do? Give her yo' ass to kiss. So why don't you do Dylan and your baby a favor and turn around and walk right back outta here 'cause you're more drama than she needs right now."

Angel clenched his jaw and swallowed hard. Outside of his sister, nobody ever stepped to him to tell him off. Most people were afraid of him and had every reason to be, but he couldn't front. Every word out of Tee-Tee's mouth had been the truth, and Angel couldn't fight it or argue with it. He hadn't been there for Dylan like he should have. Hell, he hadn't even been to a doctor's appointment with her and because of their miscommunication, he'd missed the first four and a half months of her pregnancy. And now after being so busy tryin' to prove that he was over her, he'd almost pushed her to the brink of losing their baby.

Angel couldn't fight it anymore. The hold Dylan had on his heart strings would always outweigh the strong feelings he had for Milania. But for his own sanity, the well-being of Dylan, and the health of their baby, Angel had to learn how to balance his emotions for both women without hurting them until he figured out what to do next.

It would be a difficult task, but he had to do it. The first step to doing so would be to stick his tail between his legs and leave like Tee-Tee had suggested. Maybe some time away would give Dylan a chance to cool off and clear her mind. By doing so, hopefully, she'd see that Angel wasn't trying to disrespect her but ride for his fiancée like he would've done for her.

"Just tell her I'm sorry," he said genuinely from the bottom of his heart.

"Mmm-hmm," Tee-Tee grabbed his bottle of water, turned, and walked away.

"What took you so long?" Dylan asked as he walked back into the room.

"The machine got stuck," he lied, avoiding eye contact.

Lying was something Tee-Tee hardly ever did 'cause he was a tell-it-like-it-is kinda girl, but to him, the added stress of having Angel around was just no good for Dylan in his opinion. She needed to rest and get her mind right, and with Angel all up in her grill, she would never get things back on track. For now, what Dylan didn't know wouldn't hurt her.

"Where the hell is my bottle of water?" Billie gave him a once-over glance.

"Shit, my bad. I forgot. Here, you can have mine." He tried to hand it to her.

"Do it look like I wanna taste yo' husband's dick on my lips?"

Dylan held her stomach and cracked up laughing.

"Heffa, please. You wish you could get a taste." Tee-Tee stuck his index finger in his mouth and slide it back out slowly.

"Stop. You gon' make me go into premature labor," Dylan giggled uncontrollably, still holding her stomach.

"That's his ass. He get on my nerve," Billie said, checking her cell phone which was ringing.

It was Cain calling. Instead of answering, she sent him to voice mail.

"Who was that?" Dylan asked, being nosy.

"Cain."

"Why you ain't answer?"

"'Cause he's only callin' to say something to me about going off on Becky," Billy said simply.

"Why you go off on her now?" Tee-Tee laughed.

"'Cause the kids came home today and told me that sleazeball had the nerve to ask them kids to call her mama," Billie shouted, feeling her body tense up all over again.

"Oh, hell, no!" Tee-Tee shot up. "Where my Vaseline at 'cause we about to go body slam this ho!"

"No need. I already bodied her ass, and if Cain keep callin' me, his ass gon' get it too. Besides, I ain't got time for neither one of them."

"Okay, Dylan, are you ready?" Dr. Crane reentered the room.

"Yes," she replied, excited as the nurse squeezed a cold, clear, jellylike substance on her stomach.

"I think I used some of that last night," Tee-Tee smirked, winking his eye.

"I just bet you did," Billie shot him a look of disgust.

"Do you wanna know the sex of the baby?" Dr. Crane asked.

"Ah, duh, team girl over here, holla," Dylan raised the roof.

After a few minutes of silence the doctor said, "Sorry. Seems like we won't be able to find out today. The little one is not being very cooperative, but from what I see, he or she is progressing very well."

"That's all that matters anyway," Billie gazed in amazement at the screen.

"Can I see?" Dylan said, dying with anticipation.

"Of course," Dr. Crane turned the screen to face her.

"Holy shit balls," Dylan shook her head in amazement. "I'm having a baby, you guys." She teared up.

"The heart looks good, and the spinal cord is perfect. Everything is just fine," Dr. Crane assured her once more.

"Thank you, Dr. Crane," Dylan pursed her lips together and cried.

"You're welcome. A nurse will be in in just a second with your discharge papers." He gave her a warm smile before leaving.

"Okay," Dylan's chest heaved up and down.

"You all right?" Tee-Tee poked out his bottom lip making a sad face.

"Yeah," she nodded. "I just wish Angel was here, that's all," she wiped her eyes.

Tee-Tee swallowed the lump in his throat. Maybe sending Angel away wasn't the best idea. But the deed had already been done, and if he told Dylan the truth now, she'd get upset and Tee-Tee couldn't risk her experiencing any more pain that might harm the baby.

"You know we got yo' back," Billie kissed her on the cheek, thinking it would be a cold day in hell before she spoke to her brother again.

"I know. It's just so funny that most of my life I've spent my time tryin' to find some man to take care of me, and now I have to take care of somebody else. Like, how am I gonna raise a child? Before I became a somewhat responsible adult, my role models were Britney Spears wit' her shaved head and Lindsey Lohan who now looks like something out of *The Lord of the Rings*."

"Stop!" Tee-Tee snorted. "You're going to be a great mom."

"I hope so. I just know that whatever kind of mother I'm gonna be, I'm gonna be ten times better than what Candy was to me. I'm gonna do whatever it takes to provide for my baby. I'm gonna pinch pennies, and I'm gonna save. Well, I don't really know what pinch pennies means, but I'm gonna save," Dylan pointed her index finger to prove her point. "Like, do I actually have to pinch pennies?"

"No, honey," Billie inhaled deeply. "No."

"C'mon, girl," Tee-Tee giggled. "Let's get you dressed. I know that baby of yours is dying for some Popeyes chicken."

"Hell, yeah!" Dylan pumped her fist in the air with excitement.

The clock hanging from the wall opposite Billie's bed read 3:15 A.M., but sleep was the furthest thing from her mind. After getting Dylan home from the hospital, she came home and prepared dinner for her kids since it was the chef's day off. Then she went straight to work deciding which new pieces to put on display at the St. Louis Art Museum since she was their new curator and finding donations for her Inner-City Kids' Scholarship Foundation.

This was an everyday routine for Billie. Her life was always hectic, but the sick thing about it was she enjoyed it. Billie got off on being pulled into a million different directions. It made her feel needed and like she was contributing something to the world. Unlike the 1990s R&B singer Karen White, she wanted to be equivalent to superwoman. She wanted to do it all, take care of her kids, decorate her house, be a good wife, dedicate time to her friends, and add a little sparkle to the universe through art and fashion.

Knox exited the master bath, dressed in only his boxers, and stood speechless. Since he'd gotten home from his night job as a bartender, Billie had been in bed with her glasses on overseeing paperwork for her various philanthropic work. Every night it was the same routine. He'd come home, and she'd be enthralled in paperwork. Knox was happy that she took time to help others, but Billie sometimes forgot that their relationship needed work too.

"You not done wit' that stuff yet?" Knox said, walking over to the bed and climbing in.

"No," Billie answered, not even bothering to look up.

"It's," Knox gazed up at the clock, "3:25, Billie. Enough is enough. It seem like every time I see you, you got some sort of paperwork in your hand." He took some of the papers off her lap.

"No-no-no," Billie snatched them back. "Just give me like thirty more minutes and I'll be done."

"Fuck a half an hour. I want some head now." He placed her hand on his rock-hard penis and smiled.

"Man, please, you better get yo' ass away from me."

"No, seriously, I really think you should give me some head. Jesus just put that on my heart and told me to tell you that."

"Baby," Billie doubled over laughing, taking off her glasses, "not now. I'm tryin' to finish this," she protested.

"I understand you got a lot on your plate, but Billie, c'mon, you ain't gave me no pussy in almost three weeks. Shit, in a minute my dick gon' fall off."

"You really need to stop exaggerating." Billie resumed working. "Sidebar," she quickly changed the subject. "Do you know what the twins told me today?"

"What?"

"That Becky asked them to start callin' her mommy."

"What?" Knox screwed his face up, surprised.

"Yeah, that's the same thing I said. Can you believe that heffa?"

"What you do?"

"I called and chin checked that ho. I told her she better have her own pack of wolves 'cause these bebes over here are all mine."

"Wow, that's crazy. Did you tell Cain?"

"Yeah, after I got done dealing with Dylan."

"What he say?"

"That he was gon' talk to her. Whateva *that* means," Billie pursed her lips.

"Well, that's all that can be done about it now, so don't even trip. The kids know who their mama is. Besides Kyrese, Kenzie, and Kaylee ain't going for that no way. Now back to you," Knox scooted closer. "You gon' give me some or what?"

"Really, Knox? Nooooo," Billie eased away.

"Word?" he spoke, stunned.

"I'm not sayin' it like that. It's just that I'm—"

"What? Let me guess, you too tired?" he remarked.

"Uh, yeah." She looked at him as if he were dumb.

"A'ight, Billie." He rolled over to his side of the bed.

"What?" She raised her hands up, confused.

"Ever since we got back from the honeymoon, you have shown me zero amounts of affection. Our sex life has gone down the toilet. Shit, when was the last time you even hugged me?"

Billie racked her brain and tried to conjure up a memory.

"Exactly. You can't even remember. Look, I'm not tryin' to be all up under you or no shit like that. I just want you to understand that I miss my wife. And hopefully, my wife misses me too."

"I do," she kissed him softly on the lips.

"Then show me." He tried to pull her close.

"I want to, I just really gotta get this stuff done." She pushed him away again.

"That's cool." Knox turned over, fed up.

He was over trying to get her to see that he needed her time and affection. Billie was so busy trying to be a 5-star chick that she was neglecting the one person who needed her the most. It was like once Knox put a ring on her finger, she forgot that their relationship had to be worked on every second of the day. Instead, everything was all about her.

She never asked how he was feeling or what his day was like. It was always, "I have to do this," and "I have to be here," or "the kids need this." Life was never about the two of them. All he wanted was for her to take a moment to breathe and smell the roses, but until Billie realized that with each second of the day she was pushing her husband further and further away, Knox would keep his distance and bottle his feelings up inside until they exploded.

"Yeah I like such and such yo a lot but the feeling's not as strong."

Common, "I Want You"

6

A glimpse of spring shined from the sky as the sun kissed the hood of Angel's silver Porsche Panamera 4. But warm weather didn't mean a thing to him. For several days Angel had been in a funk. News had broken that he and Milania were engaged to be married while his ex was pregnant with his baby. Every entertainment news show, blog, and magazine was covering the story. They had photos of Milania and Dylan's heated confrontation, which resulted in Milania storming out in tears.

Angel couldn't go anywhere without seeing or hearing about the so-called scandal. All of the media attention was driving him nuts. It tore him up inside that he couldn't even turn to his sister during this trying time. Billie was disgusted with him, and she had every right to be. Angel felt horrible for the way he treated Dylan. She was the mother of his unborn child. She didn't deserve that kind of treatment. Angel just had to figure out a way to get things between them back cool again because it seemed like instead of bringing them closer together, her pregnancy was pulling them further apart.

It all made no sense to him. This was supposed to be the most exciting time of his life. He was marrying one of the world's most beautiful women and becoming a father, but Angel didn't feel bliss. He felt stressed and confused. He wanted to do right by Milania and stick to his word and marry her, but every time he thought about taking that leap down the aisle, buried feelings for Dylan started to arise.

Angel pulled up to the restaurant where he was meeting Milania for lunch, turned off the engine, and stepped out into the spring air. All eyes were on him but in a good way. St. Louisians loved their hometown hero and showed him nothing but love. Angel, in turn, showed them love by hosting and donating to various charities and giving back to his community. To Angel's dismay as he activated the alarm on his car, ten paparazzi appeared and began taking his picture and asking him questions.

"Angel, how does your fiancée feel knowing your ex is using her pregnancy to tear you two apart?" one photographer asked.

"Angel, do you think your baby will be born half alien or half werewolf?" someone from TMZ asked.

"Hey, Angel, are you a fan of Glee?" another photographer questioned.

"Angel, do you think that boxing should have mandatory drug testing during training camp?"

Instead of answering any of their questions or even acknowledging their presence, he held his head up high and entered the restaurant. After checking with the hostess, Angel was escorted to his table which was in the private dining section of the restaurant. To his surprise, he found Milania talking on the phone while sitting a table with two other people.

"Miss Fairchild, the rest of your party has arrived," the hostess said politely.

"Hey, doll, he's here. Let me call you back." Milania hung up the phone.

"Hi, honey," she stood up to greet him, dressed casually chic in a white silk Elie Tahari blouse with an asymmetrical fold-over collar, black Helmut Lang shorts, and Camilla Skovgaard open-toe booties.

Her hair was pulled back into a sleek ponytail revealing her flawless skin and three-carat diamond earrings.

"What's up?" Angel looked around perplexed as she hugged and air kissed his cheek. "I didn't know we were having company."

"I'm sorry. I should've told you, but I wanted it to be a surprise. Since it seems like we're not going back to L.A. anytime soon, I planned on starting the wedding plans here. So meet Kathy, our wedding planner, and John, our new real estate agent," Milania beamed, pleased with herself.

"So nice to finally meet you," Kathy extended her hand for a shake. "I've heard so much about you."

"Really?" Angel eyed her quizzically. "I haven't heard nothin' about you."

"Baby," Milania gasped, "don't be rude."

"I'm not being rude at all. I just wasn't expecting any of this, and honestly, right now, I'm not in the mood."

"He's just a little cranky, excuse him," Milania placed her hand on the side of her mouth as if she were telling a secret.

"Baby," she ran her hand across the top of her hair trying her best not to go off, "calm down. You're probably just a little hungry. Once we sit down and start going over everything, you'll see exactly what I'm trying to do."

"I know exactly what you're tryin' to do. You're tryin' to plan a wedding, but we haven't even set a date, so how you gon' consult wit' a planner, let alone a realtor? I mean, I planned on us having a long engagement."

"What did you just say?" Milania jerked her head back, appalled. "'Cause I know damn well I didn't hear what I thought I heard."

"Chill out." Angel screwed up his face and pulled her out of the room so they could speak privately.

He was over Milania and her spoiled, divaesque ways. It was time for Angel to put his foot down with her 'cause homegirl had him past fucked up.

"I know you feelin' some kinda way right now, but don't ever play me like that in front of nobody." He shot her a look that could kill.

"But—" Milania tried to speak, but Angel stopped her.

"But nothin'. I'm talkin'. Don't interrupt me." Angel waved his hand furiously. "Look, when I asked you to marry me, I meant it, but I wasn't planning on us gettin' married so soon. I figured we'd be engaged for a few years."

"A few years!" Milania repeated, heated.

"Yes, a few years. C'mon, Milania, keep it funky. We barely know each other, and before we take that step toward being together forever, I think it's best we learn as much as we can about each other."

"You should've thought about that *before* you proposed to me," she snapped.

"You're right. I should've, but now I got the paparazzi down my back, me and my sista ain't really speaking, and Dylan won't even answer any of my calls. I mean, all of this shit is just too much."

"So what am I supposed to do now? I've already started picking out china arrangements and our color scheme for the wedding, which, by the way, will be an explosion of pink, and the realtor has found us some really breathtaking property out in L.A."

"What's wrong with the crib I already have?"

"Not to be rude but your place screams 'bachelor pad.' I think it's time to move it on up like George and Weezy."

"Yo', you start talkin' like Weezy, and we gon' have a problem for real," Angel joked.

"Shut up," Milania placed her hand on his chest and laughed.

"Look. I know that you feel like I'm rushing things, and to be honest wit' you, I am. And the reason is because I want to spend the rest of my life with you, Angel. I love you, and it's already bad enough that I won't be the first woman to bear your child. At least give me this one thing." She gave Angel a well executed expression of sorrow.

"I know. Just give me some time." Angel massaged her back.

"How much time?" Milania batted her eyes, becoming irritated.

"Not that much. Just a little."

"Okay, well, can we at least just go back in so you can see what they have to offer?"

"Yeah, give me a second. I gotta make a call." Angel reached in his pocket and pulled out his Apple iPhone 4.

"It can't wait? We've already wasted enough time as it is," she responded impatiently.

"Nah, I want to see if I can get in touch with Dylan again."

Milania's jaw unconsciously clenched tight like a pit bull. She was so sick that every conversation she and Angel had reverted back to Dylan. *Dylan, Dylan, Dylan,* she thought. She assumed that inviting the paparazzi to her showdown with Dylan and leaking her engagement and Dylan's pregnancy would help stir the pot, but all it had done was make Angel doubt their relationship. Milania had to figure out a way to get rid of Dylan for good. With her in the picture, Milania's road to superstardom and fame would always be met with road blocks and speed bumps.

"Why?" she responded, not backing down.

"What you mean, why?" Angel shot her a nasty look.

"I mean it's obvious that she doesn't want to talk to you for whatever reason," she retorted.

"'Cause she's the mother of my child, that's why, and I wanna see what's going on wit' her and my baby."

Milania inhaled deeply and replied, "A'ight, I'll see you in a second."

There was no point in starting another argument with him. Nope. Milania would bite her tongue and prepare herself for the next showdown, which was sure to come.

"Order me a Boulevard Wheat."

"Sure." She gave him a tight smile and went back in.

Angel found Dylan's name in his contacts and dialed her number, but to his displeasure, his call was sent to voice mail after the second the ring.

Dylan gazed down at her cell phone and rolled her eyes. She didn't have two words for Angel. Frankly, if she could, she would literally give him her ass to kiss. Dylan was beyond upset with Angel. She was terribly disappointed. Never in a million years had she expected him to find another chick, then chuck up the deuce like she wasn't shit, but he did.

Hell, he didn't have time enough to check on her while she was in the hospital, but now he expected her to answer his call. *Negro, please,* she thought. Plus the unwanted news coverage of her pregnancy was driving her insane. Dylan couldn't take a shit without a photographer up in her face. At this point, she wasn't concerned about how fine Angel was, how his backstroke took her to all seven continents of the world and back, how he loved her too much, how she fucked up, missed him with every pore of her skin, and would give all of her limbs to have him back in her life again.

After her health scare, Dylan was all about herself, her baby, and their future. She couldn't depend on Angel, so she decided to depend on herself. Pocketing her phone, Dylan walked out into the showroom of the bakery and smiled. There were a couple of customers in the store. Although business wasn't booming like she wanted it to, Dylan knew that her breakfast pastries, minipastries, cookies, pies, wedding cakes, coffee, and lattes were the best in town.

The way Dylan had the place decorated was utterly charming. Once customers walked through the door, they felt as if they had stumbled upon a Parisian boutique. Funky lampshades, one-of-a-kind chandeliers, and toile adorned the cozy café, along with black-and-white photos of some of her favorite fashion icons, such as Elizabeth Taylor, Rihanna, and Carrie Bradshaw.

While Dylan's cashier took care of a customer, she explained to another the ingredients inside of her famous chocolate mousse cup topped with a miniature gold Louboutin heel when she noticed, out of the corner of her eye, a familiar face walk through the door. Dylan's mouth immediately became as dry as a nun's crotch she was so shocked. She hoped that what she was experiencing within didn't resonate on her face as she and the unexpected guest locked eyes.

Memories of the way they fought, then made up, hated each other's guts, yearned for the other's touch, made love until the sun came up, and how their love was never enough crammed both of their minds. Once she wrapped up her conversation with the customer, Dylan made her way over to her guest and said, "What the hell are you doing here? I swear to God, you're like a pain in my ass that won't go away."

"I had to see if what the streets were sayin' was true," State, her ex-fiancé, shot her a sly grin.

Before Angel, State was the one who had Dylan's heart on lock. His swagger ranked at a trillion, and his accomplishments as a successful record label owner, clothing designer, restaurateur, and co-owner of the 76ers was impeccable. On top of that, the brother was fine, with a capital F. State was a six foot, 190-pound Sierra Leonean and Ghanaian hunk who repped Hackney London to the fullest. That afternoon he looked dapper as hell in a two-button corduroy Gucci jacket, tricolor wool sweater, plaid flat-front pants, and Dolce & Gabbana Oxford wingtip shoes.

"And what exactly is the streets sayin'?" Dylan placed her hand on her hip.

"That the notorious wild child, Dylan Monroe, was knocked up and off the scene for good."

"Well, as you can see, the rumor is true." Dylan rubbed her belly.

"You just had to find a way to break my heart, didn't you?" He shot her a sly grin.

"Please." She waved him off. "Your heart is made of steel. Ain't no gettin' through to that."

"You still mean as hell, I see."

"I have every right to be. You made me believe we had a future while the whole time you were married to someone else."

"When is the past gon' be the past? I mean, c'mon, that was like, what, two years ago. It's obvious," he pointed to her protruding stomach, "that you got past it."

"As a matter of fact, I did. Now have a seat, big head. My feet startin' to hurt."

"How?" He looked down at her feet as they sat down. "You wearing them thick-ass Dr. Scholl's. No way could yo' feet be hurtin'. You used to wear six-inch heels all day, er'day."

"Things have changed, honey. Nowadays, a sneeze makes my feet hurt and makes me fart."

"A'ight, Dylan, that's enough," State tuned up his face.

"Whatever, that's real," she laughed. "You want something to drink?"

"Yeah, I'll take an espresso."

"Megan," Dylan called out to her cashier, "can you bring us over an espresso and a glass of water, please?"

"Coming right up," Megan said cheerfully.

"Homegirl kinda cute." State admired her frame.

"But is as dumb as a doorknob," Dylan whispered. "The only reason I haven't fired her is because she finally discovered concealer two months ago."

"Wow," State chuckled. "The place looks good, though," he looked around the bakery.

"Yeah, but business sucks. As the economy gets worse, less customers and less orders seem to be coming in. It seems like I'm losing more money a month than I'm making, but I don't want to close the place down. It would kill me, but I have to figure out my next step because advertising and giving out free samples ain't working."

"Why don't you get you an agent?"

"An agent? What is that going to do?" Dylan eyed him, perplexed.

"With an agent on your side, you can try getting a book deal, television show, and your own products."

"Wow, I never thought about that. I always thought that that was so far out of my reach."

"Look here," State reached into his wallet and pulled out a card, "this is my homegirl Brenda. She's a literary agent. Call her up and tell her that I referred you to her."

"State, you don't have to do that," Dylan pushed his hand back.

"I want to. It's the least I can do for breaking your heart," he looked her square in the eyes.

"You damn right it is," Dylan took the card from his hand and grinned.

"So how many months are you?" State leaned back in his chair.

"Five."

"What you having?"

"Don't know. The baby was turned when we tried to see," she explained as Megan brought over their drinks.

"I see," he nodded, zeroing in on Megan's ass as she walked away.

"So where is the Mrs.?" Dylan asked, referring to his wife, R&B sensation Ashton.

"I don't know, off somewhere. We're getting a divorce. She finally got tired of trying to change me."

"Wow, didn't see that one coming," Dylan replied sarcastically.

"You real funny."

"Seriously, I'm sorry to hear that," she pretended to pout.

"Don't be. We all know marriage is not for me."

"You got that right. You know what? I think I just had an apostrophe." Dylan cupped her chin and tapped her index finger against her nose.

"You mean epiphany?"

"Yeah, that too," she pointed. "I think you're one of those people who is more in love with the idea of being married than actually being married."

"You know what, Dylan? You might actually be on to something."

"I know. Being pregnant has turned me into a fuckin' Jedi man. I swear it's like I have ESPN," she responded, not even knowing that she'd messed up.

"I totally agree," State laughed on the inside as a photographer took their photo from across the street. "I totally agree."

Shades of darkness filled the room. Angel sat alone facing the television screen with a glass of scotch in his hand. It was 2:00 A.M., but sleep evaded him. He couldn't get the scent of Dylan's perfume out of his nose or the sight of her hazel eyes out of his head. She followed him everywhere—in his dreams, when he brushed his teeth, when he bathed, walked down the street, even when he made love to Milania at night.

Angel often found himself wishing Milania's kisses came from Dylan's warm mouth or that Milania's slit was the entrance way to Dylan's honeycomb hideout. Taking a sip from the chilled glass, he watched the home movie before him and reminisced. It was the day he recorded Dylan and him in bed fooling around. Angel watched closely as she smiled gleefully and hit him in the head with a pillow. Instead of retaliating, he pinned her body down to the bed and brushed his lips upon hers.

Unable to resist the taste of his tongue, Dylan kissed his lips fervently, rotating between his top and bottom lip. Then their tongues met and heaven was exposed to their mouths. Angel couldn't get enough of her then, and the fact still remained now. No matter how hard he tried to forget the weeks and months they spent together or how much he remembered her betrayal, emotions for her still lingered on.

Now shit was all fucked up. He'd pledge his commitment to another while feelings for Dylan suffocated him to the point he couldn't breathe. Angel knew that a resolution to his problem had to come quickly, because he couldn't spend another night obsessing over Dylan's mouth, the curve of her waist, or the roundness of her hips. There was no denying it or hiding it. Dylan held the key to his heart, and yeah, he had feelings for Milania, but the feelings just weren't as strong.

But the option of breaking off their engagement wasn't something Angel was ready to do either, 'cause at the end of the day, he might carry around a love for Dylan the size of the Atlantic and Pacific oceans combined, but the fact still remained that she'd done the unforgiveable and fucked another man behind his back. Angel's ego just couldn't let that slide without feeling like an absolute punk. So here he was, engaged to a woman who only filled the void of him not being alone.

Unbeknownst to Angel, as a trickle of water from the outside of his glass slid down his hand, Milania stood silently in the doorway. Venom raced through her cold veins. Her worst nightmare had just been revealed, but she wasn't down for the count. Milania still had a couple more nasty tricks up her sleeve. Come rain or come shine, Angel Carter was going to be hers.

"All my scars are open."
Shontelle, "Impossible"

7

Brandy's chart-topping hit "Top Of The World" couldn't describe the glorious feeling inside of Dylan's heart. Despite the media frenzy claiming that State was the real father of her child after photos appeared of them chatting inside her bakery, she took State's advice and contacted agent extraordinaire Brenda Hampton. After a ten-minute conversation, they set a date to meet at House of Savoy, an Italian eatery in the heart of downtown St. Louis for dinner and drinks. Drinks meaning she'd have a cocktail and Dylan would have ginger ale.

The day of the meeting came quickly and the outcome couldn't have been any better for Dylan. She and Brenda vibed immediately. They were like long lost friends. They bonded instantly over sweets, past experiences, fashion, and men. Once Brenda skimmed through Dylan's photo book of delectable one-of-a-kind pastries, she knew that Dylan was destined to be a star.

Brenda admired her tenacity, quirky wit, energetic attitude, and her concept that would teach the everyday woman that sweets and fashion went together like Diddy and shiny suits was an instant hit. When the plates were cleared and they air-kissed good-bye, Dylan left the meeting with a literary agent and an optimistic outlook on life.

She just prayed that once the manuscript was finished that the major publishing houses would jump at the chance to sign her. But Dylan's triumphant mood changed within seconds when she exited the restaurant doors and spotted Angel and Milania walking down the street hand in hand. Dylan felt like she was in a bad 1990s teen romance where the Queen B of the cheerleading squad flaunts the fact that she's the girlfriend of the quarterback in front of the gangly, yet-if-she-just-got-a-makeover-she'd-be-beautiful nerd.

Just like in the movies, all three sets of their eyes connected and Dylan's breath faded into the night sky. Chill bumps rose beneath her cardigan-covered arms. It seemed like with every step they took, time delayed and layers of her clothes burned away. She felt like her feelings and body were exposed to the earth and people around her.

Suddenly Dylan felt sick. A sour sensation permeated the pit of her stomach. She didn't understand how something so good could be followed up by something so bad. Angel and Milania were the last people on earth she wanted to see. She just wanted peace, a space of her own to feel secure. However, the devil, karma, or the universe had other plans for her.

Plus the fact that, once again, Milania was outshining her in the style department and that crushed her heart. *Damn, do this bitch ever look bad,* she thought, eyeing her Sheri Bodell, beaded and padded cap-sleeved, silk, V-neck dress, Stella McCartney tuxedo jacket and open-toe, L.A.M.B. booties with twisted straps going down the front. Angel didn't look too bad himself. He was dressed leisurely in a blue Yankees cap, black rosary, V-neck tee, John Varvatos leather trim jacket, dirty-wash jeans, and blue Louboutin sneakers with a white sole.

The pure, unadulterated sex appeal of him put Dylan on edge. The baby could feel her anxiety too. Dylan's little one started kicking like crazy. In order to calm herself and the baby she gently rubbed her belly and whispered, *Okay, baby, Mommy's straight. You don't have to go all Street Fighter on me; Mama got this,* as Angel and Milania approached.

"Word?" Angel shifted his shoulders, disgruntled.

"What you mean, 'word'?" Dylan responded, caught off guard by his reaction to her.

"C'mon, Dylan, you already know."

"Know what?"

"That you been duckin' and dodgin' a nigga," Angel barked, becoming angrier by the second.

"And for good reason." She mean-mugged him, then eyed Milania up and down.

"I need to holla at you. You here alone?"

"Yeah, why?" she ice-grilled him, then rolled her eyes at Milania.

Dylan was determined to serve him and his chick nothin' but shade.

"Ay, why don't you go in and get us seated while I rap to Dylan real quick," he said to Milania.

"All right," she smiled.

Never passing up an opportunity to piss Dylan off, Milania placed her perfectly manicured hand on Angel's cheek, turned his face toward her, then kissed his lips in a way that foreshadowed the kind of night she wanted to have. Releasing her lips from his, she wiped the leftover lipstick residue off his mouth and smirked, "Dylan."

"Milania," Dylan snapped, sickened by the sight of her.

Milania didn't even respond. She simply grinned.

"I'll see you in a second, babe." She let go of Angel's hand and walked back toward the casino which was right next door to the Savoy.

"Man, y'all gon' stop that shit," Angel said, fed up with their nonsense.

"Pshh, please, and what is it that *you* want? I don't have too much to say to you either," Dylan snarled.

"And why is that?"

"What? You ain't get the hint yet?" Dylan rolled her neck.

"What hint?"

"That I don't want you around! I'm raising this baby by myself! You and Stankonia can continue to be the played-out version of Hov and B all y'all want and live in this fantasy world where no one else exists, but just leave me and my baby out of it!"

"What the fuck is you talkin' about?" Angel's heart raced a mile a minute he was so upset and turned on by her.

"Don't act stupid. You know damn well what I'm talkin about. Ever since I told you I was pregnant, you ain't been beat for me. All you been worried about is that bitch!" She pointed toward the casino. "You couldn't even come see about me while I was in the hospital."

"Hold up! What?" he said astounded.

"Really, Angel?" She folded her arms. "You gon' act like I'm lying?"

"I ain't actin' like shit! I came up there to see you!"

"All right, I see now yo' ass is possessed. I'm outta here," Dylan turned to walk away.

"Hold up!" Angel took her by the hand and pulled her back.

The touch of her hand sent shocks of electricity through his veins—and Milania's as well as she watched them from afar.

"Did you *really* just grab me?" Dylan pretended not to like his forcefulness.

"Shut up." He gazed down into her face.

He could vividly see all of the pain and fear she kept bottled up in her hazel eyes. He wished he could be real and tell her how he felt, take her into his arms, kiss her on the lips, and dip up outta there, but reality kept getting in the way.

"You talk too much. Now I don't know what yo' problem is or who pissed in yo' cereal this morning, but I came to the hospital. The only reason I left is because Gaylord Focker said that would be best for you. He thought me being there would cause you more stress, and I ain't wanna do that so I shook."

Dylan tried her best not to laugh at Angel's quip about Tee-Tee but failed miserably.

"Hold up, are you serious? You really came up there to see me?" Dylan said in disbelief.

"Yeah, you know I wouldn't do you like that. At least I thought you knew."

"So you mean to tell me I've been walking around feeling all mad and disappointed and shit for nothin'?"

"Yeah, toward me, but you need to throw that attitude toward yo' man."

"Oh, please, believe me, I will be."

"Now what the fuck is up with this bullshit all over the news about that nigga State being yo' baby's daddy?" He eyed her physique, taking in the fact that she'd gotten bigger.

"Exactly what you just said—a bunch of bullshit. And the fact that you're even standing here asking me about that tells me that you still don't trust me."

"I do trust you. It's *him* I don't trust," he stated bluntly.

"Well, I don't have anything to do with that," she remarked.

"Look, I know it's long overdue, but my bad for snappin' on you like that over the phone. That was a fucked-up thing to do."

"It's cool," Dylan said putting it all behind her.

"Nah, it's not. You know I don't really even roll like that. I was just upset, but anyway, how you been?" Angel placed his hands inside his pocket. "Have I missed anything?"

"When I was in the hospital I tried to learn the sex of the baby, but he or she wasn't actin' right."

"Word. So you got to see the baby?" Angel's eyes lit up.

"Yeah," she beamed. "Angel, it was so tiny and cute."

"Damn, I hate I missed it." He sighed, truly disappointed.

"Me too."

For a moment the stillness of the night and the unspoken words left in their hearts took over and they stood silent. Sounds of sirens, engines, and crickets filled the air. How Dylan wished that things between her and Angel could go back to the way things used to be before she made the worst decision of her life and cheated on him. Because to be that close to Angel and knowing he was no longer hers was pure torture.

"Well, let me get going. I don't want you to keep li'l mama waiting." Dylan adjusted the strap of her purse on her shoulder.

"Nah, you good," he said, wanting to spend a little more time with her.

"Nah, I better go," she replied, although she wanted to stay. "Besides, I gotta get home and post up. At night she get to actin' crazy."

"I thought you said you didn't know the sex?" He stared at her quizzically.

"I don't, but something's just tellin' me it's gon' be a girl. Lord knows, I wouldn't know what to do wit' no boy."

"So she's kickin' now?"

"Mmm-hmm, like David Beckham."

"Can I feel?" Angel stepped closer.

"Yeah," Dylan placed his hand on her stomach.

Angel stood still with anticipation awaiting the feel of his baby when the baby thumped his hand.

"Hell, naw," he laughed, overjoyed. He wanted to keep his hand there forever.

"I know, isn't it weird?" Dylan giggled.

"Yeah."

"Oh, I forgot to tell you that Billie is throwing me a baby shower next week."

"A'ight."

"You gon' come, right?"

"Of course, I wouldn't miss it for the world."

"Okay, it's at 2:00, so I guess I'll see you then." She stepped back, causing his hand to fall away from her stomach.

"A'ight, drive home safe."

"I will," she looked down at her feet nervously.

"I'm for real, Dylan," he placed his hand underneath her chin and lifted her head up. "Don't let nothin happen to my baby," Angel said referring to her and their baby.

"I won't, I promise," Dylan responded, knowing fully well what he meant.

"Well, a'ight, then. Have a good night." He lovingly slid the back of his hand down the side of her face.

"You too," she gazed up into his brown eyes solemnly before heading to her car.

A week later, a five-month pregnant Dylan sat comfortably eating McDonald's french fries. Bubbling hot water whooshed around her feet. She, Billie, and Tee-Tee were having a girl's day out, which consisted of a mani and pedi at La Petite Spa. La Petite was a quaint spa that offered the best manicures, facials, and massages. It was the only place Dylan dared to get her nails and toes done. She was in heaven, and she looked cute as a button in a gray sweatshirt with black lace inserts in the shoulders and black skinny-leg maternity jeans.

Dylan felt like a superstar. She hadn't been pampered in months. Her feet were in dire need of scrubbing, and her nails were a hot atrocious mess. They were chipped, and she even swore she had a hangnail or two. The only thing that was spoiling her experience was Tee-Tee's two-faced ass. She couldn't get over that he had the nerve to turn Angel away without her permission, and on top of that, not even tell her that he did it. In her mind, his ass had balls of steel to make that big of a decision on her behalf without her knowledge.

"Champagne?" one of the nail technicians asked.

"Shit, yeah." Tee-Tee reached out for one immediately.

"You, ma'am?"

"Wish I could, but I can't. Baby on board," Dylan pointed to her stomach.

"Oh, congratulations! I thought you were just . . . umm . . . okay, how about you, ma'am?" The nail tech turned to Billie.

"Yes, honey, yes. After the week I've had, I'ma need about ten of these, so keep'em coming."

"Sure thing. My name is Rebecca, if you need me," she informed them before moving on to another customer.

"Did that heffa just call me fat?" Dylan leaned over and whispered to Billie.

"I think so," she giggled.

"Bitch. I swear to God if I end up looking like Nell Carter after I have this baby I'ma kill myself," Dylan sulked.

"Shit, I'ma kill you," Tee-Tee joked.

"Was I talkin' to him?" Dylan looked over at Billie but pointed at Tee-Tee.

"Bitch, we ain't in third-grade. If you got something to say, say it to my face. Don't do me." He jerked his head around.

"Ughh, I wish he would quit talkin' to me," Dylan groaned.

"Whateva. So what's been going on wit' you?" he asked Billie, taking a sip of champagne.

"I don't even know where to start. First off, instead of getting the kids on the weekends like he's supposed to, Cain and Becky have been jet-setting around the world, leaving me to have to cancel appointments and stuff. So after he didn't get them last week, I told his ass to suck it and that he'll see them again when they're eighteen."

"Clunk!" Tee-Tee pointed his index finger.

"Well, how did that go over?" Dylan asked.

"He's been callin', but I'm not playin' wit' him. He not gon' put my kids through that bullshit. Y'all, it's just so sad. My babies just be sittin' there by the door with they bags and stuff ready to go, callin' him and callin' him, and he don't answer the phone or nothin'. Then, of course, the twins start crying and asking why their daddy won't come. And, of course, I can't say 'Your dad's an asshole,' so I'm stuck with tryin' to figure out how to explain the situation. It's all just a big mess." Billie huffed, then took a huge gulp of champagne.

"Then there's Knox," she rolled her eyes. "It's like I can't make a move without him being glued to my hip. I swear sometimes I don't know whether to blow him or burp him. Every five seconds it seem like he wanna make love or hug me or kiss me, and I don't be having time for all of that. I be having shit to do. I mean, don't get me wrong. I enjoy having sex with my husband, but don't a bitch pussy get a break, time off, sick day, *something*."

"Billie, are you serious?" Dylan looked at her like she was insane. "Y'all haven't even been married a year. Y'all still in y'all honeymoon phase. You better give that man some pussy."

"I know. I just be having so much on my plate." Billie situated herself in her seat.

"No, you're just a mental adolescent at being romantic," Tee-Tee chimed in, feeling the buzz of the champagne.

"No, I'm not," Billie disagreed. "I'm a very romantic person."

"Gurl, please, you're a high-strung type A bitch who doesn't give a damn about anything but her charity work. Part of the reason your first marriage ended is because you wasn't giving up no ass. You was too damn frigid, and by the time you did start giving up the pooh-na-ni, Cain had him a new boo."

"Okay, it's about to be a Code 10, man-down situation," Dylan sat up straight, her belly resting on her thighs. "Nigga, are you high? How dare you say some shit like that to her?"

"Don't rile yourself up, Dylan," Billie pushed her back. "I'ma body his ass myself. Just 'cause you over there takin' cum shots to the face five times a day like a Muslim don't mean I gotta be a freak too."

"Hallelu," Dylan waved her hand in the air.

"I'm just tryin' to help yo' ass so you won't lose another husband," Tee-Tee bobbed his head.

"Didn't nobody ask you for your advice, loose booty. That's yo' problem now. You always stickin' yo' nose where it don't belong," Dylan spat, heated.

"You got a problem wit' me or something? 'Cause if not, I would advise you to watch yo' mouth, 'cause if you get smart wit' me one more time, I promise I'ma turn into Wolverine and scratch yo' ass up," Tee-Tee warned.

"A'ight, bitch, you wanna go there?" Dylan said, ready to pounce. "Who told you that you could tell Angel to leave when he came to visit me in the hospital and also sit in my face and act like it never happened?"

Billie placed her hand on her mouth and gasped.

"Tell me you didn't do that, Tee-Tee," she said in disbelief. "I haven't talked to my brother for almost two months because of that."

"Once again, I was just tryin' to look out for her well-being, seeing as though their argument is what landed her in the hospital in the first place. Shit, y'all ain't gon' do me." He flicked his wrist, pissed.

"But that wasn't your place to make that decision," Dylan countered. "'Cause all that did was make me think he didn't give a fuck and cause me even more stress, so thank you."

"You know what? I ain't got time for this. I'm sittin' up here, tryin' to be a good friend to you," he pointed his index finger at Billie, "and a good cousin to you," he pointed at Dylan. "And this is how y'all do me? Forgive me for giving a damn about yo' li'l sorry-ass lives. Y'all sensitive asses ain't gon' get on my nerves." Tee-Tee grabbed his jacket and purse from the hook on the wall behind him.

"How the hell you gon' get an attitude wit' me and *you* the one that was wrong? What kind of deranged *Real Housewives of New York*, Kelly Bensimon shit is that? Just take the dildo outta yo' ass and apologize," Dylan shouted, causing people to stare.

"I wish I would. As a matter of fact, pay for your own damn mani and pedi, broke ass!" He took his feet out of the water and got up.

"I will!"

"Ya' mama!" Dylan yelled after him and crossed her legs.

"He is *such* a queen," Billie shook her head.

"Girl, he make me sick," Dylan fumed. "But, ah," she whispered, "you know I ain't got no money, right?"

Billie turned and looked at her.

"I got you, broke ass."

"It's official, you got issues."
Aaliyah, "We Need a Resolution"

8

After a full twenty-four hours of giving Tee-Tee the silent treatment, Dylan caved in and texted him.

To: Tee-Tee
Have u realized that I'm not speaking 2 u yet?
Sent: Fri, April 12, 9:50 P.M.

From: Tee-Tee
No, cuz I'm not speaking 2 u.
Received: Fri, April 12, 9:52 P.M.

To: Tee-Tee
U say what now?
Sent: Fri, April 12, 9:53 P.M.

From: Tee-Tee
U heard me!
Received: Fri, April 12, 9:56 P.M.

To: Tee-Tee
Bitch, how in the hell r u not speakin' 2 me? U pissed me off, lol!
Sent: Fri, April 12, 9:59 P.M.

From: Tee-Tee
Nooooooo, u pissed me off, coon.
Received: Fri, April 12, 10:04 P.M.

Dylan had had enough. Thoroughly amused by his so-called attitude, she stopped texting him and dialed his number.

"What do you want, li'l girl?" he answered the phone dryly.

"I can't stand you," Dylan chuckled. "So you really call yourself having an attitude?"

"Mmm-hmm." He took a long sip of chamomile tea.

"Boy, please, get over yo'self. You hurt my feelings, not the other way around."

"Ugh, okay. I'm sorry. You were right. I shouldn't have told him to leave. That wasn't my place. Huuuuuuuh."

"Thank you, and I'm sorry for being a baby bitch today. That was ignorant."

"You can't help yourself," Tee-Tee leaned back in his love seat and crossed his legs.

"Whateva," she laughed.

"But, nah, for real, the reason I was so bitchy is because I got a call yesterday from the adoption agency and the girl changed her mind and decided she wanted to keep the baby, so we're back at square one," he confessed.

"Tee-Tee, why didn't you say something?" Dylan asked, feeling horrible.

"I don't know. I guess I didn't want to believe it was true. We were so banking on her giving us the baby that we never thought she would change her mind. But it's all good. God got another baby for us . . . I know it," Tee-Tee encouraged himself.

"I'm glad you realize that."

"Yeah," he yawned. "I'll just be glad when this whole thing is over, and I have my baby in my arms."

"Me too, but guess what?" Dylan exclaimed.

"What?"

"I just got a call from Brenda. Kensington has offered me a two-book deal."

"Get it, bitch!" Tee-Tee shrieked. "How much money you gon' get? I mean, if you don't mind me askin'."

"Forty thousand."

"A'ight now!" Tee-Tee clapped. "We in the money!"

"I know. I'm so excited."

"Have you told Billie yet?" Tee-Tee asked.

"No. Have you talked to her?"

"No."

"You know you need to call and apologize."

"Yeah, I just haven't called her yet."

"Well, hold on, I'm gettin' ready to call her and press *67."

"Grow . . . up," Tee-Tee laughed.

"Shut up and hold on," Dylan clicked over and dialed Billie's number. "Hello," she said, clicking back over.

"I'm here," Tee-Tee answered.

After five rings, Knox picked up the phone.

"Hello?" he spoke deeply.

"Hey, gorgeous, is Billie there?" Tee-Tee asked sweetly.

"Hold on, man." Knox passed her the phone.

"Who is it," she mouthed.

"Yo' homeboy."

"Homegirl!" Tee-Tee yelled into the receiver.

"What you want, hag?" Billie spat, getting on to the line.

"Guuuuuuurl, you is workin' my nerves," he massaged his temples.

"I ain't got time for all the back and forth, Tee-Tee. Say what you called to say."

"I called to tell yo' funky ass that I was sorry, but you about to piss me off!" he shot into the phone.

"IDC!"

"What the hell? You mean IDK?"

"No, I mean I don't care!" Billie declared. "You *ought* to be sorry. You hurt my feelings."

"My bad, girl. You know I wasn't tryin' to. I just had a rough day that's all, but anyway, you talked to Dylan?" he asked.

"Nope."

"How her broke ass pay for them swole, crusty feet?" he joked.

"I paid for them. Who else was gon' pay for'em. You know she ain't got no money."

"She got some money somewhere. Shit, have you noticed how much weight she's gained? That bitch been over there eatin'," Tee-Tee laughed.

"YES, she *is* huge," Billie stressed.

"Right. Face lookin' like Snooki," Tee-Tee joined, causing Billie to die laughing.

"Really?" Dylan jumped into the conversation, heated. "That's really how y'all feel?"

"Girl, shut up. I knew yo' dumb ass was on the phone," Billie calmed down.

"How?"

"'Cause you the only ignorant ass that would call my house and press *67."

"Oh. Anyway, guess what, bitch?" Dylan said excited. "What?"

"I got an offer for a two-book deal with Kensington!"

"Shut the front door, lock it, and draw the blinds," Billie said, surprised. "I am *proud* of you," she cooed.

"Thanks, love," Dylan gleamed.

"Oh, we really gotta kick it tomorrow," Billie said, amped. "By the way, what you wearing tomorrow?"

"I haven't decided yet." Dylan scratched the back of her head.

"So you still don't feel bad about not inviting Candy?"

"No, I wouldn't invite her to a dogfight."

"Now, Dylan, that's not right," Billie couldn't help but laugh.

"Right, don't be talkin' about my auntie like that," Tee-Tee warned.

"Boy, boo, that heffa stole $50,000 from me—$50,000 that I need *right now*," Dylan stressed.

"That is true," Tee-Tee agreed.

"Beside, we all know the only time she comes around is when she needs pee for her parole officer," Dylan joked.

"You stupid," Billie giggled.

"I'm serious." Dylan couldn't help but laugh too.

"Look, Dylan," Tee-Tee said, "I know she's no prize, but don't you want to have a relationship with your mother? Especially since you're about to be one yourself?"

"Candy and I have never had a relationship, and we probably never will. To me, she's just some woman who shows up every couple of years to ask me for money, and to her, I'm just a chunky, naïve ATM. And frankly, I'm sick of it. Candy has been using me since the day I was born. You know I never saw a dime from the money I won doing pageants."

"Really, Dylan?" Tee-Tee said. "What the hell you gon' do with a $500 savings bond now?"

"Heffa, I won more than $500!"

"Yeah, in your mind," he teased.

"Whateva," she waved him off as if he could see what she was doing. "Anyway, Billie," she began to speak when she heard Knox say, "Let me holla at you" in the background.

"Hold on," Billie set the phone down on her lap so they wouldn't hear her conversation.

"How long you think you gon' be on the phone?"

"IDK."

Aggravated by her response, Knox inhaled deeply and shook his head.

"Why? You need to use it?" she asked.

"No, I just figured that since it was my off day and you been gone all day that we could spend some time together now, but it don't look like that's gon' happen," he said, obviously let down.

"Can you just give a minute? I'm tryin' to talk to Dylan and Tee-Tee about the shower."

"Damn, wasn't you just with them yesterday? Y'all ain't talk about that shit then?"

"Umm," Billie's eyes grew wide, "we did, but what does that have to do with anything?"

"It's good. I'm not gon' do this shit wit' you tonight. Good night." Knox left the sitting room, heated.

"Good night," she shot back, not recognizing how upset he was. "My bad, y'all," she picked back up the phone and resumed her conversation.

"Uhhhhh, don't you ever in your life have us on hold that long," Tee-Tee complained.

"Boy, hush."

"What Knox want?" Dylan asked, being nosy.

"Nothin'. Wanted to see how long I was gon' be on the phone so we could spend some together," she huffed.

"And you're still on the phone with us *because?*" Tee-Tee asked, puzzled.

"'Cause we talkin' about the shower, and besides, I'm not gettin' ready to stop doing what I'm doing to appease him. Been there, done that, and I ain't going back there no more."

"Okay, Billie, now I'm wit' Tee-Tee. Are you listening to yourself right now?" Dylan asked.

"What?" Billie replied, oblivious to her behavior.

"I understand that you got a lot going on, but damn, none of that is as important as your husband. That man halfway like yo' ass, and you over there pushing him away."

"I just don't wanna look up one day and I'm in the same position where I've given my all and this mutha-fucka decides that I'm not good enough and doesn't want me anymore. I can't go through that kinda hurt again," Billie said, put off by the thought.

"That's understandable, friend, but you can't compare Knox to Cain, especially when he's given you no reason to. Knox is a good dude who loves you and all them bad-ass gremlins you call kids. Now what you don't wanna do is take him for granted and one day wake up and realize that you've done so much damage to y'all relationship that you'll never get him back. I'm tellin' you that shit will eat you alive. Knowing you fucked up is worse than any pain Cain could've ever caused you. 'Cause when they hurt you, it stings like hell for a while, but then we remember that we are the shit and can find someone new that's gonna treat us the way we deserve to be treated. But when *you're* the reason they're gone and ain't neva coming back, man . . ." Dylan stared ab-sently off into space.

Everyone on the line became silent. Billie and Tee-Tee knew that her words of advice had all to do with her tragic ending to her and Angel's relationship. Billie didn't want to end up like Dylan. She didn't want to open her eyes each morning and close them at night knowing that the man who loved her more than life was gone and had moved on with a new chick while she sat back in agony mourning the death of their relationship.

"Since when did you get so smart?" Billie wiped a tear from her ear.

"I don't take any of the credit. I give it all to my favorite reality shows *Bethanny Getting Married* and *The Bad Girls Club*. They've taught me everything I know," Dylan stated proudly, smiling.

"You just had to go and ruin it, didn't you?" Billie shook her head.

"I'm serious."

"And that's the sad part," Billie replied with a hint of sarcasm in her voice. "Look, I'ma take your advice and get the stick out my ass and go spend some time with my husband before I end up being a Hollaback girl. Does anybody still say that?"

"No," Dylan giggled.

"Oh, well, anyway, you get the gist."

"All I got to say is you better treat that man right 'cause if you don't want him, I'll for damn sure take him," Tee-Tee jumped in.

"Heffa, please, you can forget about it. That white stallion is all mine."

"Well, go get'em, cowgirl."

"Yeeeeee haw," Billie screamed in their ear before hanging up and dashing up the steps.

Thrusting open the bedroom door she yelled out, "Babe," but got no reply.

"He must be in the bathroom," she spoke out loud to herself.

Billie walked a few steps over to the master bath. She placed her hand on the knob and turned but surprisingly still saw no signs of Knox. After checking the security monitor and viewing each room on the screen and not finding him, Billie grabbed the house phone and sat on the leather bench in front of her bed, stooped.

"Where in the hell is he at?" she wondered out loud while calling his cell phone, but Knox didn't answer.

Calling him again, Billie crossed her legs and waited with baited breath.

"What up?" he finally answered.

Billie could hear loud music and people partying in the background. "Where are you? I thought you were going to bed."

"No, I said good night."

"So why didn't you tell me you were leaving?"

"'Cause you was on the phone."

"Oh."

Suddenly an awkward silence occurred. Billie didn't know what to say or do. Knox had never been this nonchalant with her. Maybe Dylan was right. Maybe she had pushed him too far.

"You still haven't told me where you are," she finally said.

"I'm at the bar chillin' wit' my homeboys," he stated dryly.

"You know when you're coming home?"

"I'll see you in a minute."

"All right," she said, not wanting to get off the phone, but Knox had already hung up.

After waiting over an hour for him to get home, Billie became fed up and slipped on a tank top, her white cardigan, a gold-plated bib necklace, khaki parachute pants, and a pair of coral-colored suede Pelle Moda pumps. To complete the look, she threw on a couple of thick bangle bracelets, grabbed her DVF chain-link, metallic leather bag, and threw on her Lanvin trench coat. Sure she was doing a late-night creep, but Billie Townsend Christianson never left the house looking a mess.

Minutes later, she arrived at the Social House, which was a hip new bar located on Broadway in the Soulard area of St. Louis. They served great bar food, and the happy hour and nightlife were even better. It was also Knox's new place of employment. At night, he worked there, while during the day, he was a process server. Billie walked through the door and paid the entrance fee of five dollars.

She was slightly overdressed, but, oh well. Once her wristband was properly put on, she searched the crowd for her man when she found him playing pool with a hot, young white girl with boobs up to her chin. What made things even worse was the girl was dressed in a Social House uniform. Which was the equivalent of a Hooter's uniform. Deciding that she wouldn't take the ghetto gurl approach and immediately flip, Billie squared her shoulders back and sashayed over to them.

"Ahem," she cleared her throat.

Knox turned around. "What you doing here?" he asked, surprised to see her there.

"I came to spend some time with you." She looked across the table at the girl.

"Oh, I told you I was gon' be home in a minute."

"Yeah, well, I decided to take matters into my own hands." Billie blinked her eyes and smiled.

"That's what's up," Knox kissed her on the cheek. "You wanna play?"

"No, you two go ahead," Billie stepped back wondering what she should do next.

"So where were we?" The girl smooth backed her long blond hair and grinned.

"Uhhhhh, I think it was my turn," Knox replied, ready to throw down.

"Okay, hot stuff. Show me what you got."

Hot stuff? What the hell? Billie thought as Knox leaned across the table to make a shot. Although she was perturbed by his behavior, Knox's entire demeanor still had Billie on the brink of convulsions. He rocked a black V-neck tee, black Levi slim fit jeans, and all-black leather Chuck Taylors like no other. The black rosary and G-Shock watch he sported took his ensemble to a whole nother level of fly. Billie didn't know what to do, fuck him up or fuck him.

"So how long have you two been playin'?" Billie investigated.

"Since I got here," Knox responded. "Jessica thinks she can beat me in pool."

"Oh really?" Billie glared at her.

Not knowing whether she should stay or leave, Jessica stood silently with the pool stick in her hand.

"Let me introduce myself since Mr. Rudeness here didn't. Hi, I'm Knox's wife, Billie," Billie said, walking around the table and extending her hand.

"Ohhhhhhhhh, hi. I've heard so much about you." Jessica shook her hand energetically.

"Really? I've heard nothin' about you." Billie looked back at Knox, giving him the evil eye.

"Would you like something to drink? I could get you something from the bar? We have Bud Light on tap tonight for a dollar."

"No, thank you." Billie released her hand and wiped it on the side of her pants. "I'm not a Bud Light kinda girl. Besides, I don't wanna keep my husband from hanging with his homeboys. As a matter of fact, where *are* your homeboys?" she looked angrily around the bar.

"They all at home laid up with their wives," Knox stared her square in the eyes and took a swig of his beer.

Swallowing the bitter substance, he slammed his beer down hard on the table beside them and said, "Jessica, it's your turn."

"Okay," she skipped. "Eight ball in the corner pocket."

As Jessica leaned over the table attempting to make her shot and her cleavage said hello to everyone in the room, Billie felt herself on the brink of shanking everyone within a five-foot radius.

"Excuse me, sweetie, but can you give us a second," Billie said, ready to kick some ass.

"Sure," Jessica put her stick down and walked away.

"Okay, now that li'l Rachel Uchitel Jr. is gone, what's up?" Billie asked Knox with an attitude.

"What are you talkin' about?"

"Knox, please don't make me show every bit of my ass up in here. You know damn well what I'm talkin' about."

"What?" he shrugged his shoulders. "I'm up here playin' pool. It's a Friday night, I wanted to spend some time wit' you, but you wanted to gossip on the phone all night wit' yo' girlfriends, so I shook. Now I guess you got some free time on your hands."

"As a matter of fact, I do. So what's up?" She put her purse down on the table next to his beer. "You ready for me to whoop yo' ass in some pool?" Billie grabbed a cue stick.

"You don't want none," Knox said, loosening up.

"Don't talk shit," Billie exclaimed, taking her first shot and making it. "Looks like it's gon' be a long night, playboy," she stared at him then winked.

Billie and Knox knew that their moment of bliss would only last but for so long. A storm was brewing between the two of them, and unfortunately, neither of them knew how to stop it.

"All my new bitches seem to get old real quick."
Miguel Feat J. Cole, "All I Want Is You"

9

Finally the day had arrived. Dylan was decked out from head to toe. Her rocker chic haircut was freshly cut and styled to perfection. As a gift to herself, she rocked an extra cute pale pink soft chiffon dress with a one-shoulder rosette corsage detail. The hem of the dress hit her mid thigh, highlighting her firm legs and nude platform sandals.

Chandelier earrings hung from her ears while a vintage Rolex watch gleamed from her wrist, completing the look. The guests at the baby shower couldn't get over how absolutely darling she looked. Dylan, on the other hand, couldn't stop fawning over the décor. Billie had outdone herself. Outside in the center of Billie's half-acre backyard was a huge white tent. Once you walked inside, green Yoko Ono poms tied with ribbons hung from the ceiling, setting the tone for the modern, yet ladylike vibe Billie and Tee-Tee had created.

On the tables were white and apple-green linens. Towering floral arrangements of orchids and twigs played perfectly against the silver charges and menu cards. When the guests arrived, they were greeted with glasses of pink rosé and hand painted place cards. Dylan was overjoyed with how many people came out to celebrate her impending bundle of joy. All of her old club buddies were there, including Kema, Gray, Heidi, Mina, Mo, Unique, and bestselling author Chyna Black. Her hairstylist and makeup guru Delicious was also in attendance.

While waiting for the baby shower games to begin, the women stood around in their garden dresses catching up.

"Honey, you are wearing that dress for real," Gray complimented Dylan. "And I love those earrings."

"Thanks, small children made them," Dylan winked, smiling.

"You are a mess."

"So what's the T on the daddy-to-be? Is he coming?" Delicious pursed his lips.

"He's supposed to be."

"I know you are hatin' that he is with that one photo-shoot-away-from-being-Chippy-D heffa, Milania."

"I'm fine," Dylan lied. "He's moved on, and I'm okay with that. My main concern is my baby. And when the time comes, I'll meet somebody new."

"Trust me, honey, you'll find someone." Heidi finished off her third glass of champagne obviously buzzed. "Well, after you lose all that baby weight, but even then, you'll still have to go much older, 'cause these young niggas ain't tryin' to be tied down to no chick wit' no baby. Just remember to schedule a tummy tuck at the same time as your C-section," she added.

Did this bitch just call me fat? Dylan wondered.

"Right now, I don't care how old he is," Dylan continued on with the conversation. "I just wanna find a good man that can fuck me good. I mean, I wanna get fucked so good that afterward I just wanna buy him something. Be like, nigga, you don't need no tires, an oil change, nothin'."

All the women cracked up laughing.

"Now, Dylan," Kema chimed in, tilting her head to the side, "we all know that a good man and a good dick don't come in the same package."

"Who told you that lie?" Tee-Tee shot her a look. "'Cause my man puts it dooooown."

"You got that right," Gray agreed, giving Tee-Tee a high five.

"Hold up, hold up, hold up!" Kema waved her hand. "I'm not sayin' that a good nigga can't fuck you good, but ain't nothin' like a nigga that treat you like shit fuckin' you. Shit, that muthafucka will have you hemmed up in the corner shakin'."

"Got that right!" Gray waved her hand in the air.

"Girl, shut up. You making me have flashbacks," Chyna fanned her face with her hand.

"All right, enough of talkin' about penises. Where in the hell is the food?" Dylan searched the tent with her eyes.

"Calm down, greedy ass. The or devers will be out in a second," Tee-Tee explained.

"Aunty," Billie's twin daughters, Kenzie and Kaylee, skipped over, "if you're really hungry you can buy some boxes of our delicious Girl Scout cookies," Kaylee batted her eyes.

"How much are they?"

The two girls looked at each another and replied in unison, "Fifteen dollars."

"Apiece?"

"Yes!" they said at once.

"That's pretty expensive for some damn cookies, don't you think?" Dylan stared at them quizzically.

"What?" Kenzie cocked her head back. "We gotta make a profit too."

"Get yo' li'l ass away from me," Dylan tightened her lips.

"Aww, man," Kenzie groaned, snapping her fingers.

"I told you fifteen dollars was too high." Kaylee hit her sister on the arm as they walked away.

"I can't stand they li'l cute behinds," Dylan laughed.

"Ain't they a mess," Tee-Tee took a sip of champagne.

"Sidebar," Delicious tapped Tee-Tee on the shoulder. "Who is that big ole piece of meat right there," he pointed.

All of the ladies and ladyboys followed Delicious's hand.

"You can calm down, honey. That ain't nothin' but State," Tee-Tee's upper lip curled.

"Honey, he is fiiiiiiiine! Mmm, I think my panty's wet."

"I can not deal with you two," Dylan laughed, greeting State with a hug.

"What up?" He wrapped his arms around her waist.

"You, you look nice."

"Thanks, so do you," State let her go.

Delicious cleared his throat, getting State's attention.

"How you doing?" He extended his hand doing a dead-on impersonation of Wendy Williams.

"What up?" State gave him a head nod.

"Oh my God-oh my God-oh my God!" Billie came running toward the tent in a panic.

"What's going on?" Dylan turned to see what the uproar was about and spotted trouble.

"Chunky!" Candy walked across the lawn with her arms spread wide.

"Oh, hell, no!" Dylan stomped her foot.

"*Now* it's a party," Tee-Tee cackled.

"What the hell is *she* doing here?" Dylan whispered out of the side of her mouth.

She could feel the baby moving around in her stomach.

"I don't know," Billie breathed in deeply, trying to catch her breath. "Security told me that she was tryin' to use a bottle of Jack as ID to get in."

"This is *not* happening to me," Dylan tried to pretend like she was having a bad dream.

"There my baby is!" Candy stumbled into the tent with a bottle of Jack Daniels half full in hand, fixing her twisted skirt.

It took everything in Dylan not to scream.

"Candy in the ho-u-u-u-u-u-use! Watch ya' mouth!" she broke it down to the ground, popping her booty.

"Mama, what are you doing here?" Dylan hissed.

"You know yo' mama don't miss no party!" Candy wobbled from side to side.

"But nobody invited you so how did you find out?"

"Yo' mama knows everything. Shit, I know when the last time you farted. Which must have been a minute ago 'cause I smell something a li'l suspect in the air." Candy pinched her nose.

"I did not fart!" Dylan looked around, embarrassed.

"It's okay if you did, friend," Tee-Tee rubbed her arm. "We all get a li'l gas er' now and then."

"Shut up." Dylan pushed him away.

"Auntie, don't mind her." Tee-Tee hugged Candy. "How you been, girl? You look good."

"You better ask about me." Candy stepped back and posed.

She wore a black floppy hat, a halter top showcasing her newly enhanced forty-two DD implants, a zebra print pencil skirt, and patent leather, gladiator stiletto boots. Candy was the type of woman who made no secret that her plastic surgeon was her best friend. She'd had everything done: her nose, lips, breasts, stomach, butt, ears. You name it, she had it nipped and tucked. Candy looked like a well preserved wax figurine of Vanessa Williams.

"You betta work!" Tee-Tee snapped his fingers in a circle.

"And scene," Candy bowed.

"Okay, am I the only one hallucinating here?" Dylan exclaimed, feeling like she was about to cry.

"Shit, girl, quit complaining. Mama's here now, and I'ma make it all better."

"No, you're not. You're making it worse," Dylan whined.

Candy ignored her sarcasm and sauntered around the tent slowly.

"Nice decorations."

"Thank you, Candy," Billie beamed, pleased with herself. "I came up with the concept."

"No wonder I feel like I'm in the Martha Stewart section at Kmart."

"Dead!" Delicious hung his head and grinned.

"Aunty Candy!" Kenzie and Kaylee came running over.

"There my girls are! Gimmie some shugga."

The girls gladly gave her a kiss on the cheek.

"Did you bring us a present?" Kaylee asked, jumping up and down. "'Cause you know we like gifts."

"I sure did, but you got to tell me something first."

"Okay." Kaylee rubbed her hands together, ready.

"What did Aunty Candy teach you about marriage?"

"That's easy," Kenzie flicked her wrist. "Never sign a prenup."

"Y'all are growing up so fast." Candy wiped a tear from her eye. "Here you go, baby." She reached inside her purse and pulled out two mini whips. "Now, y'all go play."

"Yeah!" the twins screamed, skipping off while waving their whips in the air.

"Kenzie and Kaylee, you better bring yo' butt back here!" Billie yelled, chasing after them.

"Now I just need to know one thing!" Candy spun around, spilling her liquor. "Is this shindig open bar? 'Cause in a minute, my bottle gon' need a refill."

"Why me, God? Why me?" Dylan sighed, hoping Angel would arrive soon so she could have some kind of sense of relief.

R&B newcomer Miguel's regretful tune *All I Want Is You* thumped softly from the surround sound speakers inside Angel's penthouse suite. He stood against the window with one hand inside his pants pocket. The other held a freshly lit Cuban cigar. Buzzed from the cigar and the Jeremiah Weed sweet tea vodka he'd been sipping on for the past hour, he gazed at Milania's frame from behind.

She'd just stepped out of the shower. The sun coming through the window highlighted her creamy honey-colored skin. Methodically, she dried her entire body with a plush white cotton towel unaware that at that moment she was Angel's muse. Swaying her hips to the beat, she turned to the side and squirted lavender and vanilla-scented lotion into the palm of her hand, then sensually massaged it into her skin.

Angel watched closely as her fingertips traced her collarbone, then slid down her chest and kneaded her full breasts. Every part of her physique was taut, lean, and tantalizing. Her measurements were a perfectly crafted thirty-fourC-twenty-four-thirty-four. She possessed a flat stomach and shapely thighs. Her ass wasn't Nicki Minaj big but ample enough to fill out a pair of skinny leg jeans. No grown man with two eyes and a functioning dick could dispute how fine she was, but neither her hips nor ass could compare to Dylan's. Dylan was everything, and more, that Milania could never be.

"You must be as excited as I am," she gazed over her shoulder and smiled.

"About what?" Angel eyed her, puzzled. "The shower?"

"No, silly, about the appointment we have today at The Sheldon." She pulled her top on over her head.

"What appointment at The Sheldon?"

"The one that I told you about last week. The same appointment that I've had to reschedule now three times."

"I know that you've had to reschedule a couple of times, but I ain't know nothin' about an appointment today." Angel finished off the last of his drink.

"Well, I told you, so we can't miss it. This appointment is important because it's for our reception venue. I scheduled it for 2:30, so make sure you have everything you need 'cause the car will be here in fifteen minutes." Milania slipped on a pair of slouchy sequined pants.

"You gon' have to go by yourself, 'cause I'm not gon' be able to make it." Angel inhaled smoke from the cigar.

"Why?" Milania snapped her neck.

"'Cause I gotta go to my baby shower, that's why. What you mean?" He screwed up his face.

"You mean *Dylan's* shower?" she corrected him.

"*Our* baby shower," Angel stressed so she would get the hint.

"Whateva," Milania sat down on the bed and put on her Jill Sander's, laser-cut, wood and metal pumps. "I honestly don't give a damn if it was Mother Teresa's baby shower. Are you coming with me or not, 'cause I'm not missing this appointment."

"No, I'm not. I already told Dylan that I was coming, and I'm not gon' change that."

Milania closed her eyes. This was it. The moment she'd been dreading for months. She didn't want to have a Mel Gibson moment and flip out, but Angel was taking her there. Enough was enough. There was only so much biting her tongue that she could do. It was time for Angel to see that she meant business.

"You know what?" Milania opened her eyes and stood up. "I'm sick of y'all."

"On the real, don't get to talkin' out the side of yo' mouth wit' no slick shit, straight up," Angel cautioned, walking out of the room so he could place his cup on the dining-room table.

"Negro, pleeease! Every time I breathe, I gotta hear about Dylan this and the baby that! Don't you think I get tired of hearing about that bitch?"

"You can stop with the soap opera act," Angel reentered the room. "You knew what you was gettin' into when I told you she was pregnant, so don't start throwin' a fit now."

"Nigga, I ain't five! I'm tellin' you how I fuckin' feel, but it's obvious that you don't give a fuck! So you know what? The hell with you," she pointed her finger at his chest. "The hell with her, and the hell with that baby! As a matter of fact, I hope she lose that muthafucka!"

"What the fuck you just say?" Angel stepped up into her face, heated.

"Did I stutter, nigga?" Milania rolled her neck, unfazed. "Ever since we got here, it's been about her and that fuckin' baby! Well, what about *me* and what *I* want? Yo' selfish ass don't even take that into consideration! You just expect for me to be this ready-made stepmother to a baby that might not even be yours!"

"You pushin' me right now," Angel warned, balling his fist.

"And you've been pushing me away. I have had enough," Milania took off her engagement ring and dropped it on the floor. "Go marry that trifling, cheating-ass bitch 'cause right about now, she can have you! I'm outta here!"

Milania snatched up her purse and stormed toward the door.

"Where you going?" he yelled, racing after her.

"None of yo' damn business!" Milania screamed before slamming the door in his face.

Stunned by her tyrannical outburst and blatant disrespect of him, Angel reared his hand back and punched the wall. Fire burned through his veins. It was a dumb, irrational move that could fuck up his livelihood, but he had to take his aggression out on something before he had a serious meltdown. Angel glanced down at his hand. His knuckles were scraped and bleeding. *Fuck!* he shouted out loud. The blood on his hand only infuriated him more. He headed down the hall to the bathroom when his cell phone started to vibrate.

"Hello?" He placed the phone up to his ear.

"Where are you?" Billie asked. "The shower started almost an hour ago."

"Put Dylan on the phone," Angel replied rudely.

"Mmm, *excuse me?*" Billie took the phone away from her ear, appalled. "Dylan, come get the phone!"

"Who is it?" Angel could hear her say in the background.

"My rude-ass brother."

Dylan happily took the phone. "Hi. Where are you?" she asked.

"I'm not coming," he decided, feeling like, fuck everybody. For once, Angel was going to be selfish and put his feelings first.

"You're kidding me, right?" Dylan replied in shock.

"No, I'm not."

"But you said you would be here—"

"And you said you would be faithful, so what the fuck does that mean? Absolutely nothin'," Angel snapped, cutting her off.

As soon as the words left Angel's mouth, he regretted it, but it was too late. The damage had already been done and before he could say he was sorry, Dylan hung up in his ear. Fed up with how his day was going, Angel hurled his phone at the wall, breaking it into a thousand pieces. He wanted to fuck up some shit, yell at the heavens, curse at the wind. The shit he was dealing with was too much for even a man like him to handle.

Angel always saw himself as some kind of real-life superhero who could conquer the world. No matter what life threw his way, he always assumed he'd be able to deal with it, but being engaged to one woman while another carried his child was like kryptonite. Everything about the situation was killing him softly.

Angel plopped down on the sofa and leaned his head back. Staring at the ceiling, all he could think was this wasn't how his life was supposed to be. But nobody gave a damn about his feelings. They never took in account that he was under a lot of pressure too. After stewing in his emotions and drowning his feelings in alcohol, he gathered his emotions and stuffed them deep down into the pit of his troubled heart and headed over to the shower.

Despite what was going on with him personally, there was no way he could afford to miss such a moment in his and Dylan's life. Plus, he needed to fix the messed-up situation he'd created between himself and Dylan.

Bumping Method Man's "Break Ups 2 Make Ups," Angel pulled up to Billie's estate. Once his car was parked, Angel pocketed his keys and grabbed the bouquet of "Mango" and "Treasure" calla lilies he'd picked up for Dylan along the way. As he stepped out of his car the afternoon sun glowed against his skin.

Approaching the rear of the mansion, Angel spotted a sea of women dressed in brightly colored dresses, but amidst the abundance of beautiful faces, none stood out like Dylan's. Angel wished that he could say that he was over her, but every time he took a look at her hazel eyes and angelic smile, old feelings came flooding back. Despite his harsh words earlier in the day, she carried on as if she didn't have a care in the world.

Beams of sunlight seemed to highlight her every move. Watching her was like watching art come to life. Angel loved seeing her so at peace. It brought a smile to his face, but his smile quickly faded once he noticed State pull her to the side and give her a hug. *What the fuck?* he whispered underneath his breath, dropping the flowers down to his side. Angel felt as if he'd been gut punched. It took everything in him not to run over to Dylan and yank her up by the neck. Then he wondered if the rumors could be true. Was it all a hoax? Was State really the father of Dylan's child? Instead of lashing out and having a tyrannical outburst Kanye-style, Angel preceded in her direction as calm as he could be.

"I gotta jet," State released Dylan from his grasp.

"Well, thanks for coming, and thanks for the Fendi diaper bag and blanket."

"It was nothin'. You know despite the bullshit, I got you."

"I . . . just . . . bet . . . you . . . do," Dylan said slowly as if she'd seen a ghost.

"You a'ight?" he asked, noticing the change in her demeanor. "Please don't tell me you going into labor 'cause there is only so much a nigga like me can take."

"No . . . Angel's here," she spoke just above a whisper.

Dylan wished that she could be the type of chick that could give a fuck about the way Angel might feel upon seeing the man she'd betrayed his trust for, but the look of sadness mixed with anguish was too much for her to ignore.

"Let me holla at you," Angel stepped before her while shooting State a look that could kill.

"Stay sweet, Ma," State leaned forward and brushed his lips on Dylan's cheek. Stepping back, he shot Angel the screw face, then walked away.

"Wack-ass nigga," Angel uttered.

"I thought you wasn't coming." Dylan folded her arms and rested them on top of her protruding tummy.

"Yeah, well, I'm here now," he responded, still ticked off by State's presence.

"And what's *that* suppose to mean?" she smirked.

"It means that I'm sorry for buggin' on you like that, but that don't mean that you can just call yo'self being mad at me and gettin' smart," he joked, trying to lighten the mood.

Dylan tried her damnest not to smile but failed miserably. She couldn't stay mad at Angel if she tried.

"You look beautiful." He scanned his eyes over her entire physique.

"Thanks."

"I got these for you," he handed her the flowers.

"Awwww, thank you," she blushed, inhaling the scent. "Did you like the stuff I got for the baby?"

"I haven't opened the gifts yet."

"What you waiting on?" He took her hand and led her over to the three tables filled with presents.

"C'mon, everybody, we're gettin' ready to open gifts," Dylan yelled out to the crowd.

"So I see li'l Jon Gosselin finally showed up," Tee-Tee remarked taking a seat.

"Shut up," Dylan warned, squinting her eyes.

"Excuse me! Excuse me!" Candy trampled her way through everyone to get to the front. "I gotta sit next to the birthday girl!"

"By the way, my mom is here," Dylan whispered to Angel.

"I see." He looked at Candy, puzzled.

"Before you open anything, Mama gotta special surprise for you," Candy beamed.

"Uh, ah, Mama. I don't need no surprise. Whateva you got, take it back 'cause I don't want it."

"It's a good one, Chunky, I promise."

"No, Mama," Dylan shook her head profusely.

"Quit being so goddamn negative!" Candy stomped her foot. "You gon' ruin the damn surprise! Now shut up, shit! C'mon, baby!" Candy signaled to someone by waving her hand in the air.

Out of nowhere, Gray's uncle-in-law Uncle Clyde came across the lawn in a god-awful blue crushed velvet jumpsuit doing Michael Jackson's sideways glide, singing, "There Goes My Baby." Dylan felt like she wanted to faint.

"Honey, call FEMA, 'cause this is a disaster," Delicious laughed.

"This is *not* happening," Dylan lowered her head and looked down. "I swear to God I'm going to throw up."

"What's going on?" Gray asked, outdone as well. "Uncle Clyde, what are you doing here?"

"Tell 'em, Hot Plate." Uncle Clyde hugged Candy tightly.

"Well, after I left, I was a li'l down on my luck, but you know me. I got that eye of the tiger, honey, and one day, I was at this bar sippin' on my boy Jack," she held up her glass, "when my pussy said, 'Beep-beep-beep.' So I bent down and said, 'What is it, girl?' And she said, 'Beep-beep-beep.' And I said, 'You smell money?' And she said, 'Beep-beep-beep,' and I said, 'At the end of the bar?' And sure enough, there he was."

"Who? Clyde?" Dylan jumped in.

"No, Dick, my deceased husband."

"Ba-na-nas," Tee-Tee grinned, taking a sip of champagne.

"So let me get this straight. You met some man name Dick and married him, and now he's dead?" Dylan said, dumbfounded.

"Yes," Candy dabbed her eyes with a hundred-dollar bill. "God bless his soul. He was eighty-two years old."

"How did he die?"

"Let's just say we were in the boudoir." Candy fanned herself. "Now, I know how my mentor Anna Nicole felt when her boo passed. But thankfully, Dick didn't have any next of kin, so I ended up with everything."

"How much is everything?" Tee-Tee probed, salivating.

"Twenty-five million. Hallelujah, thank you, Jesus," Candy pretended to shout.

"Aww, shit! Get it, Aunty!" Tee-Tee danced, doing the Headache.

"That still doesn't explain you and Clyde," Dylan spoke up, swatting away a fly with her hand.

"Go head and tell 'em, Hot Plate. Tell 'em how you hooked back up wit' Daddy." Clyde curled his fingers like a cat's claws and growled.

"After the funeral, I decided to take a trip to Kentucky for the ribfest, and lo and behold, guess who was performing on the main stage? Clyde. Now, I don't know if it was my fourth glass of Jack or Clyde's sequined jump-suit, but I fell in love and ever since then, we've been inseparable."

"Show 'em the ring, Hot Plate," Clyde insisted, patting her on the butt.

"Oh, shit! How could I forget? Take that in ya' ass, Chunky!" Candy held up her hand and flashed her two-finger diamond ring made in the shape of a turntable.

"We're gettin' married!" Candy shrilled.

"Well, my day is ruined," Dylan shook her head in shock.

"*I'ma be yo' new da-dddy!*" Clyde sang like Brown from the Tyler Perry movie.

"Oh God." Dylan shook her head profusely. "Some-body get me a fan! I feel like I'ma faint!"

"You choose to give up on the possibility of love for us."
Teedra Moses, "All That I Have"

10

"I can not believe that on the day of my baby shower, the day I've been dreaming about for months, not only does Candy show up, but she's rich!" Dylan shrilled, stomping up the steps. "Rich and gettin' married again for the one-hundredth time! All I wanted was to open fabulous gifts and eat cake, but nooooo, here come Candy and all her ghetto fabulousness stealing all of my thunder yet again. And there I am drifting into the background while she makes everything about her," Dylan complained, entering the kitchen.

Not knowing what to say, Angel put down the gifts he'd brought into the house, opened his arms wide, and said, "Come here, man."

Dylan poked out her bottom lip and rushed over into his arms. "I'm sorry. I know I'm going on and on." She buried her face into his chest.

The scent of his Dolce & Gabbana Light Blue cologne was enthralling.

"You don't have anything to be sorry for. You're only sayin' how you feel." He held her close.

Angel wanted to hold her in his arms forever. She felt so warm in his arms. Dylan felt the same way. Becoming lost in his touch, she finally pulled away and said, "So, umm . . . yeah . . . you want something to drink?"

"Nah, I'm good." He placed his hands inside his pockets.

"Well, have a seat. I mean, unless you got to get home before yo' chick have a contraption fit," she probed with baited breath.

"Man, please, and you mean a conniption fit." Angel walked over to the couch and sat down.

"Yeah, that too," Dylan snapped her fingers.

It was kind of weird for him to be in Dylan's crib without anyone else around. He'd avoided it this long for fear of what might happen, but the longer he sat, the more comfortable he became. All of his worries seemed to drift away and evaporate. He would never admit it, but deep down inside, Angel knew he was home.

"I swear, the further I get into this pregnancy the more tired I become." Dylan sat down beside him.

"Put your feet up here." Angel patted his lap.

Dylan smiled and did exactly what she was told. Angel gently took off each of her heels and began massaging her swollen feet.

"Shut the front door, that feels so good." She threw her head back, relishing the feel of his hands.

"Why yo' feet so fat though?" he questioned, screwing up his face.

"Shut up!" Dylan smacked him on the shoulder. "That's what happens when you're pregnant."

"That's a damn lie. I ain't never seen no feet like these before." He placed her left foot up to his nose and smelled it. "And they stink." He held his breath.

"My feet don't stink!" Dylan held her stomach and laughed. "An-y-way, I was thinkin' maybe we should wait and find out the sex of the baby when I give birth."

"That's what's up." Angel ran his thumb up and down the middle of her foot.

"I just have one request, though. When I do go into labor, just make sure that I'm in Chanel."

"What?" Angel laughed.

"No, listen," she insisted. "I have this really cute black cashmere Chanel vintage robe that I just bought, and I feel like then is when it could be used at its best."

"I wish I could honestly say that I'm surprised. You mind if I turn on some music?" Angel looked at her.

"Nah, go ahead." Dylan set her feet down on the floor.

Angel walked over to her stereo and popped in one of Dylan's mixtapes. The first song was Lil Wayne's "I Am Not A Human Being." Out of nowhere, Angel started doing the robot.

"Challenge!" he yelled, posing in a b-boy stance.

"Oh, word?" Dylan cheesed, standing up doing the wop. After spinning around in a circle, she pointed her finger at him and said, "Challenge!"

"That ain't shit!" Angel waved her off and busted out doing the running man. He finished his routine off with the typewriter and the cabbage patch. "Now show me what you got, li'l mama!"

"Not a damn thing! I'm tired as hell." She rubbed her belly and laughed.

"You wack," Angel teased her.

"Whateva, I'll be wack," she said preparing to sit back down.

"Uh-uh, come dance wit' me." Angel took her by the hand and led her to the middle of the floor.

Seal's "Secret" was playing. Angel held Dylan close. Cherishing the moment, they swayed from side to side. Suddenly, every bad thing in the world disappeared, and it was just the two of them. What they shared was as strange as the weather, but it felt right. As time elapsed, they ventured, fingers intertwined, into her bedroom. Dylan lay facing him sound asleep. She didn't even need a cover that night. The heat from Angel's body kept her warm.

Angel lay snuggled close in front of her. His finger-tips gently traced the outline of her face. He could stare at her forever. She was the definition of beautiful. Her eyes, nose, and lips were made just for him. She was his baby, his heart, his soul, his rib. Angel just hated that things between them ended the way they had.

Maybe they could've gone the distance. She probably would've ended up being his wife. Angel couldn't even front. Dylan was already his. He didn't need a ring to prove it. But then he remembered the woman at home he'd professed his love to and realized that love wasn't as easy as fairy tales made it out to be. Resting his right hand on her belly, Angel nestled his nose on her fore-head and inhaled the rich scent of her skin until his reality turned into the place we all call dreamland.

The next morning, Angel awoke to the soothing sound of Teedra Moses' voice. That morning she sang about a lover not being ready to give his all. Angel sat up and rubbed his eyes. He didn't even remember falling asleep, let alone at Dylan's place. Swiftly, he turned his head and gazed at the other side of the bed. It was empty. The aroma of crêpes let him know she was on the second floor. Angel rose from the bed and put on his sneakers which were beside the bed and walked downstairs.

"Good morning," she smiled, warmly dressed in a black spaghetti strap nightgown.

"How long you been up?"

"Since around five. I've been working on my book." She wiped her hands on a towel.

"What book?" Angel asked, noticing the sea of food she'd prepared.

Dylan had fixed crêpes with fresh berries and home-made whip cream, poached eggs, bacon, and sausage.

"I didn't tell you. I wrote a cookbook and a got deal for it."

"Word?" He took a seat at the table.

"Yeah. State hooked me up with this awesome agent, and I pitched her my idea, and she got me a deal."

"State, huh?"

Dylan fixed him a plate and swallowed.

"Yeah."

"So, y'all close, huh?" he asked, feeling his heartbeat increase.

"I wouldn't say that." She set his plate down in front of him. "We're just cool, that's all."

"I mean, y'all must be something. He gettin' you book deals, coming to yo' job, and coming to the shower and shit."

"So that's what this is about?" Dylan scoffed.

"It's about you not giving a fuck about how I feel!" He hit the table with his fist, causing his plate to rattle and Dylan to jump. "You got that nigga hangin' around like it's all good! Shit, I'm startin' to wonder if that is my muthafuckin' baby."

Dylan instantly shrunk to two feet tall. That's how big Angel made her feel. His words made her want to die. Nothing she ever did would be good enough, and she was tired of trying to prove her loyalty to him.

"The old me would've cussed you clean out for that, but I'm not gon' even raise my blood pressure. 'Cause I'm not gon' fight wit' you. I've apologized I don't know how many times for what I did. And I know that him being around bothers you, but you've moved on."

"So what? Since I'm wit' Milania, that mean you can just throw that nigga up in my face whenever you feel like it?"

"You got a whole girlfriend at home, how you gon' talk?" Dylan shot back.

"That's different," he challenged indignantly.

"If that's what you gotta tell yourself in order to sleep at night. Look, you're doing you, and I'm respecting that. You can't be mad 'cause I'm doing me too. And I'm not going to continue to be punished for something I did almost two years ago. You're either going to forgive me or not," she said defiantly.

Angel sat silently, fuming.

"You *have* to forgive me," Dylan inched closer to him. Tears choked her throat.

"You *have* to forgive me." She cupped his cheeks with her hands and made him look at her. "You *have* to forgive me."

Angel sat helplessly, controlled by her touch.

"Please, you have to forgive me."

"I gotta go." He put his hands on top of hers and released them from his face. Feeling short of breath, he jogged down the steps, leaving her standing there hopeless.

Angel hopped in his car and pounded his fist against the steering wheel. He'd thought that being friends with Dylan would be easy, but the more time they shared, the harder it became. Sometimes he wished they'd never crossed the line and become lovers because now, there was no way they could just be friends.

Angel wasn't the type to smoke, but if he did, he would've rolled up a fatty, turned on The Cool Kids, and zoned out for the rest of the day. The shit in his life was getting more and more complicated by the second. He felt torn, torn between what his heart was screaming and what his mind kept on nagging him to do. His heart ached to be with Dylan. Somehow, she'd implanted herself there, and no matter how hard he tried to remove her, it became clearer that she was irreplaceable.

No other chick could compete with her style or grace. She was magnificent in every way conceivable, but then thoughts of her tryst would appear in his mind and Angel would remember the hollow feeling she'd also left in his heart. He couldn't risk her putting him through that kind of pain again. And yes, love should outweigh everything, but in life, you had to use common sense too, so for right now, he'd rather tread lightly than dip off into the deep end again.

Angel pulled up to the Four Seasons and sighed. All he wanted was to go inside, take a hot bath and chill, but with Milania on the warpath, that would be damn near impossible. Oddly enough, she hadn't even called his phone once. Angel figured she was just biding her time and stacking evidence against him to build her case. After valeting his car and saying what's up to the front desk clerk, Angel boarded the elevator. He stepped off the elevator, put his door key inside the lock, and prepared himself for the fight of the century.

To his surprise, Milania wasn't standing there in attack mode. Instead, he found her walking past the hallway, drying her hair with a towel. She'd just gotten out of the shower and was dressed in a big fluffy cotton robe. Little did Angel know but Milania had just gotten home too.

"What's up?" Angel said, placing his key, wallet, and phone down on the stand next to the door.

"Hey." She stopped and shook her hair so it would fall down her back.

"How long you been up?"

"Not long." She looked at him somberly. "Can I just say something to you?"

"You already did," he joked.

"Seriously," Milania licked her lips nervously.

"Go ahead."

"I'm sorry for the way I acted yesterday. I was way out of line with the stuff that I said. I was just hurt and upset 'cause I feel like it's you, Dylan, and the baby, and somewhere in all of that, I'm tryin' to fit in, but I can't and it's hard feeling like the oddball out. But, baby, I love you, and I wanna see us work but you have to meet me halfway or else we're not gonna make it."

Angel was conflicted. The words Milania spewed at him the day before still burned to the core. He couldn't see himself marrying a woman who felt that way about his child. But then again, maybe it was some heat-of-the-moment-type shit. He wasn't sure. All he knew for sure was that he was drowning. Every day he was responsible for somebody's feelings or lack of support. He wanted to appease both Milania and Dylan, but the game of tug-of-war was becoming too much, and sooner or later, Angel was sure to break. But for the sake of keeping down confusion, Angel surrendered his white flag.

"I feel everything you sayin'. I'm sorry for not taking your feelings into consideration." He kissed Milania on the lips. "I should've been more understanding."

"Thank you. That means a lot to me." She kissed him back sweetly.

"But if you ever say some shit like that to me again . . . it's a wrap," Angel said as serious as a heartache.

"Okay," Milania replied.

"Yo', I'm tired as fuck. I'm gettin' ready to take a shower and lay back for a minute." Angel began to peel off his jacket and shirt.

"Actually, we have to meet with the party planner for the engagement party today, so I'ma need you to get dressed." she said.

Milania could see steam rise from Angel's body, but she could care less. She'd come this far and no way was she gonna stop now just cause he was at his wit's end.

"Remember you said that you would be more understanding," she batted her eyes and grinned.

"A'ight, man, here I come," Angel groaned, heading toward the bedroom.

"So what are we doing here again?" Tee-Tee held his purse tightly to his side in disgust.

He and Dylan were heading into Aldi's, a grocery store where you could buy food for super low prices. This Aldi's in particular was in the center of the hood. All kinds of strange individuals were known to lurk around.

"I think I'm starting to itch." He tuned up his face. "I'm sayin' though, you got a li'l taste of dough now. Why can't we go around the corner to Schnucks?"

"'Cause the prices are better here." Dylan put a quarter into the cart to release it.

"You got to pay money just to get a cart? What kind of rigged-up shit is this?"

"Just come on," Dylan giggled, walking through the automatic doors.

Inside, they were greeted by an armed security guard.

"Okay, see now, I'm scared, and I'ma thug." Tee-Tee walked closely beside Dylan. "Thugs don't get scared."

"Will you hush?" she whispered.

"We gotta be quiet too? Oh, see, this is too much. I'm about to put my whereabouts on Facebook just in case I get shot." He pulled out his phone.

"You are so dramatic." She giggled at his silliness.

"And something told me to put on my sneakers. 'Cause if something pop off, I ain't gon' be able to do shit in these Jimmy Choo's." He held up his foot.

"Now *that* I can agree with."

Dylan was wearing a hot new pair of Sergio Rossi pumps. She might've been pregnant, but that didn't stop her from being fly at all times.

"So have you talked to Candy since the shower?" Tee-Tee asked.

"No, she's been callin' me, but I haven't answered. I can't deal with Candy and her nonsense right now." Dylan put a package of flour in her cart.

"Girl, I damn near fell out when Clyde started singing."

"That shit wasn't funny, and the sad part is I'ma have to deal with that mess all the time now."

"Honey, I would love it. It would be like a live version of *Soul Train* every day."

"Well, let him be yo' damn step daddy then." Dylan picked up some penne noodles.

"Now I know you don't think you gon' get by without tellin' me about what happened between you and Angel."

"That's because nothin' happened. He took me home, and that was it," Dylan replied nonchalantly.

"Girl, who you think you foolin'? 'Cause it for damn sure ain't me," Tee-Tee arched his eyebrow and pursed his lips together as a little Mexican girl in a pink ruffle church dress, Barbie high heels, and socks twirled around him dancing with a Teddy Ruxpin doll in her hands.

"Umm, somebody betta come get Dora the Explorer 'cause I fight kids." He tried to get away from the little girl, but she kept on following him.

"Tee-Tee, leave that baby alone. She's cute," Dylan smiled down at the little girl.

"To you. Ahhhh, ¿*Cómo estás? Quiero* Taco Bell! Nacho Bell *Grande!* Woo-hoo! Come get ya' baby!" He waved his hand in the air.

"And somebody gon' give you a kid?" Dylan shook her head, walking down the aisle.

"Bitch, I'ma be a damn good mama. At least my kid ain't gon' be runnin' around here dressed like a deranged prom queen in the middle of the damn day."

"You going to hell for that," Dylan grinned as the little girl's mother came and got her.

"Whateva. Now, what happened between you and Angel? 'Cause I know you ain't tellin' me the whole truth and nothin' but the truth."

"Damn nosy ass. He spent the night, okay." Dylan put some broccoli in her cart.

"I *knew* you still had a li'l ho up in you." Tee-Tee popped his lips.

"For your information, we didn't have sex." Dylan rolled her eyes hard at him.

"Well, it sounds like you had a boring night."

"The only reason he spent the night is because it got late and we ended up falling asleep."

"Uh-huh, sleep, my ass." He twisted his mouth to the side as if to say, "yeah, right." "You ain't got to lie to me. I know Angel got a taste of that pregnant pussy."

"You are such a douche bag," Dylan laughed. "Sidebar, did you know that Gogurt was just yogurt?"

"Girl, you 'bout to make my head hurt. Everybody knows that."

"Oh," Dylan said shocked.

"Any-who, so what now?" Tee-Tee asked as they made their way up to the checkout lane.

"Nothin'. He went back home to Milania, and that was it."

Dylan decided to keep her begging session to herself. She didn't feel like she had to tell Tee-Tee everything.

"You know, it baffles me, though, how a man can taste caviar but settle for catfish," Tee-Tee thought out loud.

"You ain't neva lied, but, honey, I'm not stuntin' Angel," Dylan lied. "My main concern is my business, finishing my book, and decorating my baby's room."

"Good girl, that's the kinda stuff I like to hear."

"It's just hard dealing with all of this."

"Honey, you don't know hard. Try auditioning for *Baywatch* and they tell you they're going in a different direction. Now *that's* hard," Tee-Tee looked at her.

"Clean up on aisle three! Clean up on aisle three," Dylan giggled.

"Why do you pick me up just to cast me away?"
Fantasia, "The Thrill Is Gone"

11

Maya Angelou's classic poem "Phenomenal Woman" came to mind as Billie stepped out of her white Bentley SuperSport and set her aching Elizabeth & James-covered feet on the concrete ground. Since six that morning, she'd been rippin' and runnin'. She'd been to one meeting after another and was tired as hell. Sista-girl needed a break and fast, but first, she had to pick up the kids from their daily afterschool program. Billie's children attended the prestigious Dwight McDaniels Jr. School of Christian Education.

After being buzzed into the building, she tiptoed slowly into the main office, trying her best to ease the pain in her sore feet. But with each step, it felt like needles were being pricked into the soles of her feet.

"Hello?" the school secretary spoke.

"I'm here to pick up Kyrese Townsend and Kenzie and Kaylee Townsend."

"Umm . . ." The secretary looked down at her dismissal sheet. "They've been picked up already."

"You say what now?" Billie's eyes bucked.

"Yes, they were picked up at . . ." The secretary looked down at the dismissal sheet once again. "It looks like 3:30 when school let out."

"By whom?" Billie's heart raced.

"Their father, Cain Townsend."

"Oh, it's about to be on." Billie went inside her purse and took out her cell phone. "He is not authorized to pick our kids up from school," she seethed with anger.

"I'm sorry, ma'am, but he said that you wouldn't mind," the secretary tried to reason.

"Don't you think that you all should've contacted me?" Billie looked at her like she was an idiot.

"We don't get involved with parental disputes, ma'am."

"Excuses," Billie scoffed. "We'll see how my lawyer feels about that 'cause I swear to God if my kids aren't back here in 10.2 seconds, me and you gon' have a dispute," she spat, walking back outside while dialing Cain's number.

"Hello?" Becky answered.

"Put Cain on the phone!"

"Billie, how many times do I have to tell you . . . stop callin' my house with an attitude!"

"And how many times do I have to tell you to kiss my ass, you ole ratchet-ass ho! Now put that asshole you call a husband on the phone!"

"I wish I would!" Becky said, not backing down.

"Okay . . . I'ma see about you." Billie chirped the alarm on her car.

She was about to make it her business to go over to Cain's house and drag Becky's ass.

"And the police are too 'cause the last time I checked, kidnapping was illegal!" Billie quipped.

"Kidnapping?" Becky shouted. "Please! You have no grounds! Cain has every right to pick up *our* kids anytime he wants! You're the silly one who doesn't want him to be involved in his kids' life 'cause he doesn't want you!"

"Hello?" Cain snatched the phone from Becky's hand.

"What made you think you could just come get the kids without my permission?"

"Billie, I don't need your permission to see my kids."

"Umm, according to our custody agreement, you do, sweetheart! You, my dear, are to get the kids on the weekends, which you barely do, but that's a whole 'nother conversation within itself!"

"Whateva. You can go ahead wit' all that."

"I just bet I can! Bring my fuckin' kids home now!" she demanded.

Cain didn't even bother to reply. He simply hung up on her.

"Stupid ass," Billie hissed, getting in her car.

Minutes later she was home.

"Babe," she yelled entering the house.

"Yeah!" Knox met her in the foyer.

"Are the kids here yet?"

"No. I thought they were with you," he replied, perplexed.

"No. I went to the school to pick them up, and Cain had already got them and didn't bother to tell me a thing. He just went behind my back and did it!"

"Have you talked to him?"

"Yes!" Billie paced back and forth.

"Is he bringing the kids home?"

"Yes!"

"Then just calm down. Breathe. Everything's gonna be fine." He rubbed her arms.

"Don't tell me to calm down!" She smacked his hands away. "That muthafucka took my kids! Maybe you'll understand how it feels when you actually have some!"

Knox felt like he'd been sliced in the throat. Before either of them could say another word, Cain pulled into the driveway. Nowhere near done going off, Billie met Cain outside.

"Who in the hell do you think you are?" she ran up on him, getting in his face.

"You better back the fuck up," he warned.

"Negro, please! Fuck you! Get my fuckin' kids outta the car!"

"*Yo'* kids?" he eyed her.

"Did I stutter? Yeah, nigga, *my* kids. Let's not pretend like yo' ass winning daddy of the year awards around here!" she yelled while Kyrese and the girls filed out of the car.

"Ay!" Knox came over to Billie. "I understand that you're mad but chill. The kids don't need to be hearing that."

"How about you mind yo' fuckin' business. This ain't got nothin' to do with you."

Knox stood speechless, only able to blink. Billie quickly realized that what she'd said was like committing the ultimate sin, but the words had already shot out of her mouth and faded into the wind.

"C'mon, y'all." Knox ushered the kids inside. "Let's give yo' mommy and daddy some time alone."

"Why? We won't be able to hear nothin' then," Kaylee complained.

"Shut up, li'l stupid girl," Kyrese snapped, irritated. He'd been putting up with his parents' battles for years and was past sick of it.

"You happy now?" Cain shouted.

"Are you?" Billie snapped back.

"I'm up. I ain't got time for this shit!" He got back inside his car.

"That's right, nigga! Run away like you always do like a little-ass fuckin' boy," she yelled as he backed out of the driveway.

Rapidly breathing in and out, Billie ran her fingers through her hair and strutted back into the house. She had to apologize to Knox. In her room she found him in their walk-in closet gathering his things.

"You going somewhere?" she asked as he whizzed by her.

"That's what it look like, don't it?" He carried a ton of socks in his arms and tossed them into a suitcase.

"Don't you think you're being just a little dramatic?"

"Nah, the question is, don't you think you've been actin' like a bitch?" he barked, pissed.

"Did you *really* just call me a *bitch?*" she cocked her head back, aghast.

"I said you've been actin' like one. There's a difference."

"I know that what I said was mean, but things between us can't be that bad for you to just up and leave."

"Tell me this." He got up in her face, scaring her. "Where the fuck have you been? 'Cause things between us been fucked up for a minute! You treat me like I'm your fuckin' employee and not your man! I'm runnin' around here askin' you to kiss me and hug me like I'm a goddamn female! And then you gon' tell me to mind my fuckin' business when it comes to them kids, and I'm the main one helping them with they homework, school projects, takin' them to karate practice, and having dinner wit' 'em every night? While you out at some gallery show or they real daddy off doing whateva the fuck he wanna do! But I don't say shit 'cause I love them and I loved you! But you don't appreciate shit, so I'ma do what I should've did a long time ago and shake!"

Paralyzed from hearing the truth, Billie stood with tears flooding her eyes. Her entire world was crumbling right before her, and she had no one else to blame but herself. For months she'd been pushing Knox away. She could vividly remember the days she'd come home from work and all Knox would want was just a little bit of her time, but selfishly, she'd push him away because she was either too tired or too busy.

Billie was so caught up in her own life that she didn't even bother to notice just how unhappy he was. She figured she'd eventually free up some time for him and things would get better before they got worse. But it wasn't just her time he craved. Knox missed the companionship they once shared.

They used to have a good time with one another. Laughter once had been a part of their daily life. When they walked, they used to hold each other's hand, but after awhile, Billie began to take all of that for granted. She began to treat her relationship with Knox as if it were a contractual agreement and nothing more. And because of that, she was left alone to forever bleed.

There they were, three friends lounging in Billie's king-sized bed wearing zebra print Snuggies, eating Hostess products while watching a marathon of *Jerseylicious*. Since Knox's departure, Billie hadn't been able to leave her room. Each day that passed, all she did was cry and stare at photographs of their wedding day. They were so happy then, but Billie, being the maniacal control freak bitch she was, ruined it all.

She saw herself being curt when she spoke to him or when she was overwhelmed and in a mood, giving him snide looks but she just couldn't control it. *Was I like this with Cain?* she wondered. Flashes of her treating Cain like an absolute idiot or them making love and her being as stiff as a board entered her mind. One time, she even told him to "hurry up and get it over with."

During their divorce, Billie had spent the entire time blaming Cain for everything, when she had faults too. The same faults she brought over into her new relationship. Billie never took the time to fix herself up because until Knox left her, she thought that she was perfect.

Now here she was, left with a cold case love and only she could be the one to solve the mystery of where her and Knox's love went wrong. The question was, could their differences be solved, and was Billie willing to take the fall?

"I think I lost him for good, y'all," she fumbled with her hands while crying.

"No, you haven't. He just needs some time to cool off, that's all," Dylan assured her, praying she was right.

"What's wrong with me? Why is it every man I get, I push him away? It's like I don't wanna be happy or something. Like, I'm sabotaging myself on purpose."

"'Cause you are," Tee-Tee said, not willing to sugarcoat the situation.

"Huh?" Billie looked at him perplexed.

"You heard me, heffa." He stopped eating his cupcake. "Sometimes you bring nonsense on yo'self. Stop tryin' to be catwoman, thinkin' you can save the world and everyone in it, and learn how to love yo' man. 'Cause to me, it seem like Knox is an afterthought. It's the kids, your charity work, us, and *then* him. Hell, what man you think gon' put up with that?" Tee-Tee glared at her.

"I'm surprised he ain't already left yo' ass. 'Cause I know I would've. Bernard would've been put the smack down if I talked to him the way you do, Knox. I don't know if it's yo' rich upbringing, but yo' snotty behind need to learn how to loosen up and realize that yo' man is your equal and not your arm candy."

"Okay, but what do I do to get him back?" she sniffled. "He won't even talk to me. When he calls here, he only wants to speak to the kids."

"Yeah, he must really love you if he still keepin' in contact with them juvenile delinquents," Dylan joked.

"Isn't he the best?" Billie sniffled. "And he fine. Oh my God, what was I thinking?" she wailed, burying her face in her hands.

"That's the point. You weren't thinkin', dummy," Tee-Tee stated matter-of-factly. "Do what I do. Start giving his ass a mouth hug er' other week and he'll be all right, trust me."

"What the hell is a mouth hug?" Billie said, disgusted.

"You know . . . and Elton John," Dylan chimed in.

"What?" Billie said, still confused.

"A blow job, bitch! A blow job!" Tee-Tee shouted, annoyed.

"Why do I hang around you two?"

"'Cause we're the only ones that can put up with yo' ass," Dylan held her head down and laughed.

"That's true. I love you, guys." Billie kissed them both on the cheek. "You're always here for me when I need you."

"That's what friends are for. At least, that's what Lionel Richie says," Tee-Tee added.

"Okay, now look, what am I gonna do?" Billie sat up and wiped her face. "I can not go another day without him. I gotta get my baby back."

"By George, I think I got it," Tee-Tee snapped his fingers. "Since Knox won't come to you, we'll go to him," he smiled deviously.

Parked on the side of the road, Billie, Tee-Tee, and Dylan sat inside Billie's car with the radio turned down low. No one had uttered a word until Dylan whispered from the backseat, "I'm hungry."

"Shhhhhhh, he might hear you," Billie replied, looking through the lens of a pair of binoculars.

"I see why he left you," Tee-Tee eyed her. "Now are we gon' sit inside this car and stalk him all night, or are you gon' go in there and say something to him like we discussed? 'Cause my booty starting to hurt."

"That ain't got shit to do wit' my seats. Blame that on yo' husband," Billie spat.

"Well, can we at least go inside and get some hot wings," Dylan whined. 'I'm hungry as hell."

"Put a cork in it, fatty. Ain't nobody in here doing nothin' until I see what's going on between Knox and that hussy he works with."

"Explain to me how you go from wanting to apologize to suspecting him of cheating?" Tee-Tee wondered out loud.

"You can never be too sure these days. Every man got a li'l ho in 'em." Billie looked closer.

"You got that right," Tee-Tee nodded in agreement.

"Both of you are retarded." Dylan rolled her eyes, dreaming of eating a burger and fries.

"Code 10! Code 10!" Billie yelled.

"What?" Tee-Tee sat up straight, trying to see what she saw.

"Knox and that tramp are walking out together!"

"Oooooh, I see 'em. What the hell? Is he walking her to her car?" Tee-Tee yelled, taken aback.

"I'ma kick his ass!" Billie threw down the binoculars and swung open the driver-side door.

"Billie, stop! You don't even know what's going on!" Dylan protested.

"Oh, yes, I do! His ass is cheating!" Billie jumped out of the car. "And I'm about to do a Lorena Bobbitt on his white ass!"

"We gotta stop her!" Dylan yelled frantically.

"This ho is bipolar as hell!" Tee-Tee opened his door and got out too.

With Dylan being almost eight months pregnant, it took her a little bit longer to make her exit.

"Aha!" Billie wagged her index finger at Knox. "You thought you had me fooled, huh?"

"What the fuck?" Knox spun around, stunned.

"Here I am cryin' over you and you foolin' around with this Paris Hilton wannabe?"

"Actually, my idol is Britney . . . bitch," Jessica spat.

"Are you insane?" Knox screwed up his face.

"No, but you must be! 'Cause if this is what I think this is, then me, the kids, and the dog gon' be gone! You betta check my credentials! I give you everything you want and everything you need!" Billie morphed into Beyoncé. "Even your friends say I'm a good woman! Now, all I wanna know is why?" She squinted her eyes like Ethel from Sanford and Son.

"Why what and what dog?" Knox said bewildered.

"That's beside the point!" Billie waved her hand. "Now, explain to me what you're doing with this bitch!"

"Knox, I'm gonna leave," Jessica said, putting her key in the door.

"Uh-uh, slut, you ain't going nowhere!" Billie charged toward her, but Knox blocked her path. "Oh, so you tryin' to play Captain Save-a-Ho?"

"If you would calm down you would know that I walked her to her car so she could get the money to pay for the Girl Scout cookies she was about to order from the twins." He pulled the sheet from his pocket.

"Oh, please, like I'm gon' believe that?"

"He got the sheet in his hand, dumb ass!" Tee-Tee spat. "Got me out here pretending like I'm Neffe for nothin! Shit, I almost broke out the Vaseline!"

"You have to know that despite whatever we're going through that I would never cheat on you," Knox reasoned.

"Oh my God. I am such an idiot," Billie said mortified.

"You ain't never lied," Tee-Tee mumbled, rolling his eyes.

"Umm, you guys," Dylan groaned, standing on the sidewalk, "either I pee'd on myself or I'm going into labor."

"I think I'm bipolar. I love you then I hate you."
Wale, "The War"

12

Dylan lay in a hospital bed, writhing in pain. She knew that going into labor would hurt but goddamn! The pain she was feeling was out of this world. It felt like someone was ripping her insides out with their bare hands. It was like a stomach and menstrual cramp had morphed into one gigantic ball of excruciating pain. Her entire body was tense and filled to the brim with pressure, and to add to her misery, she never got a chance to eat. Nobody ever told her that all you could eat was ice when in a labor. *Maybe if some mini sliders or spinach dip was available, the labor would go smoothly,* she thought.

Dylan hadn't even had her biweekly bikini wax. The baby's room wasn't finished, and she hadn't even decided on whether she'd name the baby Dahl after her grandmother or Tiffany after her favorite jewelry store. There was so much to do and so little time to do it that her head was beginning to spin.

"How you feeling, honey?" Billie patted her forehead with a damp cloth.

"Bitch, you been through this twice! You know how the hell I feel! I feel like a grenade went off in my ass!"

"Sorry," Billie winced.

"That was a dumb question," Tee-Tee said, filming the entire thing.

"If you don't get that damn camcorder out my face, I'ma kick you!" Dylan warned, trying her best to hit him.

"Ugh! Labor does not bring out the best in you." He backed up and put the camcorder away.

"Where is Angel? Did y'all call him?" she panted.

"Yeah, he should be here any minute now," Billie replied.

"Chunky!" Candy sashayed into the room dressed in a rainbow zebra print, polyester/spandex mini dress and five-inch heels.

"Who in the hell called her?" Dylan looked up at Billie.

"I did, now do something," Tee-Tee challenged, jumping at her.

"Please believe when my baby is born it's on." Dylan exhaled, then inhaled.

"Oooh, chile! You look like who did it and what foe!" Candy curled up her lip as if something smelled.

"And you look like if you had a tampon on the string, would be longer than that dress," Dylan shot back.

"Tooshay," Candy winked.

"Candy, girl, you are glowing," Tee-Tee stared at her in awe.

"Thank you," she blushed. "I just had my body twisted in all sorts of positions by a sweaty Indian man."

"Sounds like you had a good yoga class."

"What yoga class?" she shook her head.

"And there it is," Dylan scowled.

"I honestly never see it coming," Tee-Tee grinned.

"Have you dilated yet, Chunky?" Candy pulled out her trusty flask.

"Yes, six centimeters," Dylan panted in pain.

"Uh-oh, epidural time!" Candy backed her ass up. "Just do me one favor and let me be in the room 'cause I tell you one thing. I done tried a lot of shit in my day, but that epidural, baby, is the best high I ever had. That shit right there, nigga, will have you seeing purple monkeys and shit, I'm tellin' you."

"So inappropriate," Dylan inhaled deeply.

"And you five weeks early. Shit, you better take a swig of this Jack while you still can." Candy placed her flask up to Dylan's lips.

"No, thank you." She turned her head.

"Suit yourself." Candy took another sip.

"Did I miss anything?" Angel raced into the room excited, with Milania in tow.

The entire room went silent. Dylan's pain seemed to double upon their arrival. Breathing in and out, she wondered if Angel had been hit with a stupid stick 'cause he couldn't have honestly thought it was okay to bring Satan's spawn along with him.

"Okay, I know I have threw back a few, but y'all actin' like Monique and her hairy legs just entered the room."

"It's nice to meet you again, Candy," Angel extended his hand for a shake.

"No-no. That's how you get H1N1." She dodged his hand.

"All right, then, uh . . . Candy, this is my girlfriend, Milania."

"*Fiancée,*" Milania shot him a look dressed to kill.

"Well, she certainly looks like a shoe that has been worn." Candy gave her a once-over glance.

"Now it's a party," Tee-Tee chuckled, clapping his hands.

Opting not to respond, Milania searched the Internet on her phone as if none of them existed 'cause frankly, she could give a shit about Dylan or her baby. She knew she was the shit and her new, messy, just-got-of-bed look she went for with her hair proved it.

"Angel, can I talk to you for a second . . . alone." Dylan lowered her head and massaged her temples.

"Yeah." Angel turned to Milania. "Can you wait for me out in the hallway?"

"Sure." She faked a smile and walked out with everyone else.

"Are you tryin' to get cut?" Dylan said as soon as everybody was gone.

"Don't even trip. The only reason I brought her is because when Billie called she was in the car with me and I ain't have enough time to drop her off."

"Well, you better tell her to sprout some wings and fly her ass up outta her 'cause homegirl gots to go. I can't have her around me right now," Dylan breathed in and out.

"Chill. You won't even know she's here."

"For your sake I better not." Dylan gave him a glare of warning.

"You excited," he smiled brightly, ignoring her sarcasm.

"I'm scared as hell. I just pray that she's gonna be born okay."

"Or he," he arched his eyebrow.

"Team girl over here," Dylan raised the roof.

"Yo', I can't believe I'ma be a daddy." Angel beamed with pride.

"Me either."

"Dylan," the nurse said, "we're ready to give you your epidural now."

"And on that note, that's my cue to leave. Me and needles don't get along," Angel half joked.

"Scary ass," Dylan giggled.

Once the procedure was done, Angel came back inside the room alone.

"You a'ight?"

"Oh, this is a cakewalk now," she grinned.

"Wow, it's that much better?"

"What are you talkin' about? I'm at a bar right now. It's New Year's, and I am nice, word up."

"Look, why don't you try to get some sleep?"

"That's a good idea."

"I'll be right out in the hall if you need me."

Dylan gave him a slight smile and watched as he walked out of the room and into the hallway.

"We need to talk," Milania shouted as soon as he stepped out.

"You can tone all that down, sista-girl!" Billie stood up, ready to pounce.

"And you need to mind your business!"

"See? This bitch think it's a game!" Billie started taking off her earrings.

"Billie, chill," Angel ordered. "Go in the room and check on Dylan."

"You better check *her*," she warned, bypassing them both.

"Who gon' check me, boo?" Milania rolled her neck.

"This chick must wanna get smacked!" Billie spun around. "I'm talkin' to you, cocksucker!"

"Whateva. You're just jealous!"

"Jealous of *what?*" Billie looked at her as if she'd lost her mind. "Bitch, I had that bag like two seasons ago, and that I don't think I need a perm look 'cause 'I'ma model,'" Billie made air quotes with her fingers. "But I really do 'cause my edges are a mess, it's ridiculous! Nobody deserves that hair! Not even a two-dollar hooker! So once again, what you wanna do, boo? I *dare* you to pop off!"

"Girl, get yo' ass in here! You have watched one too many episodes of the *Bad Girls Club*." Tee-Tee pulled her back and into the room.

"What the fuck is yo' problem?" Angel barked.

"What is *my* problem? What is *my* problem? Nigga, you need to be askin' yo'self that question!" Milania spat out.

"Nigga?" Angel repeated, stunned.

"I don't believe I stuttered. Excuse me, ma'am," Milania addressed an elderly woman standing in the hallway. "Did you hear me stutter?"

"No, I don't think you did," the woman nervously replied, clutching her purse.

"Okay, I just wanted to make sure! Now, back to *you!*" Milania pointed at Angel. "How in the hell you gon' bring me to the hospital like it's all good? I don't wanna be a part of this shit! It's bad enough she having yo' baby, now you want me to sit around and play wait till the baby drop? You out yo' fuckin' mind!" she spat, fed up with playing second fiddle to Dylan and the baby.

"Look, I been tryin' to be patient 'cause I know this is difficult, but right now, I need you to rock wit' me. So can you do us both a favor and relax yo' fuckin' mind? 'Cause us beefin' ain't gone be good for nobody," Angel said feeling his temper rise.

Rolling her eyes, Milania sucked her teeth. The selfish part of her wanted to tell him to kick rocks, but in order for her plan to work, she had to continue to play the doting girlfriend for a while longer. Two hours later, Milania was beside herself with boredom. Her ass was hurting from the hard seats and hospital food wasn't her thing so she was starving to death too. Plus, she was missing R&B singer Ashton's after party at Lure. She didn't have time to be sitting around while Dylan pushed out her two-headed baby.

"Huh!" She crossed her legs and groaned.

"What is it now, Milania?" Angel huffed.

"What do you think? I'm ready to go home. I have a party to go to." She gave him much attitude.

"Really, Milania?" He eyed her sideways.

"Uh, yeah, really. I told you, I ain't wanna be here."

"It's not about you right now, so chill. She having my baby."

"So how long do you expect me to sit here?" Milania sat up and rolled her neck. "I'm ready to go home now."

"Angel, come on, it's time," Billie said, walking into the waiting area.

"Well, as you can see, I'm not leaving, so I don't know what you gon' do." He stood up, not giving a fuck.

"Deuces." Milania threw up the peace sign and left.

Angel wished he had the time to deal with Milania and her drama, but the birth of his son or daughter was far more important than Milania's latest tantrum.

"You ready?" He took Dylan by the hand and gazed into her eyes.

"Let's go get 'em," she smiled back, squeezing his hand tightly.

Seven pushes and many earsplitting screams later, the baby was halfway out.

"You wanna pull the baby out?" her doctor asked.

"Yes," Dylan said eagerly.

"Just reach down in between your legs and grab the baby by its arms."

Dylan did as she was told, and seconds later, her baby was in her arms.

"Hey, there, pretty gir—What the hell?" she said looking at the baby boy in her hands.

"I *knew* it was gon' be a boy!" Angel pumped his fist into the air.

It was 5:15 A.M. Angel was past tired. He was dead to the world exhausted. It felt like he'd been up forever, but the lack of sleep had been worth it. His four pound five ounce, curly haired baby boy, Mason Alexander Carter, was the apple of his eye. The infant looked exactly like him. Mason's eyes were pear-shaped just like Angel's, but the color of them was hazel just like his mother's. He had the cutest button nose and the most perfect pair of pink lips Angel had ever seen.

Angel couldn't wait to get back to his baby boy. As always when returning home, he dropped his keys and wallet on the table by the door. Milania sat on the sofa reading the latest issue of *Elle* magazine while sipping on a cup of coffee. The five-page spread she'd done a month before was in that month's issue. Determined to throw him the maximum amount of shade, she flipped the page and pretended that he hadn't even walked through the door. Not having anything to say to her either, Angel walked toward the bedroom, completely ignoring her.

She'd been on some ghetto bird stuff lately and Angel wasn't feeling it at all. At first, he thought she might've really loved him, but as time went on, he started to feel differently. All Milania cared about was her career and being featured in all of the gossip magazines and blog sites. She loved being a part of the social scene, but homegirl was starting to get the big head and forget that if it wasn't for Angel introducing her to his world, she'd still be a struggling model from Oakland, California.

After taking a steaming hot shower and placing on a white Henley Y-neck shirt, gray Obey jeans, and a pair of crisp new Nike Air Max sneakers, Angel walked to the kitchen and fixed himself a glass of ice-cold water. Milania continued to act as if he didn't exist. Finished with the drink, he put the cup in the sink and grabbed his keys.

"I know you *not* gettin' ready to leave," she snapped, slamming down the magazine.

"So *now* you wanna talk when you see I'm about to leave?"

"Don't switch this around on me!" Milania roared. "You've been gone for I don't know how long! Now you gettin' ready to leave again? Just let me know, is this what it's gettin' ready to be like, 'cause I didn't sign up for this shit!"

"Shit, if this ain't where you wanna be, then go! Ain't nobody keepin' you here!" Angel shouted, having had enough of her shit.

Milania sat with her mouth wide open. If she didn't know for a fact he could knock her out with just the slap of his hand, she would've jumped up and right hooked his ass.

"All right. When you get back I'll be gone," she challenged, folding her arms across her chest.

"Do you what you gotta do." Angel shrugged his shoulders, turning the knob.

"Wait-wait!" Milania ran after him and grabbed his arm. Her heart was pounding out of her chest. She knew that she and Angel were going through a rough patch, but she didn't realize that their relationship was actually on thin ice. *You doing too much, girl. Think, Milania, think,* she thought.

"I was just playin'. You know I'm not goin' nowhere." She tried to rationalize the situation.

"Well, I am." Angel mean-mugged her, then slammed the door in her face.

The house was completely still. It was so quiet you could hear water from the faucet drip. Billie took off her shoes and tiptoed up the steps. After peeking in on the kids and kissing their sleeping faces, she headed into her bedroom where Knox lay on his back snoring lightly. The sight of his lovely face stopped her dead in her tracks. How could she have ever doubted him? He loved her so much that it scared her.

With Cain, she always felt like she was doing all the loving and nurturing. With Knox, he loved her despite her brash, take-charge attitude. All he wanted was for her to realize that there was more to life than a bunch of art shows and organizations. Life was about making time for the ones you love and enjoying the things you worked so hard to acquire.

Billie placed her knee on the edge of the bed and crawled slowly up Knox's body. Straddling his lap, she leaned forward and kissed him softly on the lips. His eyes fluttered open.

"Hey," she spoke softly.

"What time is it?" He rubbed his eyes.

"A little after nine."

"Dylan, straight?"

"Yeah, she had a boy. His name is Mason." Billie smiled at the thought of her nephew.

"That's what's up."

"Thanks for watching the kids." Billie looked at him nervously.

"You good, but since you back, I guess I should head on out." Knox tried to get up.

"No! Wait!" Billie pushed him back down. "Stay, please." She lowered her voice. "There are a few things that I need to say."

Knox rested his head on the pillow.

"I just wanted to tell you that I'm sorry. I'm sorry for pushing you away and being such an ice queen 'cause I know that I have a tendency of being that way. I just never thought I would end up being with someone else so soon, especially someone like you who's so gentle and caring. You're my best friend, and I know that I haven't been that much of a friend to you, but I love you, Knox. And I promise that from this day on, I'm going to start putting you first. Well, you know, the kids come first, but—"

"Just shut up." He covered her mouth with his hand.

"Do you still love me?" she mumbled.

"Only on Tuesdays and Thursdays." He lowered his hand back down to his side.

A bright smile spread over Billie's face.

"It must be my lucky day then, 'cause today is Thursday," she smirked taking off her top.

"Lucky you." Knox placed his hand on the back of her neck and pulled her face close to his.

"You ready to show me how much you love me?" He kissed her lips.

"In every way imaginable." Billie unzipped his jeans and prepared herself to be taken to all heights of ecstasy.

"Even though I can do all these things by my damn
self I need you."
Jill Scott, "The Fact Is (I Need You)"

13

Despite what the haters said, Ashton was the shit. She could barely hold a note or memorize an eight-count dance step, but she had seven number-one hits, a Cover Girl contract, a clothing company, and a budding acting career. Outside of her megastar career, her other biggest achievement was marrying State. Like her, he was the best in his field. The two gave Hov and B a run for their money, but unlike America's most famous couple, Ashton and State's relationship was plagued with lies and infidelities.

Ashton thought she'd be able to keep State under control after she'd found out about his torrid affair with Hollywood's forgotten "It Girl"-turned-loving mother Dylan, but Ashton was sadly mistaken. Her threat of taking half of his $350 million empire didn't stop him from screwing around. Beyond fed up with the bullshit, Ashton decided it was time to throw in the towel and start anew.

Sure, it hurt that her marriage hadn't worked, but a bitter divorce was always good for one's career, and with all the dirt she had on State, she was sure to have the public on her side. And sure, she was in the process of moving on, but when Ashton learned of the pictures of State visiting Dylan at her bakery and him attending her baby shower, no less the scorned woman in her couldn't help but make one last return. There was no way on God's green earth that she could let him, or

Dylan, for that matter, get away with that kind of blatant disrespect.

It was time for Ashton to show them both that she wasn't just a chick who talked shit but a chick that could back it up as well. Lying flat on her stomach fully naked, Ashton enjoyed the tranquil sound of Ingrid Michaelson's voice while her masseuse gave her a deep-tissue massage.

"Your guest is here, ma'am." Her maid peeked her head inside the room.

"Send her in."

"Hey, doll!" Milania strutted into the room.

"Hey, gorgeous." Ashton lifted her head and air kissed both of her cheeks.

She and Milania had known each other since Jay-Z signed Rihanna. They'd meet at Diddy's white party in the Hamptons and had been homegirls ever since.

"Have a seat."

"Thanks, love." Milania sat down and crossed her legs.

"So how are you? I know the last time I saw you, things between you and Angel was all bad."

"Girl," Milania rolled her eyes to the ceiling, "I thought I was gon' have a situation on my hands when I got home that morning, but do you know that nigga wasn't even there?"

"Really?" Ashton's eyes grew wide.

"Yes, doll."

"Where was he at?"

"I assume with Dylan."

"Ugh," Ashton pretended to gag. "She's like a roach that won't die."

"I know. I'm so sick of that wack-ass broad."

"I swear, I don't know what the fascination is. The bitch's forehead look like a rearview mirror," Ashton joked.

"Right," Milania giggled.

"But for real, I don't know what else to do. No matter what I throw out, I just can't get rid of this ho," Milania said at her wit's end.

"You my girl, right?" Ashton arched her eyebrow.

"Of course."

"Then I got you." Ashton wrapped the sheet around her and got up. "Sit tight. I'll be right back."

Moments later, Ashton returned.

"Helga, give us a second, please."

"Yes, ma'am." Helga wiped her hands and left the room.

Ashton locked the door behind her.

"After today, you will never have to worry about Dylan Monroe's skank ass again. This right here," she held up a DVD, "is gonna solve everything."

"Is that what I think it is?" Milania's eyes brightened.

"Yes, ma'am."

"I knew I fucked wit' you for a reason." Milania jumped up and snatched the disc from Ashton's hand.

"So how are you gonna thank me?" Ashton bit into her bottom lip suggestively.

"You know we can't keep this up. You almost got me in trouble the last time." Milania took Ashton into her arms and planted a wet kiss on her lips.

"Chile, please. If I've learned anything over the last couple of years, it's that what these niggas don't know won't hurt'em."

"We're home," Dylan whispered joyfully with Mason's pumpkin seat in hand.

He was asleep. Dylan was beyond ecstatic to be home. She hadn't had a proper night's sleep since she'd gone into labor, and now she'd finally be able to rest. It had been a nerve-racking experience going into labor five weeks early and having a baby who wasn't born at a healthy weight, but they'd made it through. Mason was now a strong six pounds. After what seemed like an eternity, Dylan finally made it up the stairs to her room. It was hell carrying her purse, overnight bag, and pumpkin seat with a baby in it.

"I mean, goddamn," she huffed, dropping the bags down.

Missing her terribly, Fuck'em started barking and jumping up and down in her cage. Dylan placed Mason on the bed and ran over to Fuck'em Gurl's cage to release her.

"Hey, Mommy," Dylan held her in her arms and rubbed her back and kissed her face. "I missed you. Your brother's home. You wanna meet him? C'mon, let's go see him." She put the dog back down.

Back at the bed, Dylan noticed a note on her pillow that read:

I hope it's everything you dreamed of.
Love, Angel

"Mason, Daddy got us a present." She unbuckled his seat and wrapped him up in her arms. "But first let me introduce you to your sister." She bent down so Fuck'em Gurl could view the baby and begin to get used to him.

"Okay, now let's see what your daddy has been up to. I don't see anything in here, sooooo . . ." she thought, trying to figure out what the note meant.

"It's your room," she gasped, heading in that direction.

Dylan quickly opened the door and found that the once-empty space had been completely decorated. The walls and ceiling were made of light blue, pale yellow, and pale green square blocks with a chocolate brown border. A white, modern-designed chandelier hung from the center of the ceiling. Mason had a white crib and a lime-green toddler table with light blue stools. In the corner was a white La-Z-Boy armchair that rocked. Dylan was so overcome with emotion that she began to cry. Mason began to cry too.

"Oh, honey, Mommy's sorry. I wasn't tryin' to make you cry." She kissed him on the cheek and realized he'd pooped.

"You not cryin' 'cause of me. You cryin' 'cause you boo-booed." Dylan gently laid him down on his new changing table and pulled out a fresh pamper.

Once Mason was completely undressed she slowly peeled open his diaper and discovered a chocolate nightmare that smelled like rotten eggs.

"Oh my God-oh my God." Dylan stared at the ceiling, holding her nose. "I can't do it. Oh Lord, I can't!"

With one eye open and the other closed, Dylan looked back down and noticed Mason smiling.

"You laughing at me, man?" She smiled too, melting. "Okay, Mommy's a rock star. I can do this. Ugh," she mimicked throwing up while wiping his butt.

"Whew, I did it." She removed the dirty diaper and replaced it with a new one.

But while Dylan wrapped up the soiled diaper, she forgot to cover Mason's penis and without warning, pee spurted in her face.

"Whoa-whoa!" She tried blocking the urine with her hand to no avail.

It was like she was being sprayed in the face with a water hose. Feeling as if she were about to die, Dylan wiped her mouth with the back of her hand and recognized that she was in for the ride of her life.

"OMG, did my baby just give me my first golden shower?" she laughed. "Well, maybe second."

***

Dylan quickly learned that being a new mom was a muthafucka. She went from everything in life being 100 percent about her to dedicating her very existence to someone she barely knew. Yes, she carried Mason in her stomach for seven months and three weeks, but she soon learned that taking care of a newborn baby was a lot like dating. For the last couple of weeks, they'd spent their time feeling each other out because, honestly, she didn't know him, and he didn't know her.

Dylan would catch herself and Mason from time to time staring at each other as if to say, "Who the hell are you?" Most of the day was spent with him crying and her breaking down as well. Mason never slept during the night, and she had to feed him every two to three hours, so sleep was out of the equation. The pooping and peeing never seemed to stop. She had to constantly wash his clothes, bathe him, hold him, burp him, and love on him. Dylan hardly ever had time to eat or bathe herself.

She was utterly worn-out. Dark circles had formed around her eyes. Her hair was all over her head. Her nails were chipped, and her feet were a hot atrocious mess. Even Fuck'em Gurl was scared to come near her. Dylan didn't know what to do. She'd never seen this part of motherhood on television or in baby ads. No one ever told her it was a day-to-day struggle just to stay sane or that after giving birth, your once-tight body without blinking goes to shit or how stretch marks were scratch marks sent directly from the devil.

She couldn't even sleep on her stomach yet, because her stomach felt like a bowl of Jell-O. Yes, being a new mom was a bitch and every day Dylan was getting slapped harder and harder. On that particular afternoon, she sat on her bed trying to get Mason to nurse, but out of spite, he just wouldn't latch on. It was like he was saying, "Uh-uh, bitch." At any minute, Dylan felt like she would have a nervous breakdown.

"Girl, you ain't got that baby to stop crying yet?" Candy came in the room with a cup of Jack and Coke in her hand.

"He's still cryin', isn't he?" Dylan snapped frustrated, feeling as if she were about to cry.

"Don't be gettin' mad with me. Girl, you betta give that baby some Tussin and call it a night."

"I will not."

"Then give him a bottle." Candy sat opposite her on the bed.

"No, I'm breastfeeding him. He just won't cooperate," Dylan huffed. She felt like a complete loser. "Even while I was in the hospital he wouldn't act right."

"How have you been feeding him?" Candy ran her index finger across her grandson's cheek.

"I've been expressing my milk and freezing it," Dylan replied with tears in her eyes.

"Look, girl, you gon' drive yo'self crazy. Everybody ain't meant to breastfeed. Hell, I tried to wit' you."

"You did?" Dylan said surprised.

"Yes, and it was one of the worst experiences of my life."

"Thanks," Dylan replied sarcastically.

"No, seriously, we all have to make sacrifices, even though we may not want to."

"Mama, please, you have never sacrificed anything a day in your life." Dylan waved her off.

"Yes, I have."

"Yeah, right," Dylan twisted her mouth to the side. "Like what?"

"Like those sixteen hours I spent in labor with you even though it was Margarita Monday over at The Max," Candy said with a laugh.

"You know what? I'm over this conversation." Dylan went to stand up.

"No, let me talk to you." Candy urged her to sit back down. "Being a mother is a process . . . like Ice-T's hair. You're going to have your triumphs, and you're going to have your failures, but it's all a learning experience. No woman out here is a perfect mother. I did the best I could with you considering the kind of mother I had."

Dylan stared at her mother with tears in her eyes.

"Your grandmother Dahl, God bless her soul, hated me," Candy continued staring off absently.

"From the day I was born, she told me I would never amount to shit. And I think somewhere deep down inside I believed her. You know, it's hard tryin' to live up to someone who was so iconic, but I tried. I tried so hard to stand out on my own as a singer, but everybody always compared me to her. And after I had you, I promised myself that I would never make you feel the way she made me feel, but I ended up doing the same thing. Dylan, I tried being the best mother I could. And I know I messed up—"

"A lot," Dylan pointed out.

"You're right. I did, but know that I'm sorry for everything that I did wrong to you. And I know I never say it, but I love you, Dylan, and I'm so proud of you. You've done things that I've never been able to do. Like stand on your own two feet without help from no one. That takes a lot of guts, kid."

"Candy," Dylan cooed rubbing her mother's hand, "please don't hit me when I say this, but I think your face just moved."

"Shut up, girl." Candy slapped her gently on the hand.

"Seriously, that was like the nicest thing you've ever said to me."

"Don't go gettin' all sentimental on me." Candy flicked her wrist, then took a sip from her cup.

"I'm not. I just hope you realize that you can do stuff on your own too."

"Well, I did have one job there for a while." Candy stared off into space.

"Doing what?" Dylan asked, dying to know.

"Pretending that people had backed their cars into me."

"Check, please!" Dylan shook her head, outdone.

"Dylan, my future son-in-law here," Clyde yelled up the steps.

"Angel didn't tell me he was coming over today." She panicked, knowing she looked a hot mess.

"I called him over here," Candy announced.

"Why?" Dylan eyed her confused.

"'Cause you need a break, and hell, that's what his ass is here for, to give you a break."

"Thanks, Ma."

"You know I got you, boo." Candy rose up from the bed and looked at herself in the mirror. "I'm thinkin' about gettin' some more restylane injected into my lips." Candy poked out her lips then smiled.

"Let me tell you something, Candy. You're gettin' old!" Dylan yelled into her ear. "And yeah, I said it. You can paralyze your whole face, lift your boobs, butt, and your neck until you're six feet off the ground, but you can't stop time."

"I feel you, but I'm tryin' to be a dime piece forever." Candy snapped her fingers.

"Candy, the fresh-faced girl you were died a long time ago. You smothered her when you slept on your face for twenty years," Dylan joked.

"I swear I raised a hater." Candy popped her lips. "Now, if you'll excuse me, Clyde and I 'bout to head over to the strip club. They having a bounce-that-ass contest, and I'm determined to win."

"Just when I thought we'd be able to get along." Dylan shook her head.

"How you ladies doing today?" Angel asked, entering the room.

"I can't call it," Candy responded. "By the way," she turned to Dylan, "I put some money in your account. Don't go spending it all in one place." She winked before walking out.

"So what's going on wit' you?" Angel took his wallet and cell phone out of his pocket and put them down on her TV stand.

"Nothin', just tired."

"You know you could've called me yourself." He took Mason from her arms.

"I know, but you were just over here all day yesterday."

"What that mean? Absolutely nothin'. I'm tryin' to put in as much work as you. Just 'cause me and you ain't together don't mean that I'm tryin' only be around him a few days a week. I'ma be here every day so don't ever think that you in this alone and that you gotta do everything by yourself."

"I'ma hold you to that," she gave him a slight smile.

"Bet. Now what's up, man?" Angel held Mason up. "You over here giving yo' mama a hard time?"

"He fake. When you come around, he acts like a completely different baby."

"Say, 'I'm sorry, Mommy.'" He held Mason in front of Dylan so she could kiss him, which she did.

The closer Angel got to Dylan the more he could smell a foul stench come from her body.

"Ay, why don't you go in the bathroom and put some water on that." He eyed her with disdain.

"You tryin' to say I stink?" She bucked her eyes and smelled underneath her arm.

"I ain't tryin' to say a damn thing."

"That's fucked up." She got up, laughing.

"It's fucked up I got to smell yo' ass. Go handle that." Angel covered his nose.

While Dylan was in the tub, Angel went into Mason's room and fed him a bottle. Once his tummy was nice and full, he burped him and rocked him to sleep. In the other room, Dylan stepped out of the tub and draped herself in a towel. The hot bubble bath she took was much needed and refreshing. Her entire body felt renewed.

At that point, all she wanted to do was eat something and go to sleep, but with Mason, none of that was going down that easily. She'd probably be able to sneak a snack if she was lucky. Taking her time, she dried off and massaged on lavender vanilla lotion. Finished, she rummaged through her drawers and found a super cute pink T-shirt with the phrase "Do You Wanna Make Out?" written on it and a pair of black-and-white polka dot boxers. Unaware that she'd gotten out of the bath, Angel walked back into the room to grab his cell phone and wallet just as she was bending over to put her boxers on.

"Oh shit!" He turned his head. "My bad."

"Do you know how to knock?" Totally embarrassed, Dylan covered up her private parts with her hands.

There was no way she wanted him to see her body in that shape. In Dylan's eyes, she looked like an Oompa-Loompa.

"Get it out!" she screeched.

"You ain't gotta yell. It ain't like I never seen you naked before."

"So get it out!" she stomped her foot.

"A'ight, I'm going. Chill." Angel closed the door and started toward the kitchen.

Fully dressed, Dylan checked on Mason, who was sleeping peacefully in his crib. Being the overly cautious mother she was, Dylan placed a hand mirror over his face to make sure he was still breathing. Pleased with the results, she put the mirror up and descended down the steps to the kitchen.

"You done freakin' out, crybaby?" Angel teased, fixing himself a roast beef sandwich on honey wheat bread.

"You know what, Angel? Suck it." Dylan rolled her eyes. "As a matter of fact, you and your son can suck it. I can't believe that gettin' him to eat and sleep is so easy for you. I can't get him do nothin'."

"Don't hate. Me and my li'l man got an understanding."

"Understanding, my ass. Mason is as fake as a two-dollar bill." She pulled out a chair and sat down at the table.

"You mean three-dollar bill, don't you?" Angel sat down opposite her.

"Nooooo," she frowned.

"There *is* such a thing as a two-dollar bill. You know that, right?"

"Really?" She screwed up her face. "'Cause every time I got one, I always threw it away."

"I think I got a headache." Angel massaged his temples.

"Oh, so I got good news," Dylan danced happily in her seat.

"What's up?"

"Since my book is coming out soon, I'm going to have a book release party in a few weeks."

"That's what's up. I'm invited, right?"

"Of course. Just leave Maneka at home."

"Stop it." Angel couldn't help but laugh too.

"See? You think she look like Maneka too."

"I don't know what you talkin' about." Grinning, he chewed his food.

"Whatever. I'm tired of talkin' about Chewbacca anyway." She placed her hand underneath her chin.

Talking about Milania wasn't going to solve anything or bring her and Angel closer together, although she could tell by the look in his eyes that Milania didn't do it for him anymore. Dylan could almost bet she didn't rub his back or when he was down, tell him everything would be okay. The grass was much greener on her side, but Angel would figure that all out in time.

"You excited about your book?" he asked, wiping his mouth with a napkin.

"Yes."

"I'm proud of you."

"Thanks," she smiled, gracing him with her essence.

Angel watched her in awe. Dylan was so unaware of her affect on him. She was beautiful, and like most men, Angel admired her for her physical features, but to him, her mind was much deeper. She was a winner, and he could never ignore her. It had been an honor for him to create life with her. Now, no matter what, they were forever bonded together, and he wouldn't have it any other way.

"Well, I'm gettin' ready to take a quick nap while Lil Boosie bad ass is still asleep. When you leave, lock the door on the way out." Dylan got up and scooted the chair back in.

"A'ight. I'ma sit down here and finish eating and watch a li'l bit of this Cardinal game before I leave."

"Okay," she said going up the steps.

The thought of asking him if he wanted her to stay crossed her mind, but Dylan knew if she sat on the couch next to him for too long, she couldn't be held responsible for what she might do, so she decided that heading up the stairs was the best thing to do. Unbeknownst to Dylan, Angel was thinking the exact same thing. He truly enjoyed spending his time with her and the baby.

When he was around them, it felt like they were a real family. He was comfortable. Nothing else in the world mattered. He wasn't stressed. Everything was good. That was, until he headed back to the hotel with Milania. Nowadays, everything seemed to be an argument and the crazy amount of money she was spending on their engagement party was driving Angel up the roof.

Not up for another headache, he grabbed a throw pillow and placed it on the arm of the couch and lay down. The Cardinals were playing the Cubs, but Angel only got ten minutes into the game before his eyes became heavy and he fell asleep.

"You know what, yo? You a bitch!"
Chris Brown, "Deuces Remix"

14

"What the fuck?" Angel jumped out of his sleep.

The heart-pounding sound of someone ramming a fist into the door woke him up. Getting off the couch, Angel wobbled down the steps still trying to wake up. Whoever was at the door was now not only knocking loudly but ringing the doorbell simultaneously. The booming noise was so loud that the baby woke up screaming and hollering.

"Who is it?" Angel yelled.

"Yo' fiancée, nigga!" Milania yelled.

Angel swung open the door. Milania stood with a furious expression on her face. Her chest heaved up and down. She looked as if she'd thrown on the first thing she saw and drove over in a hurry. She hadn't even bothered to comb her hair.

"What the fuck is you doing?" He looked at her like she was insane.

"Angel, who the hell is that?" Dylan shouted from upstairs while trying to calm the baby down.

Angel didn't even get a chance to reply before Milania started going off on him.

"So not only do you spend all day over here, but now you don't even come home at night? Who the fuck do you think you are? Better yet, who the fuck do you think *I* am? If you wanna be with this bitch, then be with the bitch! But you ain't gon' fuck around on me and expect me not to say nothin' about it! You ain't that rich, nigga!"

"What the fuck are you talkin' about? I fell asleep!" he roared with anger.

"And I guess I got the word *dumb* written across my face?" Milania placed her hands on her hips.

"Right now, you do 'cause I ain't even did nothin'! If you would stop showin' yo' ass for half a second, then maybe you would see that I'm fully dressed!"

"That don't mean shit!" Milania snapped, unfazed.

With the baby in her arms Dylan stood at the top of the steps and said, "You and this trifling bitch gots to go!"

"Fuck you!" Milania threw up her middle finger.

"Okay, let me put my baby up 'cause this bitch must not know who my mama is." Dylan headed toward her room.

"Dylan, chill. Just take the baby back upstairs for me, please," Angel begged.

"I'm not playin' wit' you, Angel. You better check yo' ho!" Dylan rolled her eyes hard. "And lock my goddamn door on the way out!"

"You out yo' fuckin' mind coming over her house clownin' like that!" Angel yelled, walking into their suite.

"I *said* I was sorry." Milania sucked her teeth, throwing down her purse.

"What the fuck that mean to me? The damage already been done now!" he shouted, seething with anger.

"I thought—"

"You thought *what?*" He jumped in her face.

"Let's not play dumb. We both know she got feelings for you, so when you didn't come home, I thought you two were messin' around."

"Well, we weren't, and just so you know, Dylan ain't even came to me on no shit like that!"

"Brownie points for her." Milania clapped her hands mockingly. "So what you tryin' to say if she was on you, you would be okay wit' that?"

"Yo', I'ma be real wit' you." Angel wiped his face with his hands. "I ain't feelin' this shit no more."

"What?" Milania threw her head back, aghast.

"I don't think this gon' work." Angel paced back and forth. "I think we rushed into this way too fast, and I got a lot going on right now that obviously you can't handle."

"And you tellin' me this the night before our engagement party?" She stopped him, getting up in his face.

"The timing might be fucked up, but this how I feel."

Milania's back was up against the wall. She and Angel had fought before, and he'd threatened ending their relationship, but this time he was serious. It was written all over his face. She had to do damage control and fast. She'd come too far to lose Angel now.

"Angel, please don't do this. I love you. Please don't leave me. Don't do this to me. Not now." She forced herself to cry, but this time, Angel wasn't buying it.

"Look, I gotta go." He pulled away.

"Are you coming back?" She ran her hands through her hair like she was pulling it up into a ponytail.

"Nah, I'ma chill somewhere else tonight."

"Why?" she cried.

"I'll call you later or something." He opened the door.

"What about tomorrow? Are you even gon' come?"

"I don't know. Just give me a minute." He walked out not even bothering to close the door behind him.

Milania wiped the tears away from her eyes. This time she'd gone too far, and she couldn't put the blame off on Dylan. This time it was all her. She'd played the wrong hand and now was suffering the consequences for it. She just prayed that Angel still had a little bit of love left for her 'cause there was no way that she was going to head back to California without a marriage certificate in her hand.

The ballroom at the Four Seasons was decorated to perfection by acclaimed party designer Preston Bailey. Romantic shades of purples and gold highlighted the room. On each table were pebbled glass chargers and vibrant beaded napkin rings over brocade tablecloths. Two hundred fifty of their closest friends and family, including Giselle Bundchen and Tom Brady, were invited to dine on sumptuous Italian cuisine and later dance to a 1930s-inspired jazz band and legendary DJ Funkmaster Flex.

Running behind, Milania sat quietly while getting primped and primed for her grand entrance. Totally delusional and unwilling to accept defeat, Milania hoped and prayed that Angel would change his mind and be by her side to escort her in. She'd been calling him all day, but each time, she went straight to voice mail. Despite the nervousness that plagued her, Milania kept it cool, calm, and collected on the outside.

The only person who really knew how she felt was Ashton. They'd gone over the entire fiasco earlier that day. Milania would never discuss her business in front of the dream team of professionals who did her hair and makeup. People would sell her Social Security number to the tabloids, let alone relationship info. Milania couldn't risk it leaking to the public that her fairytale engagement was starting to crack. It would ruin her. *But then again, all press is good press,* she thought.

"So which dress are you going to wear?" Ashton asked, breaking her train of thought.

"I think the gold Marchesa." Milania pointed to the rack of her clothes.

"Luvs it." Ashton glanced down at her phone and checked the text message she'd just received.

"Amber just texted me and said she's downstairs, so I'ma head down to meet her."

"Okay, tell Miss Rose I said, 'hey, doll,'" Milania said, still on edge.

Noticing her panicked demeanor, Ashton rubbed her shoulders and said, "Everything's going to be all right. Remember, we have the golden ticket." Ashton referred to the sex tape. "And if that isn't enough, you always got me," she winked.

"Thanks, girl."

"See you in a second." Ashton made her way over to the door and opened it.

To her astonishment and dismay, on the other side of the door stood Dylan with her hand in the air, mid-knock. Instantly the hood chick in Ashton kicked into high gear. Standing back on one leg with her upper lip curled, she shouted over her shoulder, "Milania!"

"Yes!"

"It looks like you forgot to take out the trash." Ashton eyed Dylan up and down and shot her the nastiest look she could muster.

"What?" Milania met her in the living area. The sight of Dylan's face made her blood boil.

"You want me to stay?" Ashton asked, ready to throw down.

"Nah, I got this," Milania assured her.

"Girl, please," Dylan scoffed.

She wasn't afraid of either Ashton or Milania. As far as she was concerned, both of them could get it. Before leaving, Ashton shot Dylan another dirty look, then slipped past her, and boarded the elevator down the hall.

"Is Angel here?" Dylan asked dryly.

"No," Milania shot back even dryer.

"Then tell him I stopped by." Dylan turned to walk away.

"So I guess your plan was an epic failure!" Milania yelled, causing her to stop midstride.

"What plan?" Dylan spun around on her heels.

"Don't act like you didn't know that today we're having our engagement party." Milania met her in the center of the hallway.

"Actually, I didn't, so you can stop with the foolishness. I came to give Angel his wallet and his cell phone." She held it up. "He left them at my house last night."

"You can give them to me." Milania tried to snatch them from her hand.

"Did you hear anything I said? I came to give *Angel* his stuff, not you, leech. I ain't giving you shit," Dylan jerked her hand back before she could grab it. "Now if you'll excuse me I have better things to do then stand here and argue with you." Dylan tried walking away again.

"You really think it's gon' be that easy?" Milania yelled after her.

"My God! What is it now, Milania?" Dylan snapped, fed up. "I mean, damn, ain't you tired?"

"Of course I am. I'm tired of *you*. I thought by now after all the hard work I've put into gettin' rid of you, you would've been long gone by now."

"What are you talkin' about?"

"Let me it break down for you." Milania stepped up and got in her face. "I have been doing everything in my power to make you disappear, including not tellin' Angel you were pregnant after I checked his phone."

Dylan's eyes grew wide with amazement.

"Yeah, that's right, I did it," Milania basked in her glory. "And I lied to the media and told them that State was your baby's father. Oh, and that li'l lunch date we had was a setup, of course. But understand . . . I'm nowhere near done with you. I got far more in store for you, sweetheart. So if you know what's good for you, I suggest you pretend like Angel is a memory and stay the fuck away from him or else I'm going to make your life a living hell."

"What are you . . . one of Satan's babies?" Dylan's heart raced.

"No, bitch, I'm your worst fuckin' nightmare. And if you think it's a game, try me," Milania threatened.

"You're fuckin' crazy." Dylan balled up her fist ready to hit her.

"And if you even think about runnin' back and tellin' Angel anything I said, it won't matter 'cause he won't believe you. 'Cause just like I got this ten-carat diamond ring on my finger, I got him wrapped around my pinky as well."

"Is that right?" Angel said, walking down the hall.

He'd just gotten off the elevator and overheard everything, but her confession didn't mean anything. After thinking long and hard the night before at his sister's house Angel had decided to break up with her anyhow. Her confession only solidified his decision.

"Baby?" Milania quickly pulled herself together and smiled. "When did you get here?"

"I've been here long enough to hear the truth."

"Dumb bitch," Dylan giggled. "Here you go." She tossed Angel his wallet and phone and proceeded down the hallway.

"Baby, I can explain," Milania began as he walked past her and into the suite.

"Save it," Angel replied tersely. "Lying is like breathing to you. I don't wanna hear shit you got to say, and if anybody is in here, it's time for you to get the fuck out!"

Seconds later, the entire team of hair and makeup artists scurried out of the bathroom with their supplies in hand and ran out the door.

"Angel, baby, it's not what you think. Calm down," Milania tried to reason, feeling as if she was about to faint.

"Shut up! Just shut the fuck up!" Angel pointed his fingers like a gun in her face, scaring her half to death. "There ain't shit you can say! So just grab the shit you came here wit' and bounce!"

"You're kidding me, right?" Milania said, stunned.

"Do it fuckin' *look* like I'm playin'? This shit is a wrap! I should've never fucked wit' yo' ass in the first place, you trifling bitch!"

"You're right, 'cause I'm too fuckin' good for you," Milania shot back, done with pretending.

Angel instantly burst out laughing. "You out yo' mind? You *got* to be jokin', right?"

"No, I'm not! You've already served your purpose anyway! Fuck you! You can have that stank bitch if that's what you want 'cause I'm done wit' you! You'll never be nothin' without me!"

"Bitch, please! You gon' be hot a little while! I'ma be rich forever!"

"Whateva!" She went to grab her things, but Angel blocked her path.

"Where you think you going?" He looked down at her.

"I'm gettin' my stuff!" She tried moving him out of the way, to no avail.

"You ain't gettin' shit!" Angel took her roughly by her elbow and led her to the door. "Now get the fuck out!" He pushed her across the threshold and slammed the door in her face.

"I don't believe this shit," Angel huffed with his back up against the door.

He knew Milania had some inconsistencies in her attitude, but he never imagined that she was a manipulating bitch.

Dylan lay on her side sound asleep. It had been forever since she'd had a night alone to herself. Mason was at Billie's house for the night. Dreaming of being dressed in a wedding gown and walking down the aisle to an unknown man, Dylan was awakened by the alarming sound of her phone ringing. Opening her eyes, she looked at the clock and saw that it was a quarter till two.

"Hello?" She picked up the phone not even bothering to see who it was.

"You asleep?" Angel said, his voice booming with bass.

"I was, what's up?" Dylan sat up.

"My bad, I ain't mean to wake you up. I just wanted to holla at you for a second but go back to sleep."

"You good." She rubbed her eyes.

"Can you meet me outside in like five minutes?"

"Yeah."

"A'ight, I'll see you in a second." He hung up.

With the lights turned off, Dylan stood at her window. Dressed in only a metallic lace bra with a satin bow and bikini panties, she peered down at the street below. She wondered what Angel would say when he arrived. Would he blame her for her and Milania's latest showdown? She sure hoped not because another scolding from him was something she just couldn't take nor tolerate.

A flash of lightning struck the sky, igniting the nervous feeling that permeated in the pit of her stomach. Dylan loved the sound of rain and the booming crash of thunder in the air. It reminded her each time of the first time she and Angel made love. All of a sudden, the hum of a roaring engine resonated in the atmosphere, putting her on notice that he was coming.

Dylan watched closely as he swiftly parked his black 2011 Lamborghini Murcielago in front of her building. Rain carpeted the windows of his car, but she could still see him staring back at her. Dylan didn't care that it was past midnight or that a thunderstorm was raging outside her door. She had to go to him, so without hesitation or regret, she put on her black double breasted Alice + Olivia trench coat, black combat boots, and headed out the door.

A red Marimekko Kivet Stick Umbrella covered her head as she stepped outside and into the cold rain. Darkness filled the sky as the suicide doors on his car winged upward and Angel got out. His overwhelming beauty engulfed her. Despite the sadness in his eyes, he still looked deliciously good in a black Yankees cap, Armani wayfarer-style shades, 10 Deep black sweatshirt, Cheap Monday jeans, and Christian Lacroix high top sneakers.

The rain pelted Dylan's umbrella as they inched closer to one another. It was as if they were starring in their very own black-and-white film where he was Humphrey Bogart and she was Lauren Bacall. The entire scene couldn't have been crafted better if they had written it themselves. With his pants sagged low, a quiet urgency resounded in his stride as Angel approached her.

Dylan wasn't quite sure what he might do when they finally came to face-to-face. Then the moment arrived. She held her breath in anticipation of his next move. Angel took one look in Dylan's spellbinding eyes and decided he didn't want to talk anymore. They'd done enough of that to last them a lifetime. He wanted to feel whole again, and Dylan was the only person who could give that to him.

Soaking wet from the rain, he turned his hat to the left and placed his lips upon hers. Dylan felt as if she were floating on a cloud made of cotton candy. His lips tasted like midnight, while his tongue tasted like wine. There was no doubt in her mind that she could taste them forever. Angel wrapped her up in his arms. His heartbeat pounded against her chest. Unable to control her emotions, Dylan dropped the umbrella and rested her hands on both sides of his face.

Drops of rain continued to fall rapidly from the sky as Angel pressed her body against the brick wall of her building. He didn't give a damn if her neighbors or random passersby saw them. He had to have her right then and there. She felt too good in his arms for them to waste time and head inside. With precision and ease, he began to unbuttoned her coat, but Dylan stopped him.

"Uh-uh." She held his hands, still self-conscious of the weight she'd gained.

"Dylan, you're my baby. Stop trippin' off that shit. You're beautiful to me no matter what." He kissed her lips, rotating between her top and bottom one.

Feeling a little bit better, Dylan dropped her hands down to her sides and allowed him to proceed. Angel was surprisingly thrilled to find that she had little to no clothes on. To him, Dylan was perfect. Yeah, she gained a few pounds, but he liked her with a little more meat on her bones. Angel's sodden hands glided up her thick thighs and tore the sides of her panties, leaving her in just her coat and bra. But even her bra wouldn't stay in one piece for long. Since the clasp that held her breasts in place was in the front, Angel unhinged it and allowed her luscious breasts to spring forth. Taking both of her full breasts in his hands, Angel let his tongue go to work.

Dylan couldn't even think straight. His tongue was creating a world filled with pleasure, agony, and lust. With each lick, her nipples sprouted like rosebuds on the first day of spring. Through manipulating her breasts with tantalizing kisses, Angel made a trail of wet kisses up her neck and to her wanting mouth.

Just as she became one with his lips again, Angel surprised her and placed her in front of him. The next thing Dylan knew, his teeth gently bit into the side of her neck while his wet fingertips slid down her stomach and landed on the face of her pussy.

"Angel," she whimpered as he began to work his magic.

Each stroke of his fingertips caused her pussy to melt. Knowing where her spot was, Angel rotated his fingers like clockwork until the cream from her pussy mixed with the drizzling rain.

Reeling from her first orgasm in over a year, Dylan panted heavily, trying to regain her composure, but Angel wasn't having that. He wanted to hear her scream. Dying for him to enter her, Dylan undid his pants quickly. Angel's ten inches of steel caused her mouth to water on sight. Dylan had to get a taste. Easing her way down to the ground while she stared up into his hungry eyes, she wrapped her lips around the head of his dick and took him in inch by inch.

By now, Angel's eyes rolled to the back of his head. It took every ounce of his strength for his knees not to buckle. Dylan was sucking his dick *so* good. Not ready to cum yet, he ran his hand through her drenched hair and jerked her head back. As if she were as light as a feather, Angel put his hands underneath her arms and lifted her up. Dylan happily wrapped her legs around his back and held on for the ride.

Hard as a rock, Angel inserted himself deep within her honey pot. With each hard, pounding stroke, thunder clashed in the sky. While grinding in and out of her, Angel hungrily tried to lick off every last raindrop that fell onto her chest and neck. The sensation of his tongue swirling all over her body and the nonstop thrusting of his thick dick caused Dylan to scream out to the high heavens.

"Oh my God! Shit! Angel, what you doing to me? I can't take it," she moaned.

"Yes, you can," he whispered, holding her thighs. "You gon' take this dick and love it."

"I'ma take it, Daddy! I'ma take it!" She matched his thrust with her own. "Ooooooooooh, I missed you."

"I missed you too," Angel groaned, feeling himself about to cum.

What he was experiencing was far better than any fantasy he could've dreamt up or created in his mind over the past year. Dylan was made for him, and every time their bodies intertwined, that became evident. She was his other half, whether he wanted to admit or not. He was tired of watching her from afar and not being able to be her man, but after they both came down from their orgasmic high, reality was sure to set in.

Angel would remember that he'd just broken off his engagement to Milania and was in no way, shape, or form ready to commit to another woman so soon, especially Dylan. But the soft whimpers of ecstasy that fell from her lips and landed on his heart had him trapped, and in that moment, he wanted to stay in between her thighs until the end of time.

"I've never been good at sayin' goodbye."
Common, "I Want You"

15

The sun hadn't yet risen, but Angel was up and wide awake. There he was, sitting on the side of Dylan's bed, gazing down at his hands. After making love throughout the night, she'd finally fallen asleep. For months, he'd dreamed about sleeping with her. He'd yearned for it. He wanted it so much he could taste it and feel it in his veins, but now that he'd finally satisfied his craving, he wondered if he'd made the right decision.

He'd just ended things with Milania. He had no business hopping into bed with Dylan so fast. He hadn't even digested what had happened between him and Milania, and with the feelings he knew Dylan harbored for him, he was sure she'd want a commitment out of him sooner or later. But Angel wasn't sure if he'd be able to give it to her once she asked.

"What you doing up?" she asked him from behind.

"I thought you was asleep." He turned and looked at her.

"I was. Why you just sittin' there? Are you okay?" She sat up on her elbow.

"I'm good." He slid back in bed and tenderly kissed her forehead. "You?" He smoothed her bangs from out of her face so he could see her tranquil eyes.

"I'm more than good. I'm great." She leaned over and placed her lips on his.

Angel kissed her back fervently. Lost in the wonder of his tongue, Dylan closed her eyes and savored the feeling. She wished they could stay cooped up in her nest eternally. To her, lying by his side never felt so right.

"I wanted to apologize to you for the fucked-up shit Milania said and did to you," he said sincerely, feeling horrible.

"It's not your fault."

"I know. I just felt it was necessary. Yo', for a minute there, I thought you was about to hit her," Angel laughed.

"I wanted to hit her, but she's too skinny. It'd be like punching Sarah Jessica Parker," Dylan joked.

Angel died laughing. "You crazy."

"I really did miss you," she whispered, gazing into his eyes.

"How much?" He pulled her on top of him.

Mixed emotions flooded him, but he was too mentally fucked up in the head to offer her anything else besides what they shared in her bed.

"This much." She traveled down low and licked his dick as if it were a lollipop.

Angel took a much-needed breath as Dylan's warm, wet mouth traveled up and down the length of his dick. He knew that the momentary pleasure he was feeling wasn't the answer, but Angel couldn't resist, it felt so good.

Weeks later, the savory aroma of spaghetti and meatballs traveled through the air as Angel used Dylan's spare key to enter her house. Feeling like he had the weight of the world on his shoulders, he slowly traveled up the stairs and met up with Dylan, who was in the kitchen cooking.

"Hi." She wiped her hands on the pink apron she was wearing and kissed him on the cheek.

"What's up?" He kissed her back, then turned and went into the living room.

Dylan could tell by the faraway look in his eyes that he had a lot on his mind. "I hope you're hungry," she beamed, trying to brighten his mood.

Angel walked over to Mason, who was asleep in his swing, and kissed him on the forehead before responding. "I guess I could eat a li'l something." He kicked off his sneakers and sat down on the couch.

"Well, the food will be done in a minute so . . ." she responded, not really knowing what else to say.

Caught up in his thoughts, Angel picked up the remote control and turned on the baseball game. The Cardinals was playing the Red Sox that night. Dylan watched him from the kitchen and wondered what could be going through his mind. For weeks it'd been the same routine. He'd come in, take off his shoes, plop down on the couch, and become lost in the television.

Other times, he'd just lie there with his eyes closed. Ever since they made love, he seemed so blue. They barely even talked anymore. When they did, it was because she initiated the conversation. The only time they connected was when their bodies become one at night. It was like she was being shut out of his life, and she didn't even know why she was being shunned. All she wanted was for him to open up and talk to her.

She'd listen intently to every word he had to say. She'd even set the mood just so he'd feel comfortable. Dylan had it all planned out in her mind. She'd turn the lights down low, play his favorite song, and pour him his favorite glass of wine, but first, he had to be willing to divulge what panged his heart. She didn't want to become the psycho chick that made up shit in her mind, but every second that went by and he pushed her further and further away, her mind started to drum up conspiracy theories.

Like, what if he didn't love her anymore and was just too afraid to say it, or what if he really was turned off by her weight gain and found her body disgusting, or worse, what if it all were a game and he was only back with her so he could get payback and break her heart? Dylan couldn't take it. She didn't know how much longer she could continue to be the easygoing, drama-free chick in order to be Angel's girl again. The secret he was holding within was driving her insane, and she needed answers quick before she snapped.

Dylan hadn't been so excited since the birth of Mason. It was the day of her book release party, although finding a suitable outfit had been a nightmare on Elm Street. Dylan still hadn't gotten used to her new body. She went from being a svelte size four to, in her mind, a towering size thirteen. When she looked in the mirror, all she saw was a fat-bellied pig. During her pregnancy, she assumed she'd be able to lose the baby weight with a snap of a finger, but Dylan learned quickly that losing weight wasn't going to be as easy as she thought.

In between taking care of Mason, doing radio and magazine interviews, running the bakery, and spending whatever spare time she had left with Angel, Billie, and Tee-Tee, going on a diet wasn't something that even fit into her schedule. Thankfully, she had the love and support of her cousin and style guru, Tee-Tee, to help her. Because of him, she'd found the perfect Camilla and Marc, one-shoulder lace dress with an asymmetrical neck and eyelash edge at the hem.

A long, eighteen-inch ponytail braided into a fishbone and Gasoline Glamour pumps completed her look. Dylan couldn't believe her eyes when she entered the Art Dimension studio gallery where her party was being held. The entire atmosphere was so downtown New York chic. Slightly dimmed lights showcased local artists' works of art. DJ Okay spun Aloe Blacc's "I Need a Dollar" setting the mood.

All of the guests were served champagne and bruschetta. In the lounge area, guests sat and chatted while overlooking the streets below. The party was everything Dylan had dreamed it would be, and more. What made it even more special was that Angel was her date for the evening. But as usual, Angel was being his normal, quiet, and withdrawn self. He'd barely said a word all night.

"Excuse me, everyone!" Brenda tapped her glass with a fork.

"I have an important announcement to make. Months ago, I was approached by Dylan with her idea of a cookbook that combined food and fashion and I instantly loved it. I knew that her idea was special, so when she asked me to become her agent, there was no way I could say no. Well, Dylan, your hard work has paid off. Not only do you have the most buzzed about cookbook since Julia Child, but The Food Network has offered you your very own show!"

"Are you kidding me? Oh my God!" Dylan jumped up and down with glee.

"I knew we was gon' be famous one day!" Tee-Tee exclaimed, doing the dougie.

"Dylan, I am so proud of you!" Billie hugged her tightly.

"Thanks, luv."

"So, will you all please raise your glass to Dylan," Brenda continued.

"To Dylan!" the crowed cheered.

Glowing, Dylan took a sip of her champagne. Angel planted a loving kiss on her cheek and whispered into her ear, "Can I talk to you for a minute?"

"Honey, you can do whatever you please with me," Dylan flirted, licking her lips.

Over in the lounge area Angel and Dylan stood in front of a huge bay window.

"So what's up?" she rubbed his back. "You've been kind of quiet all night."

"I know this is some fucked-up timing, but I got something that I need to tell you."

"What is it? OMG!" She clasped her hand over her mouth. "Please don't tell me you're back with that crazy bitch?"

"Nah, never that," he chuckled. "It's just that I've been offered an exhibition fight overseas, and I decided to take it."

"Where overseas?" she blinked.

"Scotland."

"Wow." Dylan swallowed hard, put off by his announcement.

She knew that they weren't officially a couple again, but she kind of figured that after all the time they'd spent apart, he'd wanna spend every waking moment with her.

"You mad at me?" He caressed her cheek with the back of his hand.

"I mean, it's just kinda strange, that's all. What about Mason?"

"I already figured that part out. We can Skype every day, and I'll call you. It'll be like I'm not even gone."

"But you will be." Dylan gazed down at her feet, becoming emotional.

"You know better than that." He lifted her head up.

"But why now?" She tried her best not to cry.

"I haven't been in the ring in almost a year, and I think it would be good conditioning for me," he lied.

Angel really accepted the fight because he needed to get away, clear his mind, and breathe. Things in his life were going in every direction except straight, and he had to get things back on track. There was no way he could be the man Dylan needed when he wasn't totally sure he was prepared to be. He needed to resolve his emotions regarding Milania and process that relationship before jumping into something with Dylan.

And yes, he should've thought of all of that before filling Dylan's head with the hope that maybe they could be together, but he was a man, and sometimes men make mistakes.

"Come here, man." He took her into his strong arms.

"I'll only be gone a couple of months. Before you can say, 'ah,' I'll be back."

"Ahhhh," Dylan mocked him.

"Seriously, we gon' be straight. Plus, you got your book stuff and your new TV show to work on. I'll only be in the way. But I want you to know I'ma get you set up with an account before I leave."

"No." Dylan shook her head. "I don't want nor need your money."

"Sorry, but you don't get a say-so in this, plus, it's already been done."

"You know Billie and the kids are gonna miss you so much." She changed the subject.

"You know who's gonna miss me third as much?" He nuzzled his nose in the crook of her neck and kissed her passionately.

"Who? Tee-Tee?" Dylan joked.

"No, you, pretty girl."

"Puleese, I don't miss people. I dismiss them. When my first stepdad jetted, I was like, bye, nigga! Second stepdad, deuces!" She threw up the peace sign. "Third stepdad, don't let the doorknob hit you where the good Lord split ya'!"

"You stupid," Angel laughed.

"So when do you leave?" Dylan said seriously.

"Tomorrow."

"Wow. I feel like I've just got a scuff mark on a pair of brand-new Louboutins."

"Stop it. Everything's gon' be straight. I promise." He gave her a quick peck on the lips.

"Yeah, we'll see," Dylan replied, knowing deep down that what they shared was doomed.

Despite Angel's sudden departure, for Dylan, the show, meaning life, still had to go on. Outside of missing Angel like she missed carbohydrates, she still had Mason and a *New York Times* bestselling book to keep her happy. Dylan was over the moon when her first week sales came in. She'd sold 300,000 copies in the first two days.

Celebrities such as Jessica Simpson and June Ambrose swore by it and had already agreed to appear on her show. Dylan stood on the set getting last-minute touch-ups from the styling team before taping her first take. It was the first day of filming for her cooking show named Edible Couture. Dylan was on top of the world.

She had it all. A beautiful, chubby, baby boy, whom she loved more than her entire Chanel collection. Her career was on the rise, and the bakery was booming with business again. Money problems were a thing of the past. Not only did she have her book advance money from her deal and money coming in from her show, but Candy had put her bank account on swole by depositing a staggering half mill. She and Mason were set for life, and sure, money couldn't replace the loneliness of not having Angel around, but the accomplishment of knowing that she'd made her wildest dreams come true satisfied any feeling of separation she felt.

Sanctuaria Wild Tapas located in the trendy Tower Grove section of St. Louis was a warm, yet sexy restaurant with an alluring appeal. It was a place where you went to escape and eat amazing food in a hip environment. Seventeenth- and eighteenth-century pieces of artwork found in churches around the world were displayed on the walls for everyone to admire. Prayers over 450 years old were painted on metal in the main dining room were Dylan and her crew sat catching up.

"So how is my nephew?" Billie cut into her appetizer.

"Girl, look, I took a picture of him while I gave him a bath the other day." Dylan showed her a picture from her cell phone.

"Look at him," Billie smiled, cheerfully. "He is sooooo cute, wit' his fat self."

"I know. I can't get him off my tit now," Dylan joked.

"You silly," Tee-Tee giggled.

"No, seriously, if you had tits, I'd make *you* breastfeed him."

"Girl, I'd be happier than a make-a-wish kid at Disneyland." Tee-Tee slapped his hand against his thigh and chuckled.

"You going to hell for that," Dylan cracked up, laughing.

"In a hand basket," Tee-Tee bucked his eyes and pointed his index finger. "So, what's the T, ladies?" He took a small sip of his Cosmo.

"I promise y'all since my book came out my Black-Berry has been on another level. I've been asked to do a photo shoot with *Vanity Fair,* and Gray called me and asked me to do an interview with *Haute Couture* magazine." Dylan smiled happily.

"That's good, girl," Billie said, wiping her mouth with her napkin.

"I know. I'm just excited about my show. You know the pilot airs next week. I just hope people tune in," Dylan said wistfully.

"Girl, please. All I gotta do is make one phone call and the whole Get 'Em Girl Mafia gon' watch." Tee-Tee referenced the underground gang of gay men he hung with.

"Really?"

"Yeah, chile, we worldwide now." He pursed his lips.

"So are things between you and Knox still good?" Dylan asked Billie.

"Hell, yeah. I learned my lesson. Ain't no way I'm losing my husband again." Billie smirked, winking her eye.

"Good. I like Knox." Dylan took a small sip of her Sprite.

"Me too," Tee-Tee ran his tongue across his upper lip.

"Get stabbed with this fork," Billie cautioned, holding it up in a striking position.

"Girl, please, I ain't scared of no ghost." Tee-Tee flicked his wrist.

"Oh, I forgot to tell you," Dylan said, ecstatic. "I've been invited to Paris Fashion Week."

"Shut the front door," Tee-Tee gasped. "Girl, don't play."

"You know I never joke about panty lines, Brangelina, or fashion week."

"Aww, shit. That's what's up." Tee-Tee snapped his finger, grooving to an imaginary beat.

"And I got front-row seats to some of the shows, so, of course, you two bitches are invited." Dylan looked at both of them.

"Girl, I'm already packed," Tee-Tee replied.

"I can't go," Billie pouted.

"Why not?" Dylan questioned, disappointed.

"You know Knox and my anniversary, just passed so we're taking a vacation to celebrate."

"Aww, yeah, I totally forgot." Dylan slapped her hand against her forehead.

"Too bad. Now who am I gonna get to watch Mason?"

"Yo' mama," Tee-Tee fiddled with his salad and grinned.

"You out yo' damn mind," Dylan suddenly frowned.

"Bernard can keep him. He's a stay-at-home husband anyway. Speaking of my boo, we gettin' a baby soon!" Tee-Tee did the Cabbage Patch.

"Congratulations!" Dylan high-fived him.

"Thanks, luv." Tee-Tee batted his eyes.

"It is a girl or a boy?" Billie quizzed.

"A girl."

"Get it, bitch!" Billie threw her hands up in the air.

"So you're *sure* going to get this one?" Dylan asked, concerned.

"Yes, this baby isn't a newborn, she's six months and has been in the system since she was born."

"Well, I'm happy for you, boo," Dylan said as her food came.

"Really, Dylan?" Tee-Tee looked at her as if she had lost her mind. "Soup and a half of salad? You know we suppose to be on the Nicole Richie diet."

"Shut up," she snapped, giving him the middle finger.

"So what's going on between you and my brother?" Billie took a bite of her food.

"I don't know. We talk and skype every day, but it's like there is a distance between us. Ever since we slept together it's been weird." Dylan played with her food.

"Have you told him you're going to Paris yet?"

"No. We're going to skype later."

"Ooh, y'all gon' skype sex, ain't y'all?" Tee-Tee leaned forward, dying to know.

"Nooo, we're not." Dylan said with a deliberate emphasis on the word no.

"Heffa, please don't act demure. We all know you the biggest freak at this table."

"Okay, we might! Are you happy now?" Dylan snorted with laughter.

"Y'all are disgusting. Ugh, I feel like I need to Purell my brain," Billie scowled.

"Don't hate," Dylan smiled. "But on the real, y'all, I feel like I need a makeover or some kind of change in my life."

"Why you say that?" Tee-Tee poked out his bottom lip, making a sad face.

"'Cause I just don't wanna become one of those moms with a Kate Gosselin haircut and mom jeans all the way up to my armpits with no man," Dylan pouted.

"Girl, please, you are way too fly for that." He waved her off.

"You're not just sayin' that to make me feel better, are you?"

"I would never say anything to make you feel better," he assured her.

"I dread every moment we spend together," Billie added jokingly.

"Y'all really are my bitches." Dylan dabbed her eyes with her napkin pretending to cry.

"No, seriously, your style is so Atlantic City hooker meets Bloomingdale's, it's crazy," Tee-Tee chewed his food.

"Thank you," Dylan crossed her hands over her heart. "That means the world to me."

"Y'all are stupid," Billie giggled.

"Maybe I just need a man," Dylan sighed.

"What about Angel?" Tee-Tee inquired.

"I don't know what to qualify him as," Dylan responded.

"Well have you ever tried writing a list of all the qualities you want in a man?" Billie questioned.

"Girl, yeah. I wrote down all the qualities I wanted in a man, and in the end, I realized that muthafucka was too good for me," Dylan laughed.

"You are silly."

"I'm serious as hell."

"Well, look," Tee-Tee interjected, "while we're talkin', I'm making a visual clothing store for you right now in my head. Just tell me which shirt you want."

"Oooh, the Balenciaga one." Dylan leaned forward, eyes sparkling.

"Is that the only thing you two do is talk about clothes? I bet neither of you have read a book in the last six months," Billie challenged.

"Uh-uh, I read a book," Dylan stated proudly.

"Umm, sweetie," Tee-Tee pouted, "the instruction manual to Mason's swing doesn't count as a book."

"Why not? It was a page turner. You know, for a while there, I didn't even know where to put him in at."

"On that note, when do we leave?" Tee-Tee asked outdone.

"In two weeks," Dylan answered.

"Uh-oh, Paris better watch out 'cause *here we come!*"

"Nothin' more beautiful than knowing your worth."
Fantasia, "I'm Doin' Me"

16

"Say 'hi' to Daddy!" Dylan waved Mason's hand while he stared at the computer screen.

"Hey, man!" Angel waved back, smiling. He never got sick of seeing his son's face and truly missed being away from him.

"He's gettin' so big."

"We just went to the doctor. He weighs twelve pounds." Dylan kissed Mason on the top of his head.

"That's my boy. He gon' be a heavyweight like me."

"That's the same thing his doctor said. So how is training camp going?"

"Good." Angel yawned. "I think I'm ready."

"You better be after all of this," Dylan joked.

"Oh ole boy ain't winning at all. I got this in the bag," Angel boasted.

"You got this in the bag, huh? Let me see your muscles."

Angel proudly lifted his right arm and flexed his well-defined bicep. Dylan almost had a fit. His body was at its physical peak, and she wanted to explore every nook and cranny of it.

"I saw the segment you did for E News with Giuliani. You did good. You 'bout to be the next Rachael Ray," Angel said.

"I mean you know." Dylan turned her head, smiling. "Rachael Ray cool, but homegirl ain't got nothin' on me."

"Look at you over there with the big head. Nah, I'm happy for you, though. I always knew you could do it."

"Thanks. That means a lot coming from you," Dylan said solemnly. "I got good news." She perked up. "I was invited to fashion week in Paris so I was thinking while I'm over there I could come see you."

"Is Mason going wit' you?" Angel asked curiously.

"No, I'll be there for three days so Bernard is going to keep him for me."

"I don't know how I feel about that," Angel frowned. "What?"

"You think it's a good idea for you to be flying across the country when you got a three-month old son at home?" Angel said disapprovingly.

"Has all the rain over there made you senile or crazy?" Dylan snapped her neck. "'Cause ain't you the same person who left his newborn son for three *months,* leaving me here to do everything *by myself?* Mason is with me twenty-four hours a day. He goes to sleep and wakes up with me, goes to work with me at the bakery and at the show, then I come home and get both of us ready to do it all again the next day, so before you ask me anything about taking a three-day business trip that is going to help further my career, you need to check yo'self, home-boy!"

"You're right. I'm sorry," Angel apologized from the bottom of his heart.

After that neither of them knew what to say. Angel knew he had crossed the line big time. Dylan was an excellent mother who went above and beyond the call of duty. She deserved a break. Angel had no right coming to her like that.

"So do you want me to come or not?" Dylan said with an attitude.

"Nah, just go 'head and go to your fashion week thing. I'ma be training the whole time anyway, so it really don't make no sense for you to go outta your way to fly over here too."

Dylan's heart stopped. Her body felt frozen. She thought by now that she and Angel would have gotten past all the back-and-forth cat and mouse games but obviously not.

"So what's the deal, Angel? 'Cause you been actin' real funny here lately. Was the other night a mistake?" Dylan looked into the screen praying silently that he'd say no.

"I mean," Angel hesitated, "I thought we both knew what it was, just one night."

Dylan felt like she'd been sucker punched in the chest. All the wind had been knocked out of her. "Is that what it was?" Her voice cracked.

"Come on, Dylan, we never had any problems in the bedroom. It was the other rooms in the house we couldn't handle."

Dylan wanted to find the right words to convey how she felt, but all that seemed to come from her lips was air. For the past two and a half years of her life, she'd held out hope that Angel would see the genuine love she had for him tucked away in her heart. If given the chance, she would've given him her all, but for some reason, he just wasn't willing to receive it.

She'd tried giving him time to see that she'd changed for the better, but no matter how much she made herself available, laughed at his corny jokes, or prayed to God to send him back to her, Angel wasn't going to give in. Worn-out from fighting a never-ending battle, Dylan threw in the towel. She was done. She couldn't wait around for Angel anymore.

"All right, then, umm . . . I need to put Mason down so I guess I'll talk to you later." She looked down instead of at him.

"A'ight, I'll call you tomorrow." Angel gazed at her once more before logging off.

Sitting with his hands crisscrossed behind his head, Angel knew that he'd fucked-up royally with Dylan. Instead of being so harsh, he should've just told her the truth, which was that he was scared, scared that she might hurt him again. He was so afraid that if he allowed himself to open up to her once more, she'd trample on his heart, but this time, with spiked stiletto heels.

With every relationship he'd entered, Angel rushed in headfirst, only to be let down in the end. He was fed up with the women in his life taking his love for granted. This time, he was going to do things differently. He wouldn't jump into something new just to dull the pain. He'd face the relationship demons that haunted him with his chin up and shoulders back.

It would make him a better man. Angel got up and lay down on the bed. Gazing up at the ceiling, it suddenly hit him that the only thing that was missing was Dylan and his son. The maddening quietness which surrounded him proved it.

Dylan Monroe and Teyana aka Tee-Tee strolled Le Triangle d'Or (the golden triangle) in Paris ,where luxury goods like Piget, Louis Vuitton, Rochas, Prada, and Givenchy were the opiates of choice. They'd only been in the City of Light a few hours and had already done major retail therapy at ultra chic shops such as Tally Weijl, Zadig et Voltaire, and Dylan's favorite ba&sh. No other destination in the world could compete with Paris.

Every time Dylan got a chance to visit, she made it her business to hit up the Louvre, Notre Dame, and the historic Café de Flore. For Dylan, Paris was like heaven on earth. She was almost sure that night she would go to sleep dreaming of Louboutin and Laurent. She was très chic with her hair pulled into a French roll with side swept bangs. Dressed in a gray men's blazer with the collar popped up and the sleeves pushed back, a black T-shirt with the phrase "She Died Of Perfection" written on it, a white petticoat, white ankle socks, and tan-colored Nanette Lepore pumps with a bow accent on the toe, Dylan strolled gleefully down the cobblestone sidewalk as if she were in an opening of *The Mary Tyler Moore Show*.

A slight smile graced the corners of her lips as she took in the ambiance of the old buildings before her. The sweet smells of freshly baked croissants, blueberry scones, and apple crêpes wafted through the air tantalizing her nose. The women and men who walked by looked sophisticated and smart and seemed to live a lifestyle of leisure where time wasn't of the essence, but good food and great conversation were. This was the life, and Dylan wouldn't have traded this moment for anything in the world.

"Ahhhh, the end of summer in Paris couldn't be any better!" Dylan clasped her hands.

"I know, girl! Bonjour!" Tee-Tee waved at people as they strolled by.

"I feel like myself again," Dylan beamed, twirling around in a circle, then suddenly stopped. "Sweet baby Jesus, there it is!"

"There what is?" Tee-Tee looked around.

"Coco Chanel's apartment!" Dylan pointed with delight. "We found it!"

"Girl, I think I done died and gone to heaven!" Tee-Tee whipped out his Flip camcorder.

"Ooh, I can smell the scent of Chanel 5 from out here."
Dylan sniffed the door frame.

"Pose for the camera, girl!" Tee-Tee insisted.

Dylan threw up her hands, placed her legs together,
and cheesed.

"Ooh, Tee-Tee, we did it!" She hugged her cousin overjoyed.

"We're like so having a moment," Tee-Tee gushed.

"I know it's like kinda on another level."

"Bananas." Tee-Tee released her and stood back in
awe.

"I wish we could call Billie and tell her."

"Girl, you know we ain't got no kind of reception over
here. C'mon." He took her by the hand. "We got some
more shoppin' to do."

The Rue La La party was off the charts. In one corner
you had Lindsey Lohan dressed in an Elie Saab gown
with a scram bracelet on her ankle, and in another
corner were Estelle and Thandie Newton gossiping
like two schoolgirls. Solange was on the ones and twos
spinning "One" by Sky Ferreira. Models like Chanel
Iman and Jessica Stam partied on the dance floor. The
whole scene was a huge dog and pony show, and Dylan
loved every minute of it.

With a glass of Chardonnay in her hand, she gazed
around the crowded room. The place was packed to
the brim. The fashion industry's elite were all in attendance and celebrating the extravagant shows from
earlier that day. Dylan absolutely adored the Valentino
show. It was filled with her two favorite things in life:
ruffles and lace. Taking a sip of her wine, she wondered
how Mason was doing. She missed her baby so much
it hurt, and the pain of knowing that she was so close

to Angel but him not wanting to see her gnawed away at her insides. Sensing her sadness, Tee-Tee took her glass of champagne from her hand.

"What are you doing?" Dylan reached over to snatch it back but was too slow.

"You finna go dance," he demanded, pushing her forward.

"No, I'm not." She shook her head.

"You need to. Enjoy yourself for a change. That li'l big head baby of yours is all right," he teased.

"My baby do got a big head," Dylan laughed.

"Now go get on that dance floor and make Mama proud. Show these Parisian bitches how we do it back in the Lou!"

"Hold this." She handed him her new Carlos Falchi clutch purse and strutted over to the floor.

Unaware of her affect on the male population in the room, Dylan found her a spot with enough room and started to groove along to the bass-pounding beat of Usher's "Li'l Freak." The song was so sensual it was almost sinful. From across the room a fellow by the name of Javier Nathaniel Cruz leaned against the bar with a cup of Hennessy in his hand. For the last fifteen minutes he'd been having a conversation with a group of rail-thin supermodels when out of the blue, the most beautiful creature he's ever laid eyes upon caught his attention from the dance floor.

She was the kind of chick who wasn't in search of companionship or a man to complete her. From the way she threw up her arms, closed her eyes, and sang along to the tune, he could tell she was strictly there to have a good time. From the looks of her, he could tell she was way too fly for him, but he had to have her, so he grew wings and floated across the room to greet her. The women he'd left behind were flabbergasted that he'd left them so abruptly for an American, but he could care less. Dylan was the only woman in the room who held his attention. All eyes were on him as he walked in behind her and placed his arms around her waist.

Dylan didn't know who she was dancing with, but the scent of his Tom Ford Champaca Absolute Cologne had her open with just one whiff. In her element, Dylan ran her hand down the side of his face while moving her hips from side to side. Javier was fully focused on her sway. Then they came face-to-face. Dylan was speechless. Outside of Angel, she'd never seen a man so gorgeous.

He towered over her, standing tall at six feet two with an athletic physique. His skin was the creamy color of shea butter. He was exotically handsome in a he-could-get-it-any-day-of-the-week-type way. He rocked a low cut. Smoldering green eyes, a slim nose, a sculpted beard, perfectly plump pink lips, and pearly white teeth made up his facial features. His biceps had highs and lows like mountaintops. Various tattoos covered both his arms and hands.

The man was magically delicious in a tan, blue, yellow and black plaid jacket with brown leather sleeves, black tee shirt, fitted jeans, brown combat work boots and Ray Ban shades. From the looks of his fitted jeans, Dylan was almost sure he was working with a python. He was so fine she prayed to God that she wouldn't start drooling. Dylan looked up into his eyes and swore he could see right through to her soul, and when he gave her his ten million-dollar smile, everyone else in the room disappeared.

He didn't even have to utter a word for her to know he was the type of man she went for. Quietly, he took her hand and whisked her away to where the moon could be their guiding light. In the open warm air under a street-light, Javier leaned his back against the pole and stared down at Dylan's angelic face.

Dylan couldn't have asked for a better romantic Paris moment. What she was experiencing was unlike any-thing she'd ever seen on television. The lights from the Eiffel Tower whizzed over their heads. The humid air made love to their lips as Javier pulled her close to his chest.

"*Vous êtes beaux.*" He traced her cheek with his fin-gertip.

"I don't know what you just said but thank you," she laughed, embarrassed.

"I said you're beautiful."

"Honey, you are too." She blushed biting down on her lip.

"Thank you. So what's your name, beautiful?"

"Dylan, and you?"

"Javier Cruz, but you can call me Cruz."

"Cruz, are you French?"

"No," he chuckled. "I'm Spanish."

"Oh," she laughed too.

"I play midfield for Spain's national soccer team."

"Wow, no wonder." Dylan gave his body a lustful glance.

Cruz smiled at her appreciation of his physique.

"What you doing after all of this is done?" he asked, dying to see her naked.

"Going back to my hotel," she replied. "I'm leaving tomorrow."

"Where you from?"

"St. Louis, Missouri. You ever heard of it?"

"Yeah, some of my homeboys live out there."

"That's what's up."

"So what's the deal, Ma?" Cruz massaged her hips. "We standing here diggin' on each other. I know you wanna come back home wit' me. I promise I won't keep you up too late." He licked his bottom lip and ran his hands down her thighs.

"I wish I could, but I'm here with my cousin. I can't just leave him like that," Dylan said, flushing in distress.

Her body was screaming for Cruz to put it on her in the worst way.

"Huuuuuuuuh," Cruz groaned, becoming impatient. "What's the problem, Ma? I can see it in your eyes. You want me just like I want you. What, you scared?"

"I'm a grown woman. A grown woman ain't scared of no dick," Dylan retorted.

"If that's the case, then quit bullshittin' and come home wit' me," he said with an intense look of desire in his eyes before kissing the side of her neck.

Dylan wanted to be a lady and protest, but the flicker of his tongue on her skin had her feeling as if she were going in circles.

"All right." She backed away from him still holding his hand.

Dylan knew if she allowed him to continue, her dress would be off and she'd be fuckin' him right there on the street corner.

"Ummm . . . you're fine," she said gathering her composure. "God knows you are, but I'm thirty years old wit' a newborn baby at home whom I miss terribly. And to be totally honest, I would love to go home wit' you, but I don't think that all the muscles in the world—and believe me, you are workin' wit' a nice set of them—" Dylan ran her eyes over his arms and chest again—"could get me out of these Spanx I'm wearing right now," she said with a laugh. "But more important, I like you . . . I do, but I don't think I'm ready for any of this."

Cruz couldn't help but value her honesty. It was refreshing to meet a woman who wasn't trying to be something she was not.

"It's cool," he said with a slight look of disappointment on his face. "Can I at least call you sometime?"

"Of course."

"Well, here, put yo' number in my phone." He handed her his phone.

Once Dylan programmed her number, Cruz saved it and pulled her close once more.

"I know you're scared," he whispered into her ear. "And frankly, I'd be scared too, but it's a'ight, though." He gazed fondly into her eyes. "I'ma wait on you."

After a whirlwind trip to Paris, Dylan returned home full of energy. She was ready to conquer the world, but first she had to check her messages. Dropping her bags down by her bed, she checked her caller ID. Dylan had over fifty missed calls from Billie, Brenda, State, and numerous other friends.

"Damn, folks must've really missed me," she said out loud as the phone started to ring.

It was State.

"Dylan Monroe speaking," she answered playfully.

"Where you been? I've been tryin' to reach you for days," he said with a sense of urgency in his voice.

"Paris, I went there for fashion week. Why?" Dylan took off her earrings.

"Fuck! You don't know, do you?" State massaged his forehead.

"Know what?" Her chest tightened.

"Somebody leaked the sex tape Ashton had of us."

"What?" Dylan panicked. "You're kidding me, right?"

"I wish I was, man," State said regrettably.

"Wait," she paused. "What do you mean 'somebody leaked the tape'? It was Ashton, wasn't it?"

"Nah, she said she didn't do it."

"And you believe her?" Dylan shrieked.

"Yeah, I know when she lyin'. She ain't do it."

Suddenly, Dylan had a flashback of the night she ran into Ashton at Angel's suite and Milania's warning. *I'm going to make your life a living hell,* she remembered.

"You're right, she didn't leak the tape, but she did give it to someone else." Dylan closed her eyes and sighed.

"Who?"

"Angel's bitch fiancée from hell, Milania," Dylan seethed with rage. "She did it, and she picked the perfect time to do it. She waited until everybody got comfortable and when it would affect me the most. Right when my career has taken off because it really wouldn't have affected me beforehand 'cause I didn't have anything going on yet." She sucked her teeth.

Tears were already starting to form in her eyes. Her career was over before it even started. She didn't even have to talk to Brenda to realize it. The Food Network was a wholesome network that didn't deal or tolerate scandals. Dylan was devastated. Everything she'd worked so hard for had been taken away in a blink of the eye because of a manipulative bitch, and there was nothing she could do about it.

"I'm sorry, man. I just wish there was something I could do," State said genuinely. "You want me to come over?"

"No, I'm fine," she cried, silently. "I just wanna be by myself right now. I'll talk to you later." She hung up before he could reply.

"Mama always warned me bout boys like you."
Nicole Wray, "Boy You Should Listen"

17

Dylan sat in the center of her bed painting her toenails black because it fit her mood. For the past couple
of weeks all she had been able to do was cry and pray.
The wind had been knocked out of her, and she tried
telling herself that her bad luck would one day go away,
but no matter where she turned or ran, the gray cloud
hovering over her was still there.

There had to be more for her life than this. She'd
changed for the better, but somehow was still paying for
her past transgressions. She didn't understand why God
was being so mean to her. How could he possibly bring
her all this way to turn his back on her now? It wasn't fair,
and more important, it hurt like hell. Her entire future
was at stake. She couldn't turn on the television or go to
the grocery store without seeing her face plastered everywhere.

Internet thugs on the blog sites dogged her day in
and day out. The Food Network executives didn't want
to be affiliated with the scandal, so they put her show
on hiatus until they could figure out what to do with
her. Even her book sales had dropped. Dylan couldn't
win for losing. With all of the negative energy surrounding her, she didn't even want to leave the house.

She and Mason stayed cooped up in her room because
she couldn't bear facing the world. She'd thought of calling Angel, but every time she picked up the phone, her
silly pride would get in the way and she'd hang up. That

dreary afternoon while painting her toenails and watching one of her favorite reality shows, *Say Yes to the Dress: Atlanta*, Dylan received a phone call that would take her life into another dramatic turn. She checked the caller ID on her phone and saw that it was a local number that she'd seen a few times but had opted not to answer. She didn't want to risk it being a reporter. However, that day, something in her told her to pick up and see who it was.

"Hello?" she said hesitantly, disguising her voice to sound like a man.

"Speak to Dylan?"

"May I ask whose callin'?" She asked, deeply.

"Cruz."

"Oh, hi," she spoke in her normal tone..

"What's been up wit' you? I've been tryin' to call you."

"I'm sorry. I've just been a li'l busy," she lied.

"Well, I'm in town."

"Really?" she said surprised. "You're in St. Louis?"

"Yeah, I wanted to see you. What you doing in the next hour?"

"Nothin'. No major plans, why?"

"We was about to get some food and one of my pot'nahs was talkin' about takin' this girl he's in love with and I'm going to take the girl I'm in love wit'. Then I figured you could come too," he joked.

"That was cute." Dylan smiled for the first time in weeks.

"Nah, for real, I was wondering if you wanted to have dinner with me tonight," he said seriously, praying she'd say yes.

"I don't think that's a good idea."

"What? You gotta a man or something?" he stated, taken aback.

"No, it's not that."

"Well, what then?" he quizzed.

Dylan sat quietly, scared to tell him the real reason why.

"Is it me? 'Cause, I mean, I'm sexy," Cruz probed.

"No, it's not that either," she giggled.

"Oh, I get it. It's not about me. It's about that whole sex tape thing, isn't it?"

"So you've heard?" Dylan froze, holding her breath.

"Yeah, but I ain't trippin' off that shit. I like you, and I wanna get to know you, if you would let me." His tone was low and raspy.

Dylan couldn't help but blush.

"Real talk," Cruz took control of the situation, "I'm not taking no for an answer, so put your flyest outfit on and be ready by seven."

Dylan looked at the clock. It was 5:30. It would be a race to find a babysitter and get dressed in time, but she figured, what the heck. She wasn't doing anything else that night anyway. With no more excuses of why she couldn't say yes, Dylan opened up and said, "I'll see you then."

Dylan hung up and immediately called Billie to see if she would babysit. Overjoyed that Dylan was making an attempt at getting back to the land of the living, Billie gladly offered her help. After rushing and dropping Mason off, Dylan made it back home in just enough time to shower and dress. By 7:00 on the dot she was ready to go. Sitting by the window, she looked out in anticipation of seeing Cruz pull up.

Forty-five minutes later, her leg had begun falling asleep and she was past pissed. Cruz hadn't even bothered to call to explain why he was late. Fuming, Dylan stood up and headed toward the steps to take off her clothes, but the sound of someone ringing the doorbell stopped her. Knowing it was Cruz she walked to the door eager to give him a piece of her mind.

"Mmm-hmm?" She opened the door open with an attitude.

"My bad for being late. I got caught up." He leaned against her door frame and shot her a crooked grin.

"Frankly, I don't find anything funny," Dylan shot sternly. "It's one thing for you to be late, but to be late and not even pick up the phone is quite inconsiderate, don't you think?"

"You're right, I should've called. The only reason I didn't is because I was tryin' to get here as fast as I could."

"That's cool, but I got a lot going on in my life right now, and I don't have time for a bunch of nonsense, so please don't waste my time," she stated bluntly.

Cruz slid his arm around her waist, pulled her into him, and said, "This will never happen again, I promise."

"I know it won't, 'cause I'm not going," Dylan countered.

"C'mon, pretty girl. I said I was sorry. Let me make it up to you."

Dylan glared at him. She wanted to still be upset but the smell of cologne, the sight of his lips, and the feel of his hand on her ass made her heart pound. It wasn't fair. A man like Cruz should bear a warning. He was dangerous, and unbeknownst to Dylan, she was falling head over heels in lust with him.

"All right, but I swear this better be the best date I've ever been on."

Once Dylan found out the destination of their date, she was on fire. Instead of taking her to a five-star restaurant, Cruz took her to Atomic Cowboy. It was a bar in the heart of the city. A hip-hop festival was going on. Local rappers took their turn performing on various stages. Hipsters in attendance bobbed their heads and sipped on beer.

Hand in hand, Cruz led Dylan outdoors to the patio section where artists created murals in front of viewers. Dylan could barely walk. The entire outside area was made up of small rocks. *I could've put on a T-shirt and some jeans for this shit,* she thought. The Herve Leger iron-dust color, strapless, form-fitting, bandage dress that hit midthigh and Valentino sculpture lace pumps were no match for the elements. She was overdressed and slightly underwhelmed with his choice of venue.

"I thought we were going to dinner," she said as she walked trying not to fall.

"Nah, some of my pot'nahs up here, so I figured we'd meet up with them."

"O . . . kay." Dylan looked around, perplexed.

"There they go over there by the bar. You want something to drink?" Cruz looked down at her.

"No, thank you." Dylan shook her head trying her best not to get upset.

"I'll be right back," Cruz assured her, giving her a quick peck on the cheek.

Agitated as hell, Dylan stood at a table alone, trying her best to keep her balance. Everyone kept staring at her. She didn't know if it was because of her out-of-place outfit or the sex tape. Either way, she was mortified. She stuck out like a sore thumb. Dylan was so busy worrying about what people were thinking about her that she hadn't even noticed she'd been waiting by herself for over half an hour.

Cruz had already gotten his drink and was shooting the shit with his friends as if she weren't even there. *This fool done lost his damn mind,* Dylan thought. Tucking her clutch underneath her arm, she walked very slowly in his direction. On the way there, a rock got caught in her shoe, stabbing her in the foot.

"Goddamnit!" She wobbled, standing on one foot, wincing in pain.

Then the unthinkable occurred. While shaking her foot profusely, Dylan lost her balance and fell backward, causing her legs to fly up in the air and everyone to see her tan-colored Spanx. Right away, people started laughing and pointing while snapping pictures. Humiliated to the highest extent, Dylan put her legs down and closed her eyes.

"Just act like you're asleep. Just act like you're asleep," she whispered.

"Baby, you a'ight?" Cruz rushed over.

Dylan opened one of her eyes and glared up at him.

"Get the hell away from me," she quipped, sitting up.

"What I do? Let me help you up." Cruz extended his hand.

"I can do it myself," she hissed, slapping his hand away.

Dylan set her hand on top of the rocks and pushed her body off the ground. Wiping her hands together, she dusted off the dirt on her hands and dress.

"You sure you're a'ight?" Cruz asked with a laugh.

"And you're laughing?" Dylan shouted amazed. "No, I'm not okay. I'm ready to go home."

"Don't you think you going a li'l overboard? We just got here." He continued to laugh.

"Just take me home. I'll be at the car." She stomped away.

Cruz gulped down the rest of his drink and told his boys he'd holla at them later. Dylan leaned against

Cruz's Benz CLK 230 Kompressor wondering why she ever agreed to go out on a date with him in the first place. She had enough drama going in her life. A man would only add to it. Cruz chirped the alarm on his car. He didn't even bother to open Dylan's door.

"Wack ass," she spat, getting inside on her own. "You know what? This whole thing was a complete waste of a really great outfit. There is no love connection between you and me."

"Nope, none at all." Cruz started up the engine and sped off, heated.

"Do you know what I had to go through to even be able to go out with you tonight? First of all, you called me on short notice and asked me to go out wit' you, and since I thought you were somewhat cute, I decided to go!" she went off, staring at him.

"But I had to find a babysitter, take my son over there, come back home, take a shower, do my hair, find something that I could wear and fit in as well as get dressed, all in the matter of an hour and a half. Then you pick me up late wit' some dumb-ass excuse, and against my better judgment, I go out with you anyway. Oh, but then, guess what? The joke was on me 'cause instead of taking me to a nice restaurant like you said, you take me to a *bar*," she stressed, appalled. "And leave me alone the whole time while you chop it up wit' yo' friends! Like really, who do you think I am? Better yet, how could I have been so stupid? You are just like all the rest."

"Say that again?" Cruz barked while keeping an eye on the road.

"You heard me," Dylan whipped her neck around. "I said you're just like all the rest. A pompous ass who thinks the world revolves around you."

"Oh, word, *that's* how you feel?" he shot, getting on to the highway.

"I said it, didn't I?" Dylan shot back, not giving a fuck.

"Yo', you not even in the position to act like you such a Goody Two-shoes. I know all about you."

"What the hell is *that* supposed to mean?"

"It means you just like all the rest of these broads out here. You ain't fuckin' wit' a man unless he got a lot of money. It's strictly athletes, ball playas, and rappers for you."

"Fool, please, I'm not lowering my standards for nobody, so if that makes me a gold digger, then, oh . . . the . . . fuck . . . well, I'ma be diggin' forever. And trust, I don't need a man for his money 'cause I've always had my own, thank you very much."

"Yeah, that's right. You own a bakery," he scoffed pulling up to her house. "And a canceled show on The Food Network. Yeah, you're rollin' in it."

"For your information, I was born with money so while your ass was kickin' around balls as a child dreaming of a way out of the slums, I was gettin' waited on by butlers and maids. And this cheap-ass car," Dylan took off her seat belt enraged, "I had one of these when I was sixteen, chile, please." She got out and slammed the door.

"Don't be slamming my door!" Cruz barked out the window.

"Shut up!" Dylan threw up her middle finger and walked into her house, vowing never to see him again.

The following weekend, Billie and Dylan were at Mina's Joint Salon and Spa getting their hair and makeup done. It was early afternoon and the salon was jam-packed. Business was booming for Mina, and Dylan couldn't be happier for her. Mo, Mina's best friend, was there too getting a mani and pedi. She was seven months pregnant with her third child with her longtime boyfriend Boss.

"So how do you like being a mommy?" Mo asked Dylan.

"I love it." She gave a huge smile.

"Where is yo' baby at now?" Mo inquired, rubbing her stomach.

"At home with my mother, of all people. Can you believe it?"

"Hell, no. Yo' mama crazy as hell," Mo teased.

"What I wanna know is where the hell is Tee-Tee at? He was supposed to meet us here over an hour ago." Billie glanced at her watch.

"I don't know. I tried calling him, but he didn't answer the phone," Delicious said.

"So, Dylan, explain this to me." Mo held up the picture of Dylan falling in *US Weekly* magazine.

"Don't even get me started." Dylan rolled her eyes. "I was on a date from hell."

"Who you go out with, girl?" Delicious asked, cutting her ends.

"Cruz," Dylan replied.

"The soccer player? Oh, girl, he fine." Delicious smacked his lips together. "I would go out on a date with him anytime."

"Me too." Mo gave a sly grin.

"Then go right ahead 'cause he worked my last nerve," Dylan said.

"What happened?" Mo questioned.

Dylan gave them a quick rundown of the date. After she was done, Delicious, Billie, and Mo cracked up laughing.

"Y'all some fake asses. Ain't shit funny," Dylan snarled at them.

"Yes, it is." Billie wiped away the tears from her eyes.

"How you gon' tell that man he had a cheap-ass car?" Mo asked, still giggling.

"'Cause a nice car don't faze me," Dylan responded. "Now a nice car wit' a full tank of gas might."

"You got that right," Delicious agreed. "Have you heard from him since?"

"Yes. He's been callin' me and textin' me like crazy tellin' me he's sorry. But I haven't answered or replied back." Dylan crossed her legs. "The other day he sent me like twenty different bouquets of flowers. This fool even sent me a singing telegram."

"That's a commitment," Delicious tapped her on the arm.

"Commitment, my ass," Dylan rolled her eyes.

"Girl, you can't be playin' hard to get wit' a man who's hard to get," Mo advised.

"As far as I'm concerned, Javier Nathaniel Cruz can suck it," Dylan confirmed.

"On a brighter note," Billie chimed in, "Angel will be coming home soon, and I'm going to throw him a welcome home party. Of course you all are invited."

"You know I'm there," Delicious grinned from ear to ear. "Angel been my boo since reality shows been hot. No disrespect, Dylan."

"None taken. Angel is not my man." She tried to play it off like she didn't care when really, thoughts of him entered her mind often throughout the day.

"Well, look who's showing up late." Delicious placed his hand on his hip and watched as Tee-Tee came into the salon with a baby seat in his hand.

"Is that my nephew he's carrying?" Billie asked.

"Hell, naw. That baby got on pink," Dylan answered.

"What's up, bitches? Say hello to my brand-new baby girl Princess Gaga!" Tee-Tee exclaimed, giving them a full view of his and Bernard's Japanese adopted baby.

"Tee-Tee," Dylan started crying, "when did you get her?"

"This morning, that's why I was late."

"She's so pretty," Billie gushed, crying too.

"She is beautiful," Delicious agreed.

"Hold up. Did you say that baby name is Princess Gaga?" Mo asked.

"Yes, honey. Ain't she cute?" Tee-Tee beamed.

"She is beyond cute. She's gorgeous," Mo answered back.

After catching up with the gang and gushing over Tee-Tee's baby, Dylan's hair was done being styled. Delicious spun her around in the chair so she could take a look at herself.

"I'm the shit, bitch! I'm the shit!" Dylan danced.

"You look a'ight," Tee-Tee teased, burping his baby.

"Whatever, hater. How much I owe you?" Dylan asked Delicious.

"Two hundred dollars."

"Two hundred dollars!" Dylan threw her head back, dramatically. "Shit, with these prices, I'ma have to start gettin' my hair done in the hood."

"Don't worry. I got you," Cruz said from behind.

"Oh my God, I think I just came on myself." Delicious clutched his chest.

"Let me tell you something right now," Dylan eyed Cruz through the mirror, "I don't do stalkers, boo-boo. You will get yo' ass lit up fuckin' with me."

"You always got something smart to say. We gon' have to work on that." Cruz hit her with his infamous crooked grin.

"Is that a dimple?" Tee-Tee gasped for air. "I could totally set up a tent in that dimple."

"I'd be naked in it." Delicious licked his lips.

"Here you go." Cruz handed him four hundred dollars.

"Oh, honey, this is too much." Delicious placed his hand on his hip.

"You got my girl lookin' good, so consider the other two a tip."

"Your girl? Honey, we ain't together." Dylan took off the cape that was around her neck and stood up.

"Can we step outside for a minute?" Cruz asked with an intense look of desire in his eyes.

Dylan looked him up and down skeptically. "I'll go, but if you try anything, know that I got a can of mace on reserve and ready to go off."

"And after that, you gon' have to see about me," Tee-Tee warned.

"And me too," Billie agreed.

"I'll remember that," Cruz chuckled.

Dylan slipped on her Burberry, fur-trim, trench coat and walked with him outside. The cold November air froze her body to the core.

"Explain to me how you knew where I was at. You ain't got nobody following me, do you?" She looked around nervously.

"Nah, I called your house and some woman name Candy told me you were here."

"I'ma kick her ass," Dylan murmured.

"Why you so violent?" He got up in her face.

"I'm not. People just get on my nerves, that's all."

"Am I one of those people?" He pulled her close.

"The other day you were, yeah."

"I wanted to apologize to you for that. I've dated chicks who've dated only celebrities, and it bothered

me 'cause I didn't know if they were wit' me for me or
for what I had. And to be honest wit' you, you kinda
intimidate me. I wanted to get to know you the other
night, but what's your favorite color ain't all that original." He confessed.

"Then why didn't you just say?" Dylan asked softly.

"I don't know. I was trippin'. You gon' let me make it
up to you?" Cruz stared into her eyes.

Dylan turned her face and looked away. If she looked
at him too long she'd become trapped in his gaze eternally. Cruz was everything she didn't need. But his in-
toxicating presence compelled her to want to give in to
temptation and see where the crazy road before them
headed.

"Okay, I'll give you another chance, but if you fuck
up this time, it's gonna be adios, amigo." Dylan smiled
from ear to ear.

"Comprende." Cruz nodded.

"Could it be you're everything that these plain bitches couldn't be?"
Miguel Feat J. Cole, "All I Want Is You"

18

Feeling like a million bucks, Dylan turned from side to side and examined her outfit in the mirror. She was sure to shut the streets down in her Balmain leather jacket, white slouchy tank top, $3,500 Balmain tie die jewel-encrusted jeans, and double platform, black ankle booties by Cesare Paciotti. Opting for a less-is-more look with her makeup, she rocked a cat eye and a red lip. Dylan didn't even need to wear her Spanx that night. With all of the stress she'd been under, she'd lost five pounds.

"Goddamn!" She stepped back in awe.

"What?" Tee-Tee asked, lying across her bed.

"Look how fine I am," she grinned, then blew a kiss to herself in the mirror.

"Girl, get over yo'self." Tee-Tee waved her off while playing with Princess Gaga.

"Now you sure you gon' be able to handle Mason and Princess Gaga?" Dylan got his attention.

"Do you see these hips?" Tee-Tee stood up. "These are childbearing hips. I was built for this."

"Well, let me get up outta here. I told Cruz I would meet him at Lola at nine." Dylan grabbed her Chanel cassette clutch. "Bye, bye, Mason." She leaned over on the bed where he was lying and kissed his chubby face.

"Be good for Aunty." Dylan stood up straight and looked at Tee-Tee. "You really think I should go?" She hated leaving Mason.

"Girl, if you don't get outta here . . . Go out and enjoy yourself. Hell, get you some, 'cause yo' ass need it."

"Shut up," Dylan laughed. "Okay, I'm gone."

Dylan rode down Washington Avenue in her 2011 Jeep Wrangler Unlimited looking for a parking space. Everybody and their mama was out. Traffic was at a standstill from people cruising, trying their best to be noticed. After what seemed like forever, Dylan found a parking space around the corner from the bar and got out.

She'd never been to Lola so she didn't quite know what to expect, but upon walking in, she was impressed. From its funky décor to its live band, Lola was a place that celebrated St. Louis culture. They offered hand crafted cocktails, organic martinis, succulent nosh and jazz, hip-hop and funk music weekly. In the main bar and dining area Dylan found Cruz sitting at a table for two alone. He immediately spotted her and got up to greet her.

"For a minute there I didn't think you were gon' come." He hugged her.

"I'm a woman of my word." She hugged him back, trying her best not to kiss his lips.

There were no words to define him except Cruz was fine! Everything from his eyes, to his smile, and the way he talked was charming. She just prayed that this time his personality would shine through because being good looking wasn't enough to keep her interested.

Determined to be on his best behavior, Crux pulled out her chair.

"Why, thank you," Dylan smiled, sitting down.

"You hungry? You want something to drink?" he asked before retaking his seat.

"I'll have an apple martini, please."

"A'ight, I'll be right back." Cruz headed toward the bar. This time he made sure to return in a swift manner.

"Here you go." He handed her the drink.

"Thanks." Dylan took a sip. "This place is nice." She set her drink down on a napkin and looked around.

"Yeah, I heard it's real laid-back and chill. Some burlesque dancer name Lola Van Ella suppose to be performing tonight."

"I've never seen a burlesque performance before." Dylan smiled at him.

"Me either." Cruz made himself more comfortable by folding his arms on the table. "So, Miss Dylan, tell me something about yourself."

"What do you wanna know? You already know pretty much everything."

"I mean, I just wanna know more about you. I already know that you're a single mother and a pastry chef, but I wanna know what you dream about, what you hope for," he said gravely interested.

Taken aback by his question, Dylan thought carefully before answering. "I guess I just want something different, something more. Some sort of counterintuitive love."

"Meaning?" he quizzed.

"Meaning, I don't know what I want." She laughed, throwing up her hands. "I only know what I don't want, and that's to be unhappy. I just wanna be happy. What about you?" She took another sip of her drink.

"This may sound corny, but on the real . . . I want you."

Dylan cocked her head to the side mockingly.

"You don't even know me."

"I know enough to know that I'ma make you mine."

Dylan gulped because she could see his words coming true.

"We'll see about that." She blushed, turning beet red.

"Excuse me," the MC said into the mic. "I want everyone in the house tonight to welcome Lola Van Ella to the stage!"

Dylan and Cruz, along with everyone else in attendance, gave her a rousing applause as she sashayed onto the stage. She was dressed demurely in a vintage black sequined dress from the 1930s with her blond hair pulled back. Catcalls and whistling floated through the air while Lola grabbed a chair and placed it center stage.

Then her sultry voice sang into the microphone the words, "Whatever Lola wants, Lola gets." The crowd went wild. Shinnying, she eased her way down in the chair, slid up her dress, crossed her legs, and ran her free hand down her exposed thigh. Dylan's eyes grew wide with surprise. With the crowd in the palm of her hand, Lola put the mic back on the mic stand. Her eyes smoldered as she gradually began to unbutton the side of her dress.

A guy in the audience roared in anticipation of what was to come. Using her dress as a shield, Lola turned around and wiggled her butt to the crowd. Turning around, she covered her front with the dress and seductively put her index finger in her mouth. Dylan looked over at Cruz. Catching her gaze, he looked back at her and arched his eyebrow. Dylan lowered her head and laughed.

Then Lola gave the crowd what they'd been waiting for. In the midst of dancing, she threw the dress to the side and revealed a pale-pink fringed bustier and thong set. Lost in the beat, she locked eyes with a woman sitting near the stage and began to unzip the front of the bustier. Slightly uncomfortable, the woman gazed off to the side, then back up at Lola.

Dressed only in fringed pasties and her thong, Lola shook her bosom with reckless abandon, then dropped down low and rolled her ass. All you could hear was screams from the spectators, they were so into her routine. Dylan couldn't even hate. Lola knew how to shake her moneymaker. Once her routine was over, Lola bowed while the crowd stood on their feet giving her a stirring applause.

"That was something," Dylan said, sitting back down.

"It was," Cruz agreed.

"You like that kinda shit, don't you?" She gave him a mock-glare and grinned.

"What man doesn't? I would especially like it if it were you doing it," he flirted.

"For the right amount of money I'll take my clothes off right now," she joked.

"Promise?"

"You're a mess." Dylan smiled feeling her temperature rise.

Two hours later after sharing memories and details on what the other wanted in a mate, Cruz walked Dylan to her car. The full moon up above shined its light directly down on them as she stood in between his legs. His hard dick pressed against her thigh. Cruz's lips were inches away from hers. Dylan's heart thumped loudly in her chest. In never failed. Whenever they came in contact, her blood pressure rose, and her palms began to sweat.

No other man had this affect on her except Angel. Was this a sign? Could Cruz be the new man in her life? Dylan didn't know the answer. All she knew was that he was there making her feel as light as a feather. Cruz was never the type of man to be afraid of a woman, but with Dylan, he found himself swept up in her beauty to the point he couldn't even put together sentences correctly.

It was hard for him to control himself when he was next to her. But he couldn't let the chance of being her man slip away. She was the kind of woman he only saw in romantic comedies. She was shy, funny, smart, and sexy as hell but could give you attitude at the same time. She didn't throw herself on him or come across needy. Dylan was wifey material. She just had to open her heart to the possibility because something behind her hazel eyes was keeping her feelings at bay.

"Give me a kiss me," he demanded in a low tone.

Dylan tried to kiss him on the cheek, but Cruz surprisingly took her face into his hands and made her kiss his lips.

The kiss was juicy and passionate. Fireworks exploded in their mouths as their tongues danced. After kissing for what seemed like hours, Cruz gave her one last peck on the lips.

"Well, that was rude," Dylan stated not knowing what else to say.

Cruz just looked at her and grinned. He could tell that she was shaken.

"What?" she said with a sudden fierceness. "You think I've never had a kiss like that before? You think that's gonna make me take my top off? I mean, even if we were to have sex—which we won't . . ." she rambled anxiously.

"Well, you raised the subject." His hands roamed her back as his tongue created havoc on the side of her neck.

Her skin reminded him of sweet butterscotch candy. Dylan unconsciously released a soft moan. The commotion he was creating in between her thighs should've been illegal. Placing her hand on his chest, Dylan pushed herself back. She needed a moment to gather her emotions and breathe before she was butt naked on the avenue.

"What's wrong?"

"Nothin'," she fibbed.

Cruz just stared at her. It fucked him up how she tried to act like she couldn't see that they belonged together.

"Come here." He reached out for her hand.

Dylan placed her hand in his and inched closer.

"I like you," he confessed, holding her in his arms.

"I know you do." She looked down at her feet.

"Then what's the problem?" He bent down some and cocked his head to the side so he could see her face.

"I'm just afraid," Dylan said in a trembling voice.

"Shit, I am too, but I'm diggin' the hell outta you," Cruz said firmly. "And I ain't never felt this way about no other female before."

"What's so special about me?" she asked curiously. "You can have any woman you want."

"I like you 'cause you don't take none of my shit. You say what's on your mind no matter how embarrassing it may be. Most important, I like a strong woman who can stand on her own two feet and despite what's going on wit' you in the media, you still standing tall. I like that." He stroked her cheek gently with the tip of his finger.

"And I like you." She finally opened up the doors to her heart and allowed Cruz in.

"You got the sexiest lips I've ever seen." He traced her mouth with his eyes. "Since the first time I saw you I wanted to kiss you."

"You have my permission." Her voice shook slightly.

Cruz leaned down and brushed his lips upon hers. His soft kisses sent tingles all over her skin. Their kiss seemed to go on forever. The wicked taste of his tongue drew Dylan deep into his web. With every stroke of his tongue, Dylan could visualize the beginning of something new.

***

"What do you think?" Tee-Tee pranced around the shoe department at Nordstrom's.

He was trying on shoes for Angel's coming home party. All eyes were on him. He'd just tried on a pair of Chloe, over-the-knee, grey leather boots that not many could afford. As usual, he was dressed in women's clothes. He was rockin' the hell out of a crème blazer, slouchy cashmere tank top, and black leggings.

"I like'em." Bernard answered unenthusiastically, holding the baby. He hated all of the attention they got when they went out.

"But you don't love them?" Tee-Tee's left hand rested delicately on his hip.

"I said I like'em," Bernard replied, wishing he'd make up his mind.

"But not as much as you loved the other ones?" Tee-Tee referred to a pair of Christian Louboutin, nutmeg-colored, suede, over-the-knee platform boots.

"Ooh." He bent down and picked up one of the Louboutins.

"Okay, the house is on fire. I only have time enough to grab a Diana Ross CD and one of these boots." He pointed at his right foot and held up the Louboutin. "Which one do I take? Go!" He pointed his index finger at Bernard like they were on a game show.

"I would think you would grab the baby first." Bernard gave him the screw face.

"After that?" Tee-Tee flicked his wrist in a dismissive way.

"The brown ones," Bernard answered dryly.

"Because the gray pair washes me out?" Tee-Tee squinted and pursed his lips.

"Babe, either way, you look good. Everything you try on looks hot on you."

"Awwww, boo, look at you being all sweet to me."
Tee-Tee leaned over for a kiss, but Bernard pulled his
head back.

He loved Tee-Tee with his all of his heart, but being
an openly gay man in St. Louis, a still somewhat con-
servative city, was hard to deal with. Bernard hated the
stares and the whispers they got whenever they went
out. On occasion, they'd even been called fags, and being the alpha male he was, Bernard handled his business when it came to bigotry. But he couldn't fight the
world, so he figured, why bring on added attention if it
wasn't necessary?

"You actin' funny," Tee-Tee said, rattled.

"Nah, I'm just ready to go." Bernard partially told the
truth.

"Then give me a kiss." Tee-Tee stuck out his lips and
tried once more.

"I'm good." Bernard turned his face and noticed a
middle-aged woman giving them the stink face.

"Really, Bernard?" Tee-Tee snapped, standing up
straight.

"Pound it out." Bernard made a fist.

"You out yo' damn mind." Tee-Tee looked at him
like he was crazy. "So what? Since we out in public you
can't give me no kiss?"

"You know it's not like that," Bernard tried to reason.

"Uh-uh. Just stop talkin'." Tee-Tee stuck his palm in
Bernard's face. "I need some time for this wound to become a scar." He spun around dramatically, whipping
his hair like Willow Smith.

Bernard bounced Princess Gaga on his knee and
shook his head. He didn't feel like it, but for the rest
of the day he and Tee-Tee would be arguing. He just
hoped that eventually Tee-Tee would see his point of

view. If not, this would be something that haunted
their marriage forever.

   Thanksgiving had come and gone, and Dylan still
hadn't received news on whether The Food Network
would renew her show. Thank God her bakery was still
pulling in major revenue. The public was fascinated
with her and wanted to catch a glimpse of the woman
who wore the scarlet letter on her chest. The paparazzi
stayed camped out in front and in back of the building.
Disinclined to being vilified or made fun of in the press,
Dylan continued to hide in shame.
   She ran the bakery by phone. She trusted her em-
ployees completely, and so far, they'd done a great job
keeping the business intact. The vagueness of where
her entertainment career was heading still haunted
her. Sleep evaded her; she couldn't eat and she'd begun
to have migraine headaches. Dylan was in so much
pain that Billie had to come get Mason because she was
unable to take care of him.
   Lying in bed with the lights turned off, Dylan lay
sound asleep with the covers over her head in Cruz's
arms. Since their date, he hadn't left her side. Any time
he could spend with her and Mason, he cherished. The
fact that they hadn't had sex didn't even cross his mind.
When it happened, it would only be an added bonus.
She was special, and Cruz wanted to take his time with
her.
   He wanted to show her the world and everything it
had to offer. Often he wondered why it'd taken him so
long to come across a woman like her. She made him
want to be better. He could see himself settling down
and becoming a family man. The bad boy in him still
lingered in his veins, but Cruz was doing a good job at
keeping him hidden.

Awaking, Dylan opened her eyes and smiled. She loved waking up beside Cruz, plus the medication she'd taken had kicked in and kicked her migraine to the curb. Dylan ran her index finger lightly across Cruz's lips. All of a sudden, he'd taken her finger in his warm mouth, licked it, and slid it out, then began kissing the palm of her hand.

"You nasty," she teased.

"You like it." He kissed her hand once more. "You feelin' better?"

"Yes, thank God." She sat up.

"I got a surprise for you." He climbed out of the bed.

Dylan watched as he lit candles that had been strategically placed around the room while she was asleep.

"I know that wit' your headaches light can be a bit much, so I decided we'd do everything by candlelight tonight."

"Did you really?" She blushed, feeling tingly inside.

"I got something else for you too." He went into the bathroom and drew a steaming hot bubble bath.

Once the tub was filled, Dylan went inside and closed the door. Undressed, she stepped into the water and sat down. The soothing hot water felt wonderful on her skin. Covered by a sea of bubbles, she called out for Cruz to come in. To her surprise, he walked inside with no shirt and just his jeans and sneakers on. Jesse Boykins III "Come To My Room" serenaded them while he sat on the side of the tub.

"Before you get to trippin', it's not what you think. I just didn't want to get my shirt wet while I bathe you."

"Who said I was gon' let you bathe me?" she smirked.

"You ain't got no choice." Cruz picked up a bar of soap, dipped it into the water, and lathered it in his hands.

256   Keisha Ervin

Dylan watched closely as his long fingers glided across her chest and down to her breasts. Cruz playfully toyed with her nipples while placing wet kisses onto the side of her neck. Dylan wanted him so bad her head began to spin. Then his hand slipped down her stomach and said hello to her clit. With every caress, she melted like chocolate. Needing her as much as she needed him, Cruz scooped Dylan up into his arms and carried her back to the bed.

Her glistening wet body lay before him, dying to be sexually pleased. Cruz couldn't get the rest of his clothes off fast enough. The scent of her skin was inebriating. He kneeled on the bed. His eyes devoured her inch by inch. Lifting her leg, Dylan ran her toes up his sculpted chest. Cruz took her foot into his hands and kissed all the way from her ankle to the inner part of her thigh.

Dylan closed her eyes and clutched the sheets. Cruz was kissing her thigh as if it were her mouth, and she cherished every second of it. With her thick thighs in the cusp of his strong hands, Cruz glanced up into Dylan's eyes, smiling. The look of sheer desire on her face said it all. She was dying for him to plant his face in between her thighs.

With velvet ease, Cruz's tongue licked the lips of Dylan's pussy. Her back instantly arched. Each flicker of his wet tongue felt like electricity. After succumbing to orgasmic bliss, Dylan lay on her side. Cruz swiftly placed on a condom. Lying behind her, he entered her from behind.

"Ohhhhhhhhhhhhhhhhhhhhhh," Dylan moaned, closing her eyes tightly.

Cruz's dick was creating a world of havoc and torture on her insides. With each stroke, Dylan lost more of her control. Her body was so hot. The lips of her pussy felt so weak. She ran her tongue across her upper lip, then bit her bottom lip. Cruz gripped her thighs and thrust his dick in deeper. He wanted to get to the very core of her.

Pure lust fueled his desire to fuck her until she screamed out his name. Each touch of her skin sent searing flashes of heat through his veins. Rocking to the beat they'd created, Cruz and Dylan tried their best to suppress the impending orgasm that was rapidly approaching. Neither wanted the stirring commotion in their private parts to end.

But as always, the moment where an explosion of fireworks went off inside their bodies happened.

"Cruz!" Dylan screamed out in agony.

As the dust cleared, Dylan's body quaked in the aftermath. Cruz planted sensual kisses along her neck and shoulder as his muscles began to relax. Dylan turned around and faced him. Cruz smiled. The look in her eyes spoke volumes. She wanted more, and he was just the man to give her what she wanted.

"Don't leave while you're hot that's how Mase screwed up."
Kanye West, "Devil In A New Dress"

19

Billie had outdone herself. She'd invited twenty of Angel's closest family members and friends to Sleek, a restaurant found exclusively at Lumière Place Casino & Hotel downtown. Internationally renowned Chef Hubert Keller was the proprietor. He and his team had created a chic and stylish dining experience that patrons loved. The restaurant and ultra lounge consisted of custom butcher-block tables, semiprivate dining areas, and a "liquor library" visible from virtually anywhere in the restaurant.

Being the loving sister she was, Billie rented out the private dining section for their pleasure. That night, they would dine on Steak Tartare, gnocchi, panned-seared scallops, and Kobe beef. For dessert, Billie had the kitchen prepare one of Angel's favorite's: crème brûlée. Fresh from his flight, Angel stood off to the side talking to Knox when he spotted Dylan coming his way.

Angel couldn't believe his eyes. Dylan was doing the absolute most. Long, wavy curls framed her face. She'd lost most of the extra baby weight she'd gained and was wearing the hell out of a backless, silk, gray Thayer halter dress. The dress featured a deep V-neck which exposed her bronze, luscious breasts. At the skirt of the dress was a thigh-high split that showcased her toned legs. To complete the ensemble, she wore a Felix Rey lace clutch and Giuseppe Zanotti laser-cut high heel sandals.

Angel couldn't have been prouder to call her his son's mother. Her presence took up all the space in the room. She unknowingly captivated everyone in her path. For weeks, he'd been yearning to see her face in the flesh. Skyping and talking on the phone every day just hadn't been enough. Now he would finally have her all to himself, and Angel planned to make the most of the moment.

"Hi," she waved awkwardly.

"You can do better than that. Give me a hug." He scooped her up in his arms, twirling her around in a circle.

Placing her back down, he whispered in her ear, "Damn, you smell good."

"Thanks." She pulled away from him anxiously.

Dylan hadn't expected for the feelings she'd buried to resurface upon seeing his face. She thought that she'd moved on, but the hold Angel had on her seemed to be indestructible.

"You look good. How was your flight home?" She tried to make idle conversation.

"It was cool. I can't wait to see li'l man later on."

"Yeah, about that—" She looked down shuffling her feet.

"Hold up." He cut her off. "There's something I need to do. Can I have everyone's attention?" he said, walking to the center of the room.

Everybody stopped doing what they were doing and gave him their full attention.

"While I was gone I had a lot of time on my hands to think. With the kind of lifestyle that I live, things can get kind of lonely at times. You can become very homesick, but I realized that I'm most happy when I'm here with Dylan and my boy, who, by the way, looks more and more like me every day," he bragged.

"Get back to the point!" Billie yelled from across the room.

"My big head sister, y'all!" Angel joked, pointing at her.

"What I'm sayin' is . . ." He placed his hand inside of his pant pocket.

"Dylan, you're my best friend, and I can't think of—" He stopped mid-speech and gazed lovingly into her eyes, but Angel's words became lost when he noticed some dude walk in behind Dylan and wrap his arms around her waist.

Avoiding Angel's eye contact, Dylan swallowed the huge lump in her throat. She had seen the look of pain in his eyes. She'd planned on telling him about Cruz, but every time they talked, the words just wouldn't come out.

"Umm . . . Dylan, you're a great mom." Angel took his hand out of his pocket.

"And I can't say thank you enough for taking such good care of our boy. Salute!" He held up his glass.

"Salute!" all the partygoers yelled.

Dylan felt like shit. She never wanted him to find out about Cruz this way. But she'd given him his chance, and he'd passed. She couldn't live her life waiting for him to figure out whether he wanted her. Like a kid in trouble, Dylan held her head down as Angel approached.

"You wanna introduce me to your friend?" he asked stone-faced, gulping down the rest of his drink.

"Cruz, this is Angel, Mason's dad, and Angel, this is Javier Cruz." Dylan pointed back and forth between the two men.

"Her boyfriend." Cruz stuck out his hand for a shake.

"I'm sorry, yes, my boyfriend." Dylan blinked her eyes nervously. "He plays soccer for Spain," she added, as if that would make things better.

"What's up wit' you?" Angel gave him a head nod instead. "Let me holla at you for a second, Dylan," he said, turning his back and heading toward the bar.

"I'll be right back," Dylan assured Cruz by rubbing his forearm.

Angel gazed absently out at the casino. A million thoughts ran through his mind. He'd fucked up royally by taking his precious time with Dylan. He'd been a fool to think he'd return and she'd be waiting with open arms in anticipation of him saying they can be together now. He just assumed that she'd hold on a little while longer, but evidently, she'd grown tired of holding out for hope for something that was so unsure.

"I'm sorry I didn't tell you about Cruz sooner." Dylan stood beside him.

"Is it serious?" Angel stared straight ahead.

"It's starting to be," she uttered, unable to breathe.

"You happy?" he asked after a pause.

"Yeah . . . I am."

"Then that's all that matters," Angel uttered, feeling like he'd been stabbed in the chest 150 times.

Dylan was at a loss for words. She'd dreaded this day for weeks.

"I just—"

"It's cool, Ma." Angel finally gave her eye contact.

Tears filled Dylan's eyes as she gazed back at him. She could feel pieces of her heart break with every breath she took. This was it—the moment where reality became really real. She'd given him her heart on a silver platter, and he'd sent it back with not even a glance. It was unfortunate, but she'd moved on, and now Angel was left suffering the consequences of his decision.

"I better go." Dylan blinked away her tears, swallowing hard. "I just stopped by to say hi." She placed her clutch underneath her arm. "Mason's at home with my mom if you wanna pick him up."

"Most definitely. I was planning on gettin' him for a few days, if you don't mind."

"Of course not." She bit her bottom lip. "He misses you."

"I miss him too." Angel stared directly into her eyes.

"You ready, babe?" Cruz put his hand on the small of Dylan's back.

"Yeah, see you later," she said to Angel before walking off.

Angel leaned against the bar and reached inside his pocket and pulled out a small box. The velvet burned against his skin. He'd planned on giving her his all that night. He was done with running and hiding. Dylan was his, and no amount of reasoning was going to change that. The ten-carat Harry Winston diamond ring he'd picked out was sure to prove it, but now, shit was all fucked up.

Angel wanted nothing more than to turn back the hands of time. He would do it just to make her his baby again. He would apologize for putting her through the agony of seeing him with Milania when all he really wanted was to be with Dylan. He'd hold her in his arms for all the lonely nights she spent alone. But now, everything he wished for would never come true. Dylan belonged to another, and the thought of what he and she could've been was now just that—a mere thought.

Alone in their room, Kenzie and Kaylee sat on the floor playing Barbies. Their room was adorably cute. The walls were painted hot pink with huge white polka dots. Sheer curtains graced their windows. On one side of the room was a bookcase with storage shelves hidden down below. Both girls had their very own antique daybed with beautiful shades of green, black, and white pillows and matching covers on the beds. A custom-designed rug with a flower insert lay in the middle of the floor. To complete the room were two nightstands and two dressers with an array of stuffed animals on each.

"So you be Chris Brown, and I'ma be Rihanna," Kaylee said, handing her sister a black Ken doll and a pink Corvette.

"Why I always gotta be Chris Breezy?" Kenzie spat back with an attitude.

"'Cause you got him down pat, plus I gotta use the rest of the Barbies to be the paparazzi when he go in for questioning."

"All right," Kenzie pouted, dressing the Ken doll in its Clive Davis Grammy Pre-Party outfit.

"I know you gon' tell me what Jaden said to you at recess," Kaylee popped her lips.

"He asked me would I sit with him tomorrow at lunch." A smile spread across Kenzie's face.

"Oooooooooooooh, you gotta boyfriend! You gotta boyfriend!" Kaylee bounced up and down. "I can see it now. Y'all gon' be the new Nas and Kelis when we get big!"

"They gotta divorce, dummy!" Kenzie pushed her sister in the arm.

"Oh," Kaylee twisted up her lip. "My bad."

"Aha!" Kyrese kicked open their door. "I'm tellin' Mama!"

"Tellin' Mama what?" Kenzie rolled her neck.

"That you got a boyfriend, li'l ugly girl." He kicked over their dollhouse.

"No, I don't!" she yelled, whacking him in the leg with her hand.

"Yes, you do." He sat down on her bed. "Who is he?"

"I'm not tellin' you," Kenzie snapped.

"You might as well tell me 'cause you gon' get in trouble anyway."

"He's not my boyfriend. He's just this boy that's in my class that I—"

"Loooooooove?" Kyrese crossed his hands on his chest and batted his eyes.

"I don't love him!" Kenzie shouted, flushing with distress.

"Have you kissed him yet?" Kyrese probed.

"No," she said defiantly.

"What you waiting on?"

"Are you retarded? I'm nine."

"And you've never kissed a boy?" Kyrese bucked his eyes.

"No. Have you kissed a girl?"

"Yeah, like when I was five. What can I say? I'm a ladies' man." He popped his collar. "So I would advise you to kiss him tomorrow at lunch or else he's gonna think you're a lesbian."

"He's not going to think I'm a lesbian."

"I thought you were," Kaylee spoke up. "Look at the sandals you have on," she pointed at Kenzie's Birken-stocks.

"Shut up, li'l stupid li'l girl!" Kenzie threw the Ken doll at her but missed.

Before Kaylee could retaliate, the doorbell rang.

"I'll get it!" Kenzie ran down the stairs.

At the door, she set her hand on the knob and said, "State yo' name, fool!"

"The original Sasha Fierce."

"Tee-Tee!" Kenzie beamed, opening the door.

"You look cute, pretty girl." He kissed her on the cheek. "But why you got on them Birkenstocks?" He tuned up his face.

"Huh?" she groaned, rolling her eyes. "My daddy bought me these."

"Yo' daddy was tryin' to be funny then." He came inside and took off his coat. "Where yo' mama at?"

"Her and Knox in the room taking one of they grunting naps again."

"Oh, God," Tee-Tee chuckled, rolling his eyes to the ceiling. "Go knock on they door and tell her I'm here."

"Okay." Kenzie spun around and ran back up the steps.

Half an hour, later Billie strolled down the stairs feeling as light as a feather.

"Somebody just got some." Tee-Tee arched his eyebrow while on the phone with Dylan.

"Sholl did," Billie glowed, dressed in only a silk robe and high-heeled, slide-in sandals with fluffy white fur on the toes. "What you doing over here?" She sat down next to him on the couch.

"Hold on. I'm finna put Dylan on speakerphone." Tee-Tee pressed a button.

"Hey, sexy!" Dylan spoke to Billie.

"Hey, gorgeous," Billie spoke back.

"Listen, y'all." Tee-Tee crossed his legs and tucked an imaginary long strand of hair behind his ear. "I don't know what the hell Bernard problem is. Lately, he don't wanna show me affection in public. Do you know this Negro tried to give me a fist pound the other day?"

"What's wrong with that?" Billie shrugged her arms.

"First of all, gay men don't fist pound, and second of all, gay men don't fist pound."

"Maybe he doesn't like PDA," Dylan said.

"I mean, since I've known him, he's never really been big on public affection, but that just makes me feel like he's ashamed of me—hell, of us." Tee-Tee's bottom lip trembled.

"Bernard is head over heels in love with you. You know that." Billie pulled him into her arms and hugged him.

"I know. It just hurts my feelings, that's all."

"It would hurt my feelings too," Dylan agreed. "Just talk to him."

"I am." Tee-Tee pulled himself together.

"Now on to me, bitches. I think I'm in love," Dylan shrilled.

"With who? Cruz?" Billie asked, surprised.

"Yes! I mean, like I've never felt this way before about any other guy except your brother, of course. But this shit right here, y'all, is deep. It's like keep-the-baby-type love deep."

"Oh, shit, you serious," Tee-Tee perked up.

"I told you."

"What's so special about him?" Billie wanted to know.

"He's so arrogant but in a good way. And I think I'm a little bit smarter than he is. You guys have no idea how good that makes me feel," Dylan gushed.

"I can only imagine," Billie said sarcastically. "Seriously, don't you think you might be jumpin' the gun here? Y'all only known each other five minutes. I personally feel like it's not so much love that you're feelin' but the good dick that's got you infatuated."

"You may be right. All I know is I'm happy, and I haven't felt this good in a looooong time," Dylan stressed.

"I say go for it," Tee-Tee encouraged her. "You only live once."

"Thanks, luv."

"Let me ask you this," Billie said skeptically. "Can you honestly say that things between you and my brother are over for good?"

Dylan paused. She knew that she'd be hit with that question sooner or later but still wasn't quite prepared to answer it.

"Yeah . . . I've finally come to the conclusion that what we had wasn't meant to be," she tried to convince herself.

"We'll see," Billie replied doubtfully.

After much debate, Dylan decided to give her first television interview since the whole sex-tape debacle. The backstage area of *The Wendy Williams Show* was filled with pandemonium. Stagehands and producers were feverishly running around everywhere. Dylan sat anxiously clutching her hands together tightly in the green room. For years, she'd dreamt of this moment. She was finally going to come face-to-face with one of her biggest idols, Mrs. Wendy Williams herself.

Dylan had even worn one of her best outfits in hopes that she'd be the first celebrity guest to receive a diva fan given out by the talk-show host, Wendy Williams. Homegirl was laid-back but cute in a blue jean button-up with the sleeves rolled up. The shirt was tucked inside a black, sequined pencil skirt. And since Wendy was a shoenista like herself, she rocked one of the hottest pair of Louboutins she had. They were the simple yet classic nude platform pumps. They accentuated her bronze-colored legs perfectly.

"Miss Monroe," the stage director poked her head inside, "it's time."

"Okay." Dylan got up apprehensively. "Wish me luck," she said to Cruz who accompanied her on the trip for moral support.

"You're gonna do fine." He kissed her tenderly on the lips.

Dylan savored his taste.

"Thanks, babe." She stepped back and looked into the mirror, hoping her nude-colored lipstick hadn't smeared.

"You straight," he assured her.

Dylan just stared at him and smiled from ear to ear.

"I love you," he admitted, feeling like it was the right time.

Dylan stopped dead in her tracks. Her mouth wanted to say, "I love you" back, but Billie's words haunted her brain. Were they moving too fast? Were her feelings really love, or the newness of being in an uncomplicated relationship? Most important, could Dylan utter those three words without feeling like the other half of her that belonged to Angel wasn't dying? Hoping that she'd be certain about her feelings soon, she told him that she loved him too and left the room. Cruz stared closely at the monitor and watched as Wendy announced Dylan to the audience. Right as her interview began, his cell phone rang. It was Ted, his agent.

"What's up, Ted? You got good news for me?" Cruz answered energetically.

What he'd failed to tell Dylan was after his poor performance at the World Cup, Spain had opted not to renew his contract. For the last couple of months, Cruz and his agent had been doing their best to get him on another team, preferably the LA Galaxy. That way, he would be closer to Dylan.

"Sorry, man. All the teams that we discussed have passed." Ted said regrettably.

"Fuck!" Cruz barked, pacing the room.

"I'm sorry, man. I tried," Ted said sincerely.

"I know, so what now?" Cruz stood in one place.

"I suggest we hold off for a second and restrategize."

"I agree," Cruz sighed. "Look, I'm at a taping right now with my girl, so I'll just give you a call later."

"All right, I'll call you back if anything changes."

"A'ight." Cruz hung up.

"That was sooooo freakin' awesome!" Dylan shrilled with delight, rushing back into the room. "How'd I do?"

"Damn," Cruz wiped his hand over his face, "I didn't even get a chance to watch."

"Why not?" Her smile faded.

"My agent just called."

"And said what?" she quizzed.

"It's nothin'. Look, you ready to go?" he asked with an attitude.

"Yeah," Dylan said, caught off guard. "Let me just tell everyone thank you and I'll be down."

"A'ight, I'll be in the car." He walked past her abruptly.

Dylan grabbed her purse dumbfounded. *Did that really just happen?* she thought. Despite Cruz's unexplainable change in demeanor, Dylan was determined not to let him or anyone else ruin her day. She'd gone through too much and come too far to let the devil win, so she held her head up high and left with a gigantic smile on her face.

"Baby girl got all the right weaponry."
Mos Def, "Ms. Fat Booty"

20

Dylan was back on top. Her appearance on *The Wendy Show* had received rave reviews and was its highest-rated episode in its history. Dylan's honesty about her past and how she'd changed her life resonated with fans worldwide. With the general public back on her side, the network decided to put her show back in production, and it became the number-one show in its time slot. Baby Mason was crawling and eating baby food. Dylan couldn't have been happier.

Things between Dylan and Cruz, however, had been less than perfect after their trip to New York. When they talked on the phone, their conversations seemed forced. Cruz acted like he didn't even want to talk to her half the time. They barely spent any time together and when she did get to see him, they either sat in silence or had mind-numbing sex. Although the sex was amazing, the whole situation was getting tiresome quickly. She cared for him and wanted to see things work, but the secret he was carrying around was tearing them apart. Wanting to see his face, she picked up the phone and called him.

"Hello?" Cruz answered after a couple of rings.

"Hey," she said softly, "you busy?"

"Nah, just lying down watching television," he said lazily. "Why? What's up?"

"I just wanted to see if you wanted to come over."

"I'ma fall back tonight and stay in the crib," Cruz replied with no kind of hesitance.

"Okay. I'll just talk to you later then," Dylan said hurt.

"A'ight. I'll call you." Cruz hung up feeling a ton of guilt.

He wanted to spend time with her 'cause he loved her, but the shit with his career was fucking him up. Soccer was his life, and without it, he didn't know what his place in the world would be. In dire need of fresh air, Cruz threw on his coat and drove to Club Amnesia to meet up with his pot'nahs.

In front of the club he valeted his car. The chicks in line couldn't take their eyes off him as he headed toward the door. He was thuggishly handsome in a black Chicago Bulls cap, all-black wafer shades, unbuttoned stone-washed denim shirt with a black T-shirt on underneath, black-fitted jeans, and Deion Sanders sneakers. Not one to don a lot of jewelry, Cruz wore a simple diamond necklace and a diamond pinky ring.

Receiving special treatment because of his star status, he entered the club without paying or showing an ID. As Cruz walked inside, the dark atmosphere hit him instantly. The only source of light came from the neon lights on the ceiling which were concealed by sheer fabric. Amnesia was off the chain that night. Women of all different sizes, shapes, and persuasions were in the house.

Ready to let off some steam, Cruz posted up in the VIP section with his boys and a slew of scantily clad women dressed in spandex and faux leather. Bottles of Nuvo, Grey Goose, and Patrón had already been ordered. Cruz leaned back on the couch with his legs cocked open and took one of the bottles of Goose to the head. Then out of nowhere, he locked eyes with a thick redbone.

She was built like a stallion. Dressed in a silver metal, backless halter top and black cotton booty shorts that kissed her hips and blessed her ass cheeks, she stepped onto the mini stage located in the center of the VIP section. Never breaking eye contact with him, she wrapped her fingers around the pole and started to do a sexy dance where she rolled her hips in a suggestive, circular motion.

Hypnotized by her thighs, Cruz took another swig from the bottle. Then the girl began to bounce her ass like she was in a Luke video. From where he was sitting, Cruz could see the crease of her butt cheeks. Her ass reminded him of Kim Kardashian. Suddenly, within a blink of the eye, the chick had leaped onto the pole. Next, she slowly slid down it with her legs spread wide open.

The sight of her fat pussy print had his dick on hard. His homeboys immediately pulled out a stack of dough. Dollar bills poured over her body like rain. But money wasn't on the girl's mind. She wanted Cruz in the worst way. Stepping down off the stage, she glided her way in between his legs.

Cruz took off his shades and glared into her eyes. This girl was risky business. She was the type of broad that, if given the opportunity, would suck the skin off your dick. The bad boy in him wanted to indulge in the nasty fantasies that played out in his head, but flashes of Dylan's face entered his mind. He couldn't play her out like that, especially after just professing his love to her.

Cruz watched closely as the redbone turned around so her ass could face him. After that, she sat down on his lap, her plump ass grinded hard against his stiff dick. Mesmerized by her moves, he thought about pulling a Lil Wayne and being single for the night. Dylan never had to know. He could take the chick into the bathroom and get one off, then cancel her ass like Nino.

But is busting a nut really enough to jeopardize my relationship with Dylan? he thought. While Cruz contemplated right and wrong, he had no idea that photographers had been taking his picture the entire time. Missing his baby, he tapped the girl on the thigh and signaled for her to get up. Disappointed, she watched as he told his boys he was about to shake.

Drunk, Cruz stumbled out of the club and to his car. Before he knew it, he was in front of Dylan's crib. After what seemed like a five-minute walk, he made it to her door and rang the doorbell. Knocked out, Dylan jumped out of her sleep when she heard the sound of someone ringing her doorbell repeatedly.

"What the fuck?" she said, getting out of bed.

Dressed in only a T-shirt and panties, she headed to the door with a wooden bat in her hand.

"Who is it?" she asked, standing in a batting stance.

"It's me, baby, open the door," Cruz's voice slurred.

"What are you doing here?" She put down the bat. "I thought you were staying home." She unlocked the door.

"I wanted to see you." He hugged her, engulfing her sweet scent.

"Are you drunk?"

"Shhhhhh." He placed his index finger up to her mouth, silencing her. "Don't tell nobody," he grinned.

"Ugh, you smell like peanuts and gasoline." She tuned up her face, fanning her nose with her hand.

"Just come lie down with me, baby." He took her by the hand and led her up the stairs.

In her room, Cruz plopped down on the bed fully dressed. Dylan didn't even get a chance to pull the covers back on his side of the bed. Rolling her eyes, she sat down on the edge of the bed and took off his coat and shoes.

"That's why I love you," he confessed. "You make sure I'm straight. Come here." He pulled Dylan on top of him. "You gon' give me some?" he asked, rubbing her ass.

"Yeah, nasty." She straddled him, then kissed and licked his neck.

Cruz ran his hand up her back, pulling her shirt off along the way. Dylan's full breasts dangled in front of his face. He wanted to place them in his mouth, but the alcohol had taken full control and before either of them knew it, he'd fallen asleep.

"Ain't this about a bitch. Cruz!" She shook him. "Wake up!" She shook him again but still got no response. "I don't believe this shit."

Dylan got off of him and put her shirt back on. Since she wasn't about to get any, she slid underneath the covers and drifted off to sleep as well.

Dylan got up the next morning around ten and checked her e-mails and favorite blog sites. This was a part of her daily routine. To her surprise, the cover story on Mediatakeout in bright bold red letters read: "Javier Cruz Caught In The Club Creepin'." Dylan instantly clicked on the headline. The next page revealed several photos of Cruz in the club with slutty women surrounding him. One picture in particular that really caught her attention was of a curvaceous woman who looked like she could be found in a Gucci Mane video, giving him a lap dance. *WWED! What would Elin do?* Dylan pondered. Livid, she headed over to the bed and shook Cruz so hard that he jumped out of his deep slumber.

"What you doing?" he questioned, pissed.

"So while I was at home last night missing you, thinking you were at home, you up in the club chillin' wit' a bunch of raggedy bitches?"

"What are you talkin' about?" He sat up, placing his feet on the floor.

"Don't play stupid! The shit is all over the Internet! Got me over here lookin' like a Got-damn dummy!"

"It ain't even like that. I just got a lot on my mind," he said, still visibly sleepy and drunk.

"Shit, I can't tell." Dylan folded her arms.

"Dylan, I do. I got a lot going on right now." Cruz's head was spinning.

"You got so much going that you gotta have bitches dancing on you?" Dylan yelled, outraged.

"I got drunk," he yawned. "We was just partying and shit got out of hand."

"Whateva." She flicked her wrist.

"Look, come here." He grabbed her hand and made her sit down on the bed.

"I didn't know how to tell you this 'cause I was embarrassed, but Spain didn't renew my contract and nobody else wanna pick me up. The shit been fuckin' wit' my head, and I ain't wanna come across as a fuckin' bum to you."

Dylan shook her head and inhaled deeply, unmoved.

"You know what? This is the same ole shit all over again. I understand how you feel. For a minute there, I thought my career was over, but I never took that out on you or treated you different. I've been with somebody who constantly pushed me away and only dealt with me when they felt like it, and I'm not doing that again for you or nobody else. And besides that, you suppose to be my man, but you all in the club with another female on yo' lap. What kind of shit is that?" Dylan stared at him feeling as if she'd been backslapped.

Cruz sat silently knowing that nothing he said would make things better.

"So," Dylan inhaled deeply, "I think for a little while we need to take a break."

"You for real?" he said astonished.

"Yes, before you can be the man I need you to be, you have to be happy with yourself." Dylan hated to be blunt, but it was time out for playin' games.

"If that's what you want. You're right. I fucked up."

Cruz put on his shoes and coat. Standing before her, he gazed deeply into her eyes and said, "You know I love you, right?"

"I guess."

"I'ma call you later." He kissed her sweetly on the forehead.

"Mmm-hmm," Dylan rolled her eyes, knowing she wouldn't be sitting around waiting for the phone call.

The 1980s pop sensation Vanity 6 hit "Nasty Girl" thumped through the speakers inside of Tee-Tee and Bernard's bedroom. Their room was like a playland full of fantasy and debauchery. On the wall behind their bed was a colossal-size mural of a woman with wild hair. The comforter on their bed was a full-body-sized portrait of the same woman. In front of their bed was a black-and-white checkerboard-designed fireplace with pink logs that glowed in the dark. They even had a life-size horse, mannequin, and DJ booth in their room.

Tee-Tee sat at his hot-pink vanity table putting on his face. There was an important staff meeting at work that day that he had to look his absolute best for. Putting a splash of pink blush on his cheek, he watched out of the corner of his eye as Bernard came out of the master bath dressed in nothing but a towel. Since their tiff at Nordstrom's, Tee-Tee had been giving him the silent treatment.

"You look cute." Bernard went in for a kiss, but Tee-Tee turned his face.

"You sure you don't want me to put the chain on the door, Mr. Clark, or better yet, draw up the blinds?" Tee-Tee sneered.

"What's that supposed to mean?"

"It means that yo' ass is afraid to kiss me in public 'cause you're ashamed of who you are. And before you say a damn thang . . . yes, I went there." Tee-Tee rolled his eyes.

"You take it there all the time. That ain't nothin' new, and FYI, *I'm* the one who chin checks niggas on the regular when they look at us crazy or when my mama refers to you as 'my friend.'"

"That's different. I can't fight yo' mama. I mean, I could, and Lord knows sometimes I want to—"

"You can stop now," Bernard warned.

"Whateva. Sometimes you wanna fight her too." Tee-Tee couldn't help but laugh.

"This shit is stupid. Buying some ridiculous, over-priced shoes ain't a defining moment in our life that needs to be sealed wit' a kiss. To me, that's a bunch of extra shit." Bernard dried off.

"If you think this is about some shoes, then you must be dumber than you look. This is about you being too afraid to acknowledge me in public as your wife! There is always gonna be people out there that judge or call us names, but you know what, Bernard? We can't stop living because they're ignorant. All we can do is live each day to the fullest and cherish every moment that we have together. What I tell you when we got married? It's us against the world, baby. But I can't live for both of us." Tee-Tee got up and left Bernard there to ponder his words.

"I got another man but he ain't like you."
                    Tweet, "Call Me"

21

"And action!" the director of Edible Couture said, pointing his finger at Dylan.

"Hey, material girls and boys!" Dylan smiled warmly into the camera. "I'm Dylan, and you're watching Edible Couture—"

"Cut!" the director yelled, satisfied with the take. "That's great. We got it!"

Pleased as well, Dylan smiled and prepared for the next take. While the stage crew set everything up, she stood still going over her lines while the on set makeup artist touched up her lipstick. Little did Dylan know but Cruz and the crew had a huge surprise in store for her.

"All right, Dylan." The director sat back down in his chair. "We're ready for you to tell the viewers what you're preparing today."

"Okay," she nodded.

"Quiet on the set!" he shouted. "And action!"

"Today, we're going to prepare shortbread cookies in the shape of a Louboutin platform heel. We're even going to create the brand's signature red—"

"Baby?" Cruz interrupted her.

"Huh? What?" She glanced to her left, surprised. "What are you doing here? I'm taping." She looked at the crew, mortified.

"I came here to tell you how much I love you." He took her by the hand as the cameras continued to roll.

The few weeks they'd spent apart had been torturous on him. Cruz was willing to do any and everything to get her back. He'd realized that having a successful career was one thing, but having no one to share it with was something he wasn't willing to do.

"You're the best thing that's ever happened to me. And after doing some soul searching, I realized that I'm good by myself, but I'm greater when I'm with you, so Dylan Dahl Monroe," he took her by the hand and got down on one knee, "will you do me the honor of being my wife?"

"Umm . . ." she said speechless, "I don't know what to say," she said with a hint of panic in her voice.

"Say you'll be my wife," Cruz responded simply.

Overwhelmed with emotion, Dylan gulped. She wasn't sure if she was ready to be Mrs. Javier Cruz, but the look of sincerity in his eyes spoke volumes. Cruz really did love her, and he'd be a great husband and stepfather to Mason. She honestly didn't have a reason to say no, and she didn't want to embarrass him in front of everyone by saying no, so she opened her mouth and said, "Yes."

Darkness swept over the horizon as Angel pulled his car onto the lot of Dylan's show. Raindrops pelted his windshield. He could barely see through, it was raining so hard. But rain wasn't going to stop him. He'd tried playing the background and being respectful of Dylan's relationship with Cruz, but now, shit was getting out of hand. There was no way she could be serious about marrying him when all Angel did was think of her.

She had to still think about him too. All he could see was her for him. She'd become his addiction in more ways than one. Angel was going mad without her. Every meal he ate brought back memories of her. Since he couldn't physically be around her, he watched old home movies, trying his best to recapture the time they spent together.

At night, he lay staring at the wall, envisioning her soothing eyes. Without her, his whole life had been off track. He needed his baby back ASAP. No other man on God's green earth could love her more than he, and he was determined to prove it.

Angel hopped out of his car and chirped the alarm. Within seconds, he was drenched from the rain, but that was the least of his concerns. Donning a black skull cap, white V-neck tee, black trench coat, True Religion jeans, and black leather combat boots, Angel walked briskly around the lot trying to find her trailer. People buzzed by him hard at work.

"Ay!" He stopped a random guy. "You know where Dylan Monroe's trailer is?"

"Yeah, it's straight ahead. It's the last one on the left."

"Good lookin' out." Angel patted him on the back and kept it moving.

Finding her trailer, he stopped at the door. On the way there, he'd planned his speech out to a T; now, he was at a loss for words. What if she turned him away? It would kill him. Never the one to back down from a fight, Angel pulled open the door and walked in. Dylan's back faced him. She was dressed in only a white cotton robe.

"Is it time already?" she asked, turning around, thinking it was her assistant.

Shocked to find Angel instead, Dylan looked at him, confused. He was soaking wet. The T-shirt he wore clung to his chest, exposing the outline of his pecs.

"Is it true?" he asked, breathing heavily.

"Is what true?" she said softly.

Angel invaded her personal space and lifted her left hand.

"I guess so." He dropped her hand, going numb.

All of the air in Angel's lungs escaped. It was like he was being suffocated. Dylan stood up.

"What do you want me to say? You fucked me, then went to Scotland for three months. You knew how I felt about you, but you didn't care." Tears immediately formed in her eyes.

"That's not true," he tried to explain.

"Save it!" Dylan put up her hand, crying. "You can't keep doing this to me! When you want me, you want me, and when you don't, you don't! That's not fair to me, Angel! And this constant tug-of-war on my heart is too much!"

"I know it is, baby, and I'm sorry." He held her face in the palm of his hands.

"No, you're not!" She pushed him away. "Ever since we broke up, I've been tryin' to make you see that I'm different! That I've changed, but you just couldn't put the past in the past! You just kept on punishing me, and my dumb ass just kept coming back for more!"

Angel pulled her back into his embrace. Water dripped from his hat and chin onto her robe as they stood face-to-face.

"I love you, and I don't give a fuck what you say. You're my girl, and I'm your man. I need you, Dylan." He dropped down to his knees and wrapped his strong arms around her slim waist.

Angel's face rested on her stomach. Within seconds, Dylan's entire being was reduced to a mere puddle. Her mind was screaming at her to put up a better fight, but the temptation of feeling him enter her wet slit had taken over. Angel silently slid his damp hands up her robe and caressed her thighs.

Tears filled every crevice of her face. She could feel them in her nose, cheeks, and even her mouth. With each touch, Dylan's breath escaped her. Their bodies were so close that no air could pass between them. Caught up in the moment, Angel lightly kissed Dylan's thighs while she looked on with a look of sorrow in her eyes. She hated that the warm, succulent feel of his lips sent sparks through the most sensitive parts of her.

Angel untied Dylan's robe and admired her belly button. He could stare at her forever. She was perfect. Not willing to waste any time, Angel pulled her down to him and lay her body down. The coldness from the floor sent chills up Dylan's spine. Angel couldn't unzip his jeans fast enough. He was dying to feel the creaminess of her pussy on his dick. Fervently, he kissed her mouth while inserting himself deep within.

"Ahhhhhhh," Dylan moaned.

With each thrust she tightened her pelvic floor. The sensation was enthralling. Then their lips fused together again. Pinning her legs back, Angel slowly grinded his dick in and out of her. Dylan could feel each mind-blowing stroke all the way down to her tippy-toes. Wanting more of him, she held his ass in the palm of her hands and pushed him in further.

"Mmmmm," Angel groaned. He was drowning in her wetness.

"I'm about to cum, baby," he moaned.

"Me too," Dylan shrilled, holding on tightly.

Spent from their sexual romp, Angel and Dylan lay panting heavily. Dylan gazed off absently. She felt like shit. Thoughts of Cruz flooded her mind. He loved her so much, and if he ever found out about what just happened, they'd be over for good.

***

"What's wrong wit' you?" Cruz asked, taking a sip of his wine. He and Dylan were having a nice romantic dinner at Mosaic, a modern fusion restaurant. "You haven't even touched your food."

"I'm not that hungry." Dylan picked at her pot stickers.

"You sick or something?" He took one off her plate and ate it.

"I guess you could say that." She set her fork down and rested her hands on her lap. The guilt Dylan felt was tearing her up inside to the point she felt queasy. Thankfully, she had the noise of the restaurant to drown out her thoughts.

"Order a 7 Up. That'll make you feel better."

"I'm not thirsty either," she frowned.

"So I was thinkin'," Cruz took another sip from his glass, "instead of us having a long, drawn-out engagement, why don't we get married in a month?"

"A month?" Dylan blurted out loudly, causing other patrons to stare. "Are you insane?" She softened her tone. "I'm not gettin' married in a month."

"Why not?" He shrugged his shoulders. "My homeboy Lamar Odem and Khloe Kardashian did."

"Unless you plan on marrying me for publicity, then I don't think that's a good example."

"Well, I don't wanna wait. Besides, when I start playin' for the LA Galaxy, I wanna be able to introduce you as my wife." He stared at her and smiled joyfully.

"You got a deal?" Dylan perked up.

"Yep. I signed with the Galaxy today."

"Congratulations! I knew you could do it." She reached her hand across the table and placed it on top of his.

"Thanks, but dig on this." He held her hand. "I gotta start by March."

"Wow." Dylan sat back, stunned.

It felt like she was being hit with a ton of bricks all at once. She hadn't even come to terms yet that she was engaged. How in the hell could she go from *that* to planning a wedding in a month? Plus, she still had to mentally deal with her and Angel's unexpected rendezvous and the repercussions it could have on her and Cruz's relationship.

"Don't you think we might be moving too fast?" she finally said, trying her best to vie for more time.

"No. I say, why wait? We gon' get married anyway, so why put it off?"

"I just don't know." She shook her head and bit her bottom lip. "I have so much on my plate as it is. I have my baby and my bakery and my show, and I still have to promote my book. And on top of all of that, plan a wedding. I mean, come on."

"That's what's wedding planners are for," Cruz reasoned.

"You just got an answer for everything, don't you?" Dylan said sarcastically.

"Hell, yeah," he laughed. "You know me. When I want something I get it, and I wanna marry you and have you as my wife by the end of this month. So what do you say?"

Dylan held her breath. Her life had somehow become a merry-go-round, and no matter how badly she wanted to get off, she couldn't. She was backed into a corner, and the old Dylan that she'd buried was starting to emerge. She didn't like it, but life was like a game of survival of the fittest. If she kept on giving reasons about why they shouldn't get married, Cruz would know something was up and start asking questions.

There was no way she could have any of that, so Dylan did what Dylan knew best—and caved in.

"Okay." She threw up her hands. "You win, but I have to have Mindy Weiss as my wedding planner if we're going to do this."

"You can have whoever you like." Cruz smiled, pleased.

Dylan, on the other hand, was even more nervous. Her throat felt like it was constricting with each breath.

Everything's going to be fine, Dylan, she thought. *You have nothing to worry about. Cruz loves you, and you love him. What happened between you and Angel the other night was just a mistake. It didn't mean anything. And besides, it'll never happen again.*

Since the age of ten, Dylan had dreamed of the day she'd be able to try on a Vera Wang wedding dress. The moment was as magical as she'd seen it in her head. The staff catered to her every need. On arrival, she, along with Billie and Tee-Tee, were served champagne and caviar. Dylan, Billie, and Tee-Tee all held hands upon entering the showroom. Once they stepped foot inside, they all simultaneously gasped.

The gowns were breathtaking. All they could do was stare with their mouth's wide open in awe. Mrs. Wang's fall 2011 collection was to die for. Dylan was like a kid in a candy store. She couldn't wait to try on as many dresses as possible. Tee-Tee felt the exact same way. An hour later, they'd had a full fashion show, but Dylan still hadn't found the perfect dress.

She didn't want your typical run-of-the mill gown. She wanted something whimsical, glamorous, and totally unexpected. She wanted to stand out. Then it happened. Mrs. Wang herself entered the room. Dylan had to place her hand on the wall to steady herself in case she became faint.

"I have the perfect dress for you," Vera smiled as one of her consultants revealed the gown Dylan had been dreaming of.

Within seconds, Dylan was dressed and zipped up. Tears filled her eyes as she stepped out of the dressing room. Billie covered her mouth and instantly started to cry.

"You better work, bitch!" Tee-Tee gave three snaps in a z formation.

"Dylan, you look beautiful." Billie hugged her.

"Do I really?" She stood in front of the mirror and looked at herself.

"Yes."

And Billie was right. The dress was everything that Dylan wanted, and more. It was playful, romantic, and very high fashion. This was it. She didn't have to try on another thing. This was the one.

"I think you need to rock your hair in a supertight chignon." Tee-Tee surveyed her up close. "Ooh, and a smokey eye will set this dress off right."

"I agree," Dylan replied as she heard her cell phone ring.

"Someone hand me my phone, please."

Billie went inside of Dylan's purse and took out her phone.

"It's Angel," she said, handing the phone to Dylan.

Feeling like her secret had been exposed, Dylan quickly took the phone and sent his call to voice mail. He'd been calling her nonstop since they slept together, but Dylan just couldn't bear talking to him or see him. When he came to pick up Mason, she made it her business to be gone and for her assistant to interact with him. In order to adjust to her new life, Dylan had to keep her distance. If she came in contact with Angel, she'd have to face reality, and the reality of them being together was too far-fetched. She was marrying someone else, and she couldn't just break off her engagement without hurting Cruz in the process. She cared for him too much to do that to him.

"I'll call him back later." She tried to play it off.

Never missing a beat, Billie walked up behind Dylan and looked at her through the mirror. "You're going to make an exquisite bride."

"Thanks, luv," Dylan beamed.

"You know I always thought . . . we'd be picking out dresses for you to marry my brother." Billie toyed with the fabric of Dylan's veil.

"Really?" Dylan spun around, shocked.

"I'm not gonna lie. At first, I was like, hell, no, this will never work, but after you got pregnant, I saw a difference in you. And I realized how much you really loved him. I mean, I always knew how much he loved you, but just seeing it from both sides was huge to me. So I say all of that to say," she looked Dylan square in the eyes, "are you *really* sure want to marry Cruz? 'Cause this is a huge decision you're making."

Dylan wanted desperately to tell her friend how she really felt, but if she let her feelings out to even one soul, her tower of cards would come crumbling down. She had to stand by her decision. She couldn't keep on beating a dead horse in the head. She and Angel were over. History.

"I know." Dylan turned back around and looked down. "And yeah, I'm . . . sure." She looked up. "Cruz is a good guy. It started off rocky, but he's good for me."

Billie could tell Dylan wasn't telling the truth, but she wasn't going to press the issue. If marrying Cruz was what she really wanted, then she'd be happy for her no matter what.

"Then that's that. I'm gonna shut my mouth and support you 100 percent." Billie zipped her lips and threw away the key.

"Thank you." Dylan gave her a quick smile.

"Now, let's try on some veils." Billie patted her on the butt.

"Yea!" Dylan jumped up and down with glee.

"I've got a tight grip on reality but I can't let go of what's in front of me here."
Paramore, "The Only Exception"

22

After a full month of picking out table linens, a DJ, lighting, flowers, and more, all of the planning was done. It was the night before Dylan's wedding. She and Cruz, along with their immediate family and friends, were joined together at Lola's for their rehearsal dinner. Lola had become a special place for them. It was where Dylan and Cruz had their first official date and fell in love.

Everyone in attendance sat together at a long rectangle-shaped table feasting on everything from mussels, Smoked Salmon Carpaccio, and Cobb Salad. There was an open bar so guests devoured bottles of wine and champagne. The atmosphere was cheerful. Excitement filled the air. Cruz hadn't been able to keep his hands off Dylan the entire night, he was so excited.

Dylan was excited too. After meeting Cruz's family and seeing how warm and accepting they were, the weight on her shoulders melted away. In less than twenty-four hours, she would be Mrs. Javier Nathanial Cruz, and for the first time since their engagement, she was content with that. Apparently Angel had accepted it too because the phone calls had stopped. When they did, Dylan's whole world shut down. That feeling of it really being over ate her up to the core, but she soon came to terms that it was for their own good. They couldn't keep on going round and round in circles. Someone had to let go eventually.

"I'd like to make a toast." Bernard stood up with a glass of champagne in his hand. "Through my wife, Dylan, you have become a great friend to me. You're like my little sister, and I love you, word up. But I would like to dedicate this toast to my ride-or-die chick, Teyana." He looked down into Tee-Tee's face.

"Lately, we've been fighting a lot, and it's all because of me. At first, I was being stubborn, but I understand how you feel, Ma, for real. That's why . . ." he reached down for Tee-Tee's hand and pulled him, "I wanted to do this." Bernard took Tee-Tee into his tattoo-covered arms and planted a juicy kiss on his lips.

"All right!" Dylan clapped her hands along with everyone else.

"Oh, Bernard . . ." Tee-Tee hit him playfully on the chest. "You really *do* love me."

"You my boo, girl." He kissed him once more.

"That was so cute," Dylan smiled.

"You're cute." Cruz gave her a loving kiss on the cheek.

"Thank you." She touched the side of his face and kissed him back on the lips.

"Did I tell you how stunning you look tonight?" He pressed his forehead against her's.

"Yes," she giggled. "And if you want me to continue lookin' this way, I'ma have to go to the powder room and freshen up."

"Go 'head and do yo' thang." Cruz stood up and pulled out her chair.

Dylan picked up her purse and walked toward the restroom. Strolling through the crowd, she eased her way up the stairs when all of the air in her lungs evaporated. Her eyes had grown to the size of saucers. It was as if she'd seen a ghost. Angel was coming her way.

For a second, she thought about turning around and running. But where would she run to? With nowhere to run or hide, Dylan stared at him. Their eyes instantly locked. Dylan swallowed hard. Goose bumps covered her arms. She felt trapped.

Time stood still as Angel inched closer and closer. The flame that stayed lit for him in the pit of her stomach was turning into a raging fire. Everything about him was decadent and alluring, from his bald head, to the toothpick that hung from the corner of his mouth, down to his size eleven feet. His whole swag was off the meter. Angel captivated every woman's attention in the room, whether they were with their man or not. He made the Crooks and Castles sweatshirt, crisp, dark blue denim jeans, and six and a half-inch wheat Tims he donned look effortless.

And, yes, Angel knew he had no business just poppin' up unannounced. But he had to see Dylan one more time before their lives changed forever. She was his, and he was willing to make a fool out of himself if need be in order for her to see that his words were true.

"Can I talk to you for a second?" His tone was low but commanding.

"Umm . . ." Dylan looked over her shoulder to make sure the coast was clear.

"Yeah," she replied, seeing that it was.

Since privacy was of the essence, Angel led her inside the ladies' restroom and locked the door behind them. The entire restroom was the color black and the lighting was dim.

"What are you doing here?" she questioned, perturbed.

"You wouldn't answer any of my calls, so I decided to cut out the middle man and step to you directly," Angel said firmly.

"But I'm having my rehearsal dinner for my wedding," Dylan stressed. "My fiancé is a few steps away. I can't deal with this shit right now." She paced back and forth, frantic.

"Well, when?" Angel interrogated. "You can't keep on runnin' away from what happened."

"You can't tell me what to do," Dylan snapped defiantly.

"Seriously, Dylan."

"I am being serious. I'm gettin' married tomorrow. What about that don't you understand?" she questioned, about to flip.

"You don't wanna marry that man. I mean, he cool and all. But he ain't me."

"Why would I go through all of this, then, if I didn't really want to marry him?" Dylan retorted indignantly.

"You tell me," Angel responded coolly.

Dylan stood silent. She knew the answer to her own question. She wanted to prove to herself that she could move on too. That she was loveable and not the same tainted woman from years before. But somehow, the rug had come out from underneath her, and she now floated on clouds made of air.

"What exactly is it that you want from me, Angel?" Dylan asked, fed up.

"You already know." Angel leaned against the wall.

"Know what? That we've been going back and forth doing this same, tired, two-step for two and half years now? Well, guess what? My fuckin' feet hurt, and I'm over it!"

"You don't mean that."

"Yes, I do." Dylan tried to convince herself.

"No, you don't, so stop pretending like you do. You love me just like I love you."

"I gotta go. Cruz is waiting on me." Dylan turned to walk away.

"Come here," Angel ordered.

"What is it, Angel?" Dylan stomped her foot like a child.

Angel stepped into her personal space and gazed down upon her face. "I love you, and there's no way gettin' around that. You're my baby."

"No, I'm not." Tears flooded Dylan's eyes.

"Yes, you are. I want you back. I want me, you, and Mason to be a family for real."

Dylan's heart dropped to her knees. "I can't do this. I gotta go." She turned around.

"Where you going?" Angel grabbed her forcefully by the arm and pulled her into his embrace.

"Let me go. You're hurtin' me." Dylan tried to pull away.

"No." Angel leaned down and tried to kiss her.

"Are you crazy?" Dylan yanked her head back.

"What you think?" Angel attempted to kiss her once more.

"You're not gon' keep doing this to me! You're not gon' keep building me up just to let me crash back down!" She pounded her fist into his chest.

"I won't," he promised.

"Yes, you will! 'Cause as soon as I do or say something that reminds you of what I did, you're gonna push me away again!"

"I'm over that shit, I swear to God." Angel softly kissed her neck.

"Bullshit. Get off of me." Dylan placed her hands on his chest and pushed him.

"I love you." Angel ignored her protest and kissed her lips intensely.

Weighed down by the commitment she made to Cruz and love she kept locked away for Angel, she slapped him. But her hit only invigorated Angel. As Dylan tried

to strike him yet again, Angel restrained her by grabbing each of her arms. Not one to back down from a
fight, Dylan did her best to break loose from his grasp,
but her attempts were futile. Angel was ten times her
size and twenty times stronger.

"Just let me go," Dylan begged, still trying to escape.

Using brute force, Angel lifted Dylan up and held her
in his arms. His hands rested on her butt as he sat her
down on the sink. Dylan tried to force him off of her,
but the cream building between her thighs caused her
to stop putting up a fight. Then their mouths met. At
first, their kiss was rough, but after a brief moment,
their mouths formed an untamed rhythm.

Caught up in the sweetness of his tongue, Dylan
parted her thighs, allowing him to come closer. This
shit was crazy. She wished that she could stay there
with him in between her thighs forever. Angel knew
just what she liked. She could almost feel him biting
the lips of her pussy as she screamed out his name.
Dylan wanted to do everything her body was yearning
for, but a loud knock on the door brought her back to
reality.

"Dylan, you a'ight?" Cruz asked, concerned.

Dylan stared at Angel with fear in her eyes. "I'll be
out in just a minute!" she answered, never taking her
eyes off him.

"I'ma wait on you out here."

"Okay."

Dylan dropped her hands down to her side.

"You don't have to do this," Angel finally said.

Dylan didn't utter a word. The tears that slid down
her cheeks relayed her emotions. Closing her eyes, she
licked her bottom lip. She could still taste Angel on her
tongue. Everything inside her was saying stay there
with him, but the man outside the door needed her

more. Closing her legs, Dylan picked up her purse and hopped down.

Angel stood back and watched her with tears in his eyes. He wasn't the type of dude to cry, but Dylan was breaking his heart. If it were any other woman, he would've loved her, left her, and moved on to the next one, but Dylan was different. She was his baby, his rib, the mother of his child. He couldn't just let her walk away without giving it his all. But now, her decision was final. Cruz was who she had chosen.

Dylan stood at the door with her hand on the handle. This was it. If she walked out the door, her choice would be set in stone. Choosing what was right over her own selfish desires, Dylan plastered on a fake smile and pulled the door back and walked through.

"Time to get up, Chunky!" Candy turned on the lights inside Dylan's bedroom.

"Huh?" Dylan opened her eyes in a daze. It had taken her forever to fall asleep. All night she kept thinking about Angel.

"Why do I have to get up?" Dylan pulled the covers up over her head.

"Umm . . .'cause it's your wedding day. The most important day in our lives." Candy snatched the covers back.

"You mean *my* life, don't you?" Dylan said in a sarcastic tone.

"I know what I said. Now here." Candy set a tray on Dylan's lap with a silver dome on top.

"Eat up." She lifted the lid and revealed a bottle of Jack. "Breakfast of champions!"

"You never cease to amaze me," Dylan huffed, not knowing whether to laugh or cry.

"I'll take that as a compliment."

"Where my baby at?" Dylan sat up and stretched her arms.

"Clyde in there playin' wit' 'em. Oh, before I forget, I also got you this." Candy handed Dylan a long jewelry box.

Dylan's eyes sparkled as she opened it. Inside the box was her grandmother Dahl's vintage Chanel bracelet.

"Candy!" Dylan cooed, becoming misty eyed.

"Don't go gettin' all sappy. It's just jewelry." Candy downplayed her token of affection.

"It's gorgeous though. Thank you." Dylan gave Candy a warm smile.

"Yeah, yeah, enough of that. Eat up. Your hairstylist and makeup artist will be here soon."

By midafternoon, Dylan was dressed and at the church. She and Cruz were having a Latin Catholic ceremony because of his family's faith. Seated in a chair, Dylan tapped her foot anxiously. She wondered if everyone could see on her face the panic she felt on the inside. All morning long she'd been trying to keep it together, but the closer the ceremony came, the more she unraveled.

"Girl, it's a full house out there!" Tee-Tee pranced in the room dressed in his caramel-colored bridesmaid gown.

"Really?"

"Girl, yeah. I can't wait to get this show on the road." He snapped his fingers.

"Well, it's time," Mindy Weiss, Dylan's wedding planner, said.

"All right now!" Tee-Tee tooted his lips and popped his booty.

"Where's Billie?" Dylan looked around.

"Right here, darling." Billie waved, coming into the room.

"Can you all just give me a minute please?" Dylan's voice cracked.

"Sure, sweet thang." Tee-Tee rubbed her back, then left.

Billie grabbed her bouquet and turned to leave as well.

"Ah, uh, not you, Billie. You stay." Dylan clutched her hands together tightly.

"Is everything okay?" Billie asked, seeing the frustration on her face.

"Yeah. I'm just nervous, that's all. I've never done this before," Dylan nervously grinned.

"Are you *sure* you still want to? 'Cause we can leave right now if you like."

"Don't be silly." Dylan got up. "Come on. Let's put on my veil."

Dylan had decided on a cathedral veil. It complemented her one-shoulder, ribbon-detailed, dropped waist, watercolored gown perfectly.

"Look at you." Billie stared at her in awe. "In a few minutes, you'll be Mrs. Javier Cruz."

"I will be, won't I?" Dylan's voice trembled.

"You ready?" Billie extended her arm.

"As ready as I'll ever be." Dylan linked her arm with Billie's.

Pachelbel's "Canon In D" serenaded the crowd while Kyrese walked down the aisle holding baby Mason in his arms. Mason was the ring bearer. Kenzie and Kaylee soon followed, dropping white rose petals along the way. Then it was Billie and Tee-Tee's turn. The palms of Dylan's hands were saturated with sweat as she watched them head toward the altar.

"Okay, Dylan," Mindy smiled. "It's that time."

Dylan simply nodded. Before she could take another moment to breathe, the church doors swung open. All of the guests were up on their feet. Dylan didn't even realize she'd begun to walk until she got halfway down the aisle and noticed her mother giving her the thumbs-up. Dylan ignored Candy and continued to walk. Somehow she made it to Cruz in one piece.

"You look beautiful," Cruz whispered, taking her hand.

"Thank you," Dylan replied, handing Tee-Tee her bouquet. He was her matron of honor.

Dylan and Cruz turned toward the priest and shook his hand. Then the ceremony began.

"Javier Nathanial," the priest said, "will you now take Dylan Dahl here present for thy lawful wife, according to the rite of our holy Mother the Church?"

"I will," Javier replied, proudly holding Dylan's hand.

"Dylan Dahl," the priest looked at Dylan, "will you now take Javier Nathanial here present for thy lawful husband, according to the rite of our holy Mother the Church?"

"I will," Dylan's voice cracked.

"Javier, repeat after me," the priest continued. "I, Javier, take thee Dylan Dahl for my lawful wife, to have and to hold from this day forward."

"I, Javier, take thee Dylan Dahl," Cruz smiled brightly at Dylan, "for my lawful wife, to have and to hold from this day forward."

"For better for worse," the priest gazed down at his Bible, "for richer or for poorer, in sickness and in health, until death do us part."

"For better or for worse, for richer or for poorer, in sickness and in health, until death do us part," Cruz said with all sincerity.

"Dylan, now it's your turn." The priest glanced up at her. "Say, I, Dylan, take thee Javier Nathanial for my lawful husband, to have and to hold from this day forward."

Dylan didn't know if she could do it. She began to feel faint. The entire room was spinning in a million different directions. She couldn't even focus her gaze on Cruz.

"Dylan?" the priest said, getting her attention.

"I'm sorry. Can you repeat that?" Dylan blinked her eyes profusely, trying to regain her vision.

"Say, I, Dylan, take thee Javier Nathanial for my lawful husband, to have and to hold from this day forward," the priest repeated.

"I . . . uh . . ." Dylan rubbed her forehead. "Dahl. I mean Dylan. Take thee Javier Cruz—"

"Nathanial," the priest whispered.

"My bad. Uh . . , whew, it's hot in here." She fanned herself with her hands.

"Do you need some water?" Cruz asked, concerned.

"No, I'm fine." Dylan shook her head. "I, Dylan, take thee Javier Nathanial . . . I'm sorry what was it again?"

"For my lawful husband, to have and to hold from this day forward," the priest said once more, becoming impatient.

"I swear I'm gonna get it right this time," Dylan said with a laugh. "For my lawful husband, to have . . ."

Then the strangest thing happened. Not a single word would come out of Dylan's mouth. She glanced to her right at Cruz. He smiled lovingly back at her, waiting for her to finish. But the words were stuck on pause in her throat. This was all wrong. He wasn't the man she was supposed to be dedicating her life to. The man she longed for, would die for, was Angel. Not able to continue her charade any longer, Dylan looked at Cruz apologetically and whispered, "I'm sorry."

"It's okay," he assured her.

"No." Dylan held her head down and began to cry. "I can't do this."

"What?" Cruz eyed her, confused.

"I can't go through with this." Her voice rose.

All of the guests gasped.

"Are you *kidding* me?" Cruz screwed up his face, heated.

"I'm so sorry." Dylan's bottom lip trembled as she pulled her hand away from his.

"Billie . . ." She turned to her friend. "Where is he?" Dylan referred to Angel.

"At the airport," Billie replied in shock. "He's heading back to California."

"Which airline is he taking?" Dylan asked in a panic.

"American Flight 57."

Dylan gathered the bottom of her gown in her hand and prepared to run.

"And where do you think you're going?" Cruz's mother blocked her path.

"This has nothin' to do with you," Dylan declared.

"This has *everything* to do with me. Who in the hell do you think you are?" Mrs. Cruz pointed her finger in Dylan's face.

"Uh . . . ah, bitch!" Candy rose from her seat. "You got the wrong one! Now I would advise you to step aside or else it's gon' be wrestle mania up in this piece!" Candy said, ready to throw down.

Instead of waiting on Mrs. Cruz to move, Dylan pushed her out of the way. The entire congregation was in an uproar.

"One of y'all get my baby!" Dylan yelled over her shoulder.

"If you find him, you better cling to him like a Chanel bag," Tee-Tee shouted.

"I will!" Dylan replied with a huge smile on her face.

"Dylan!" Cruz called after her. "Dylan!"

As Dylan ran at top speed, she could hear the echo of his voice behind her. But she couldn't stop running if she tried. The love of her life at any minute was about to board a plane back to California. She couldn't let him leave without him knowing how she truly felt.

"Well, we ain't about to let all these flowers go to waste," Uncle Clyde stood up. "C'mon, Hot Plate." He extended his hand to Candy.

"Aww, Daddy, you wanna get married now?" she gushed.

"Might as well. It's already paid for," he shrugged.

"You always puttin' that mind of yours to good use. C'mon, Daddy."

Outside the church, the sun shined down on Dylan's face. After hopping into the back of the limousine, she told the driver to head to Lambert Airport. Twenty minutes later, she ran into the airport with her veil flying in the air behind her. People were gawking and staring at her, but she didn't care. She had to get her man. Angel held his carry-on bag in his hand. He'd just finished going through security and was putting his shoes back on when he heard a familiar voice scream his name.

"Angel!" Dylan yelled, trying to get to him, but security stopped her.

Angel stood up straight and looked at her. He wondered if his eyes were playing tricks on him. Dylan was standing there looking like an angel sent from heaven in her wedding gown.

"Let me go! I need to speak to him!" Dylan tried to break through, to no avail.

"Do you have a ticket?" the security officer asked, restraining her.

"No!" Dylan elbowed the security officer in the stomach.

"Well, then, you can't go through!" he coughed.

"Let her go, man," Angel insisted, walking her way.

The security officer released Dylan, then straightened his shirt as he ice-grilled her and said, "I got my eye on you."

"What are you doing here?" Angel asked, stunned by her presence.

"I couldn't go through with it."

"I see." He eyed her up and down.

"Angel," Dylan said cautiously, "I love you too. You're the only one for me." Dylan broke down and cried. "And if you still want me . . ." she inhaled, "I'm yours."

"Come here."

Dylan stepped closer, unable to look him in the eyes.

Angel placed his index finger underneath her chin and lifted her head up. "You're all I've ever wanted."

Dylan glowed with pride. Angel took her into his arms and hugged her so tightly she could barely breathe. With her arms wrapped around his neck, Dylan planted a deep, sensual kiss on his lips. A thunderous applause resounded around them. From that moment on, they were one. The material girl had met her match, and there wasn't anything about him that she was willing to let go.